FINDING TRANQUILITY

A LOVE STORY

LAURA HEFFERNAN

EMPRESS BOOKS

For Lee and Alex

And for Didi, wherever you are.

PROLOGUE

<u>Prologue: Christa</u>

September 2019

I didn't realize today was the eighteenth anniversary of my death until I caught a flash of the burning towers on CBC. As always, my heart skipped a beat when I thought about what would've happened if I'd gotten on my flight that day.

Like the final scene in *Say Anything*, maybe I'd have defeated my fear of crashing once the fasten seatbelt light went off. Maybe I'd have convinced myself that everything would be okay. But then the terrorists would have taken over. Could I have been brave like the passengers on United Flight 93? Could I have stood up, wrestled the terrorists to the ground, and reclaimed the plane? Someone on board might've known how to fly, and with my help, the flight could've landed safely, saving thousands of lives.

It was a lovely fairy tale, but I doubted it. If I'd been on the plane, I'd have spent my last moments picturing Jess's face, thinking of how I'd apologize for our argument when they finally released us, and planning our new life together in Los Angeles. Not knowing that death hovered, my goal would have been to sit quietly and hope no one noticed me.

Starting in 2002, I celebrated September 11 as my birthday. Quietly, without fanfare. I'd go to a bar, find a dark corner, order a drink, and contemplate my existence for a few hours.

This year was destined to be different. My morning started in chaos and had gone straight downhill. After a broken coffeemaker, a housekeeping plague, allegedly haunted rooms, and a headache the size of Quebec, if I made it out of the hotel before midnight, my birthday drink would be a triple shot. But first, a zillion crises at work demanded my attention.

The cell phone permanently attached to my hip rang. Again.

Make that a zillion and one crises. I pulled the phone from its holster. "This is Christa McCall."

"Christa, it's me." The head of my housekeeping staff. In her nervousness, the woman switched to her native French. "I don't know what to do. Three of our maids called in sick, and we've got forty guests scheduled for early check-in for the conference starting tomorrow. I called everyone, but no one's picking up."

Ugh. So much for relaxing with a cup of coffee any time soon. This day would never end.

"Did you try Happy Housecleaners?" Sometimes, a local company sent people out last minute to help in a pinch.

"*Oui,* but they're slammed, too. There's some kind of bug going around, and two hundred delegates are landing in Montreal today, planning to drive up here. Every timeshare in town is about to be occupied, and everyone needs to turn over their own rooms as fast as possible."

Of course they did.

"Well, I've cleaned toilets before. I can do it again." I sighed. Happy "birthday" to me... "I'll be there as soon as I convince

Mrs. Radimsky that Room 213 isn't haunted. Meanwhile, call everyone else on the schedule to see who wants overtime. Give them an extra vacation day, too, if you have to. As soon as a guest checks out of a room, we need to be ready to flip it."

I hung up and returned to the front desk, where one of our regular customers loudly objected to the room she'd been placed in. The first time ever the woman showed up without a reservation, and naturally, conferences ate up all but one available room.

It never rains, but it pours. What a day.

"I'm very sorry, Mrs. Radimsky, we're just slammed today. There's nothing—"

"Thirteen is bad luck. You will put me in another room! Any other room will do."

"I wish I could, but unfortunately, we don't have any other rooms right now. Everything is booked."

The sixty-year-old woman drew herself up to her full height of four-feet, eleven inches, narrowed her eyes, and glared up at me. All of a sudden, I felt five years old, being scolded for climbing the neighbor's tree to rescue the Frisbee my older brother Brad told me not to play with.

"You will find me another room, or I will find myself another hotel and casino to spend my money in. Are we clear?"

"Yes, ma'am, of course. Again, I'm sorry. Why don't you go over to the café and have anything you like, on me, while we work this out." I pulled the clerk aside. "Find any other guest who's arriving today, preferably someone we don't have a relationship with, and put them in room 213. Give Mrs. Radimsky their assigned room, and send up a fruit basket and a gift certificate to the spa. Make sure housekeeping knows to make the new room a priority."

By the time four o'clock rolled around, I wanted nothing more than a long, hot bath and a stiff drink. I considered not even going back into the office to pick up my purse, because someone might come up with another fire to put out. But in the end, only six people delayed my exit. Practically a record.

On the way out, I held the door open automatically for an approaching guest, a woman with long, sun-kissed blonde hair tapping on her phone instead of looking at the objects in her path. She dragged a suitcase behind her with the other hand, and I signaled a bell boy silently to offer assistance.

The woman nearly walked into me before she looked up from her phone. She was beautiful, but her blue eyes, full lips, and snub nose weren't the reason my heart stopped at the sight of her.

"I'm sorry, ma'am. Excuse me."

The woman's eyes met mine with a startled expression, and her mouth formed a silent "O" shape. At the same time, I drew in a sharp breath. Tears formed at the corners of her eyes, puddling in her thick, dark lashes. Lashes I personally knew to be fake, having seen her attach them a thousand times while lounging on our bed.

Fucking fuck.

I froze, both knowing and fearing what the woman would say next. Indecision seized me. I wanted to run, wanted to pause this moment forever until I escaped. Silently, I cursed myself for daring to wonder what the fates could do to make a bad day worse.

"Holy shit." The color drained from Jess's face. "Is that really you?"

PART 1

BRETT

Above all, don't lie to yourself. The man who lies to himself and listens to his own lie comes to a point that he cannot distinguish the truth within him, or around him, and so loses all respect for himself and for others.

— Fyodor Dostoyevsky

CHAPTER ONE

September 2001

Sweat poured down my forehead. I gripped the armrests and squeezed my eyes shut, trying to remember the mantra I'd been trying out. Oh, right. *Serenity now. Serenity now. Serenity now.* Just because it was from *Seinfeld* didn't mean it couldn't work. In my imagination, my seat rocked and tilted, any moment prepared to plummet out from under me to certain death thirty thousand feet below.

Repeating the words in my head didn't help, so I said, "Serenity now," to see if hearing the chant did anything to lessen my utter dread. It didn't.

"Excuse me?"

I cracked one eyelid. Beside me sat a woman, probably about ten years older than me. She sat so composed, so calm, she must do this all the time.

"Sorry, ma'am. I have a slight...ly paralyzing fear of flying."

Her brow wrinkled, crackling the edges of her foundation

and suggesting she'd actually lived a few more years than I originally guessed. "But we're not even on the plane yet."

I nodded. "Yup. I'm so afraid, panic starts in the waiting area. S-sorry."

With effort, I sat up and undid my death grip on the armrests. At this hour, the terminal was slowly coming to life. Kiosks were opening, lights coming on at more and more gates, travelers starting to wander in, some bleary—eyed while others clutched coffee cups like a lifeline. The hush permeating the air when I arrived shortly before seven a.m., as if no one wanted to dispel the early morning magic by speaking, was mostly evaporated by now. In a few hours, it would be nearly impossible to connect that Logan with the bustling hub it turned into.

About a dozen people scattered around our gate. A group of businessmen huddled around their laptops in one corner. A family with a toddler sat against the far wall. One of the children howled, ignoring her father's attempts at comfort. Poor kid. She must not want to fly, either. A few single travelers waited throughout the seating area. Hardly any, really. I wondered if the entire flight would be this empty. Maybe I'd get a row to myself and quake with terror in peace.

A stewardess stood behind the podium, talking quietly into the phone. I gazed at the wall, my eyes tracing the letters in United's logo over and over, trying to control my breathing. Every time my gaze strayed to the plane outside the gate, my whole body tensed.

"It'll be okay," the woman beside me said. "But we're boarding soon. You may want to head to the bathroom before takeoff, take some deep breaths, splash cold water on your face."

"G—good idea." I struggled not to give voice to my fears. "Thanks."

A howl rose from the family in the corner as I walked away, slow so my legs wouldn't shake. Poor kids. In the bright fluorescent lights of the men's room, I looked even worse than I felt.

Sweat stains soaked both sides of my shirt from the armpits down. Way to make a great first impression at my job interview.

An interview I didn't want to go to, but my wife's parents had arranged it. Jess loved the idea of trading Boston's weather for the sun and fun of Los Angeles, but I hadn't been sold on the idea yet. I hadn't been sold on anything. It didn't matter. My whole life, I did what people expected of me, whether I wanted to or not. Moving to the west coast was par for the course.

Pulling a bit of fabric from my pocket, I blotted my clammy hands before realizing what I clutched. The silk square my wife had given me the night before.

"I have a present for you," she'd said with a grin, handing me a flat, squishy package with a bow on top. "A going away gift."

"Jess, you didn't have to get me anything," I'd protested.

"I know," she said. "I wanted to. I made it this afternoon."

She'd made... what? I eyed her suspiciously. "I thought you stayed home from work because you were sick."

She'd stuck her tongue out at me. "After lying on the couch all morning drinking tea, I felt well enough to sit up and move a needle and thread. A bit of bad shrimp doesn't make me totally incapable of doing anything."

Curious, I'd peeled the tape from the wrapping, leaving the bow where it was, and pulled out a large white rectangle. It looked vaguely familiar. I peered closely at the fabric, at the white whorls throughout. Up close, I recognized it.

"Is this from your wedding dress?"

"It is," she said. "I knew you'd be nervous about your flight and the interview, so I made you a pocket square for your suit. I thought you'd like something to remind you of the happiest day of our lives."

Sometimes, I loved her so much, emotion overwhelmed me. Tears had formed in my eyes. "Oh, Jess, you shouldn't have destroyed your dress for me. You loved that dress."

She'd shrugged. "It's no big deal. Someday, we'll cut it down to make a christening gown for our kids anyway, right? Besides, I took it from the lining. No one would ever know."

I'd pulled her close, breathing in the scent of her, as if I created a physical imprint of her to carry with me. She put her arms around me, breathing deeply.

"I love you," I'd said into her hair. "Thank you so much."

"You're welcome." Her voice cracked slightly. "I love you, too."

Now I held the square over my face and inhaled deeply. Lilac and jasmine from her perfume combined with the vague undertones of the unique scent of Jess to soothe me. Not enough to go back out there, but enough to take another breath and confront my reflection.

My face matched the colorless bathroom walls. I glowered at the bathroom mirror, hating the face reflected there. I wasn't unattractive, or scarred, or pimply, or even the wrong weight for my frame. Nothing like that. The face simply didn't reflect the way I saw myself. In the mirror, I saw the man who played football because it was expected, dated the prom queen because it was expected, and chose the career path of least resistance, going into computers because Dad said it was the way of the future and I didn't know what else to do.

As soon as I hit puberty, I grew a beard to hide the too-heavy brow, the angles of my jaw. My face wasn't what I should see in the mirror. It didn't reflect me, who I needed to be. The beard looked horrendous, took me further from my true self, but it removed the need to stare at myself for twenty minutes every morning while shaving.

Jess hated the beard. I hated it too, but I couldn't explain to her what it is—what she was, even. Camouflage. A way for me to hide.

I loved Jess with all my heart, but our marriage was a mistake when we said "I do" and a mistake now. Marrying me was, quite simply, the worst thing Jess possibly could have done. I shouldn't have proposed, should've broken up with her instead, but everyone expected us to get married. I really did love Jess, so figured if I went with it, we'd eventually be happy.

I needed to man up and get on the plane, go to the interview. Since I couldn't be honest with her, or even myself, at least I could be the husband my wife deserved.

The guy from the waiting area entered the bathroom, interrupting my loathing. To hide that I'd been examining my face, I washed my hands again, keeping my face averted. When I turned to find the hand dryer, our eyes met in the mirror, and I paused. His eyes were as red as mine. Something twisted in my gut.

"You okay, man?"

He shook his head. "It's hard, saying good-bye to my kids. They're only going to visit their grandma for a week, but we couldn't afford the extra ticket. I knew the separation would suck for them, but I didn't realize how hard it would hit for me."

The electric hand dryer clicked off, and Alanis Morrisette's voice filled the restroom, pumped in on tinny speakers. Of course. Just the song I needed. Halfway through the first verse, the shakes returned. Sweat poured down my face. Perfect. I couldn't do this. Before Alanis got to the end of her question, I started to bolt.

A voice stopped me. "What about you? You a'ight?"

"No. I am one hundred percent terrified of flying. The last thing I want in the world is to get on that flight."

He gestured at the speakers. "Isn't it ironic? I'd give my left nut to board."

Something in the back of my mind clicked. I didn't want to fly. I didn't want to go to Los Angeles, didn't want to interview, didn't want any of this. And this guy did. Before I stopped to think about it, I wiped my wet hands on my ass and pulled my boarding pass out of my back pocket.

"Here."

"What?"

I shook the pass at him. "Take it. Get on the plane. Go be with your kids."

"No way, man. I can't."

"Sure you can. Consider it a... random act of kindness. Today's your lucky day."

He stared at me for a long moment. I didn't flinch. "You're like a fucking fairy godmother, aren't you? I can't believe it. Thank you!" A moment later, this stranger wrapped his arms around me in a hug so tight it brought tears to my eyes.

"You're welcome."

"Give me your address. I'll pay you back when I can."

I shook my head. "Someday, when you're in a better place, help someone who needs it. And be good to those kids."

He made it halfway out of the restroom before turning back and offering a fifty-dollar bill and a business card identifying him as Dan. "You ever need anything, dude, look me up."

If I didn't take it, Dan would never get on the plane and I risked changing my mind. "Sure thing. Have a safe flight."

Flashing me a thumbs-up, he vanished. I waited by the sink, wondering how pissed Jess would be when she found out what I'd done. But I couldn't get on the plane.

When I got back to the terminal, the people in the waiting area were boarding at the gate to my right. I slowed from a sprint to a walk. Behind me, a stewardess spoke into the intercom. "Last call for Flight 175 to Los Angeles. Passenger Cooper, please proceed to the boarding area immediately. Paging Brett Cooper. Your flight is about to take off."

The thought of boarding a plane made me hyperventilate again. A chill went down my spine that wasn't just from the air conditioning hitting the sweat on my brow. I couldn't do it.

Dan trotted up to the gate and handed her my boarding pass. "I'm Cooper."

No turning back now. What I'd just done was probably illegal. Time to go home and face the music. Thinking about the chilly reception awaiting me, I shivered.

Sorry, Jess. If you need to leave Massachusetts, we can move some-where within driving distance.

I couldn't get on the plane, but I also couldn't head home and tell my wife what I'd done. Not without a plan. Instead, I turned off my cell phone and left the airport. The MBTA would take me downtown, where I could walk around until I figured out what to do. Later, I'd catch a train home to face my wife. Try to figure out how to tell her that this wasn't the life I wanted, that I couldn't take the job in Los Angeles. That I was sorry she'd gotten herself chained to me, that she should walk away and be free.

Without a second glance, I allowed my feet to carry me toward the airport shuttle. At the last minute, I decided to take a more scenic route. When the shuttle stopped at the waterfront, I found a water taxi to drive me across the Charles River into downtown Boston.

"Hey, man," the driver said. "You need a lift?"

Wordlessly, I pulled a twenty from my wallet. It grew damp in my still-wet palm. He stepped back, pulling my suitcase into the tiny watercraft. I settled into a seat, my eyes skipping over the water. In the morning stillness, the quiet waves soothed me.

"I hate to disturb ya, buddy, but where we goin'?" the driver asked.

"Anywhere," I said. "I just can't go home yet."

"Downtown it is." Once we pulled away from the dock, the driver left me alone with my thoughts.

When my flight took off without me at 8:14 a.m., I sat on the boat, letting the waves relax me. My body finally unclenched, the shaking stopped. A plane flew over the water, a streak against the morning sky, and I waved, pretending Dan and his family could see me.

The water taxi dropped me off downtown, near a sea of office buildings. Living in a suburb, I didn't spend enough time in Boston proper to have a destination in mind. All I knew was that I didn't want to get on the T and go back to Jess. How do you say, *Honey, I don't want to come home,* to the person you love most in the world?

This life was all wrong. I was all wrong. But the last thing I wanted was to hurt Jess. I simply didn't know what to do. My feet carried me up and down the streets until I spotted a coffee shop next to a hotel, with waitresses pouring coffee at a long bar and televisions playing nothing more earth-shattering than the latest Red Sox recap.

After I settled onto a stool, a waitress brought me a menu. Although not hungry, I ordered scrambled eggs and coffee. My plane wasn't expected to land for about six hours, so that left time to get my thoughts in order before Jess would start to wonder why I hadn't called yet.

At 8:46 a.m., phones started beeping and whispers spread through the room. Someone changed the television on the wall from ESPN to CNN. On the screen, plumes of smoke billowed out of the World Trade Center. Was it a trick? Something like Orson Welles' *War of the Worlds?* For a long minute, the only sounds in the room were forks clattering against plates, glasses thudding onto tabletops, and the reporters on the television, saying horrible words, filling me with terror yet failing to penetrate my brain at the same time. No one spoke.

Everyone in the room sat in collective horror, eyes glued to the TV. We watched, transfixed, a dozen people watching as one entity. What was going on? The word "live" in the bottom told me this wasn't some horrifying dream.

At 9:03 a.m., another airplane flew into the second tower. An older lady in the corner shrieked and fainted. A waitress ran to help her. A child started crying, then another. Water streaked my cheeks, but I didn't know when the tears started.

Some people pulled out their cell phones and started making calls. Scattered mentions of friends, family in New York flew about the room, interspersed with the questions, the fear.

"The signal is jammed," the woman next to me said. "I can't get through. Of course."

"Do you have friends in New York?" I asked, more out of reflexive politeness than a desire to swap stories.

"No, but my sister flew out of Logan this morning." She barely looked at me as she kept hitting redial. "Nothing. Dammit."

"I'm sure your sister's fine," I said. "Those planes probably came from JFK."

"Sure, but I won't be able to relax until—" Her phone beeped in her hand, cutting her off. "Oh, thank God! It's her. Still at the airport. Her flight was delayed due to a mechanical issue."

Before I responded, the woman bolted from her stool, gathering her belongings and rushing toward the door, presumably headed for the airport to hug her sister. The scene must be madness. I hoped she made it safely.

I turned back to the TV, but my mind went back to the people on the plane. Where did the planes come from? Who were the passengers on board? No one could've survived a plane hitting a building at hundreds of miles per hour. Had I seen any of those people at Logan before I left? The man in line ahead of me at Starbucks, the woman buying a book where I picked up gum from the newsstand? What about the other passengers on my flight? Were Dan and his family still in the air, blissfully unaware of what was happening and planning their first trip to Disneyland?

The room buzzed with whispers, but no one moved. When the news reported a third plane crashing into the Pentagon and a fourth crashing in a field in Pennsylvania, some sick, tiny part of my mind envied the people who'd managed to escape their miserable lives to find something better in the world beyond.

What kind of asshole was I, thinking about myself in the middle of a national tragedy?

I wasn't hungry anymore, but since I didn't know what else to do, I stayed in the coffee shop, soaking in other people's reactions. Waitresses moved like zombies, no one knowing what was happening or why. Rumors flew around the room. It must be terrorists. Such a thing couldn't be an accident. Were we in danger? What if someone attacked Boston? More planes were missing, someone said, and they were headed for the state capitals.

The place slowly filled with people, everyone in a similar state of shock. People who were afraid to get on the T in case terrorists struck again. Meanwhile, horror continued to unfold on the screen. We were powerless to tear our gazes away from it. I should go home and hug my wife, tell her what I did, apologize. She'd be so happy I wasn't in the air, nothing else would matter. Until I told her why I'd run away.

Nearly three hours later, indecision still glued me to my seat when the newscasters released information about the four hijacked planes: American Airlines, Flight 11. American Airlines, Flight 77. United Airlines, Flight 93. United Airlines, Flight 175.

My flight.

CHAPTER TWO

Shock waves racked my body, causing me to double over. Tears streamed down my face, beneath the collar of my shirt. I couldn't breathe. I choked, clawing at the top button until it popped open.

The woman in the seat beside me at the airport, dead. The flight attendant chatting with the gate attendant before going to prepare the plane, dead. The cute kids in the corner, dead. Everyone on the plane plunged into the south tower, their lives extinguished in an instant. Everyone except me.

Dan. Holy fuck, I killed Dan. He never would've been on the plane if it weren't for me. His death was my fault. Despair overwhelmed me.

I should be dead. Brett Cooper was supposed to be on Flight 175, sitting in seat 23A. Brett Cooper is dead. I'm dead.

With a gasp, I shoved myself away from the counter, dropping a twenty into the soggy mess that used to be my eggs. In a daze, I wheeled my suitcase to the attached hotel, plunked cash on the counter, then asked for a room. Mechanically, I followed the clerk's instructions to the elevator, stepped off at the third floor, and staggered down the hall. Finally, I dropped onto the bed and allowed CNN to fill my brain with information.

A couple of hours later, I turned it off, unable to watch anymore. My entire body shook. My thoughts whirled.

Jess wrote down my flight information. I should've been on the flight. The only person in the world who knew I didn't board that plane was dead. Tears welled in my eyes at the thought of how easily I could've been among them.

The media would release passenger lists from all of those flights. My name would be on one of those lists. I'd checked in for the flight, shown my driver's license. Dan only showed my boarding pass—no one checked ID at the gate. My parents and brother would see my name, think I was dead. They'd never learn the truth about me.

As soon as she verified the flight number, Jess would think I died on that plane. She'd call my parents, and she would grieve. My parents and Brad would comfort each other; they'd be fine. One day, Jess would move on. She'd find someone more open, less conflicted. Calling her now, telling her I was okay, felt like the most selfish thing I could possibly do. She was so much better off without me. They all were.

Our marriage could never last, but if I went home, we'd try. I'd pretend nothing was wrong, we'd even have kids to see if that helped fill the void inside me. What was worse: the pain of losing me now, in a heartbeat, or the pain of losing me slowly over the next twenty-five years? She deserved to be free, to find someone who was free to love her. Jess's future children deserved a better father. I couldn't love a family when I didn't know how to love myself.

For weeks before the interview, I was tense. I'd thought being married would make me feel like I fit in, like I was the man my brother Brad always told me to be. I wanted to be what Jess needed, but my unease with myself—with my body—kept growing. Faking contentment it didn't help. Starting over somewhere new might be the answer, but deep inside, I doubted it.

As we'd driven up I-93 to Logan airport, Jess had remained quiet, lost in her thoughts. Part of me wondered what she was thinking, if she realized our marriage was wrong, if she ever noticed *I* was wrong. But mostly I'd wondered what would happen if I got on the plane, got off in Los Angeles, headed for Mexico, and never turned back. She'd be better off without me.

Jess wasn't happy. She pretended things were good, and I knew she wanted to make it work, but her posture told me she sensed my weirdness. She didn't understand it, but she reflected it back at me, anyway. Things kept getting more awkward.

She deserved better.

She'd snuck a glance at me, which I saw reflected in the passenger's side window. I waited. If she had something to say, we had another five miles for her to get around to telling me.

"I got a letter from UCLA's School of Medicine yesterday," she said finally.

"Oh, yeah?" My heart sank, although I tried to sound excited for her.

I didn't want to move to Los Angeles, didn't want to live in the land of perfect beach bodies, glowing tans, and tofu. I also didn't have the slightest idea how to tell my wife that I had been hoping not to get the very job I'd been about to fly out to interview for. But if she got into medical school, everything changed. It would be much more difficult to stall and avoid the move without pissing her off. I might have to make a decision I'd been terrified to make.

"Yeah. I'm in!"

"That's amazing, Jess! I knew you'd do it!" Although a pit was growing in my stomach, I grasped on a tiny strand of hope. "What about the financial aid package?"

Jess furrowed her brow, attention suddenly very intent upon the road. "They offered me a small scholarship."

"How small?"

"The cost of living is lower in Los Angeles—"

"—than in New York City and Boston and San Francisco and

virtually nowhere else in the United States. We've been over this. How much, Jess?"

Jess cleared her throat. "Five thousand a year."

"That's it?"

"We may qualify for low-cost student housing, but otherwise, yeah. That's it."

What a shitty financial aid package. Okay, we wouldn't have to move. A wave of relief hit me before I realized it made me a total ass for being glad we couldn't live out my wife's dream. Maybe I should encourage her to go without me. She'd be happier in the long run.

"That's less than Boston University offered. And if we stay in Boston, I have a job and we have a place to live and we have friends and—"

"We're buried in snow every winter and we forget what the sun looks like and, God, I'm sick of having this same conversation. I want to move to L.A., Brett. Whether you get the job or not. I want to go to UCLA and get an M.D. and get a change of scenery at the same time. We'll figure everything else out once we get there."

I didn't answer. Instead, I focused on the city skyline drawing near, my gaze planted on the window as we curved down the ramp connecting I-93 to the Mass Pike. What if I told her how I felt? Would it make anything better?

"Please say something," Jess had said.

No, it wouldn't.

The car entered the Ted Williams Tunnel. We'd be at the airport in less than ten minutes. I didn't want to leave for three days after telling her how scared I was that our fledgling marriage might be over already. Or telling her how messed up I was.

When I got back, I'd make an appointment with a therapist and find a way to work everything out. It was the only solution. Otherwise, this awkwardness between us would continue to grow until one of us snapped.

"I'm sorry, Jess. Just nervous about making the flight. We left the house late, and I've never flown before."

"No, I'm sorry," she said for the four hundredth time. "I've been having trouble getting out of bed in the mornings."

"It's not you. It's fine. It's hard for me to make life-changing decisions when I'm afraid I won't even make it onto the plane. I don't know what I want. But I don't think racking up a ton of debt is the best way to start married life, do you?"

"Do you think being poor and miserable is the best way to start married life? Working at a crap nine-to-five job knowing I'll never make anything of myself?"

The car pulled off the highway, so I didn't answer while she maneuvered through the cloverleaf making up the airport, other than to point at the exit for my terminal.

Jess took a deep breath. She sounded much less pissed when she spoke again. "One thing at a time, okay? I'll look into grants and scholarships while you're gone. This job is a huge jump for you. If you get it, that'll make our decision much easier. Let's see what happens."

"Yeah, okay," I said dully. "Let's wait and see."

My flight took off in less than an hour. Getting to my gate in time wasn't guaranteed if the security lane got backed up.

"Do you want me to park and walk you to the gate?"

The last thing I needed was to argue about our future while waiting to board. "No, I'm fine. I'll see you when I get home. Pull in over here and I'll jump out."

Before she shifted into park at the curb, my door flew open. I jumped out of the car, hoping it looked like I was worried about being late and not trying to escape our conversation. I grabbed my suitcase from the trunk, then leaned through the front driver's window to kiss her cheek, almost as an afterthought.

I started to walk away, well aware that she held her head rigid, didn't turn to let me kiss her lips. She must be really angry. Poor Jess. She deserved better.

"Brett!" she called. I stopped and turned around. "I love you!"

"I love you, too, Jess!"

I blew her a kiss, turned, and disappeared into the crowd. If I'd known I would never see her again, I'd have stood watching until she drove out of sight.

As terrible a tragedy as the crash was for the rest of the world, for me, a golden opportunity presented itself. This was my chance to start a new life, without hurting Jess any more than absolutely necessary. My wallet held cash for the trip, not a ton, but some. I could walk away. Jess could be free. I could be free.

A COUPLE OF HOURS LATER, I made myself get up and leave the hotel. Nearby, I found a consignment shop where a forty-year-old woman with blood-red nails and a black bob stood behind the counter. She offered me a hundred bucks cash for all three suits in my suitcase.

"That's it?" I asked.

She rifled through them a second time. "If you wanted to leave them here until they sold, you could probably get more, but you said you need the cash now."

My eyes met hers in a silent plea. Mascara caked her lashes, muddying, rather than enhancing, her hazel eyes. She probably wouldn't appreciate the make-up tip, though.

"Okay, fine," she relented. "I'll give ya fifty cash and a hundred in trade if you throw in the suit you're wearing. Plus another fifty for the suitcase."

The carry-on sized roller bag I'd packed to take on the plane served no purpose in my new life. Jess's parents bought us this gorgeous leather set for a wedding present. Intact, the whole set must've cost them a couple grand. At the time, it was a much better gift than the life insurance policy my parents gave us. But I didn't need the reminder of my old life, and I no longer owned enough clothes to fill it.

The woman coughed, derailing my train of thought. "It's the best I can do. Take it or leave it."

I rolled the bag around the counter, handle pointed toward her. "I'll take it. Thanks."

An hour later, I wove through a sea of pedestrians on the sidewalk, carrying a slightly-worn red backpack full of jeans and T-shirts and wearing a brand-new fake Boston Red Sox cap bought for ten bucks from a street vendor, pulled low over my now beardless face. The extra cash in my wallet added a spring to my step.

Someone shoved a microphone under my nose. "Sir, what do you think about today's shocking terrorist attacks on the World Trade Center?"

Behind a fake-tanned, overly-made up woman with perfect hair stood a man holding a camera displaying a solid red light. My heartbeat pounded in my ears. Oh no. I couldn't afford to get caught on video while fleeing from my old life.

I pulled the cap lower over my face and planted my gaze firmly on the sidewalk. "No comment," I mumbled before I took off into the crowd.

Block after block passed in a blur before I stopped to catch my breath. I had no way of knowing how much time passed. What if they used the footage? What if Jess saw it? Would she recognize me?

Something in the backpack dug into my hip as I walked. I welcomed the pain, the chance to feel something for the first time in days.

It was time to come up with a long-term plan. Staying here forever wasn't an option. Too expensive, too close to home, too much chance I'd run into someone who knew me or Jess.

I slowed to a walk, moving up and down the sidewalks, trying to figure out where I'd wound up. Street signs provided little help since Boston streets liked to tell a person the name of cross streets only, not the name of the street you're actually walking on. There weren't any gas stations in this residential area, so I kept going. Boston was a walking city. Even if most people were inside, mourning or glued to their TVs, I'd eventually find another person to give me directions back downtown.

The sun rose high in the sky before I turned down a random street and spotted a small park at the end of the row of brownstones. The pinprick in my hip grew more obnoxious. The name of the park told me nothing; I wasn't familiar with this part of the city. Finally, I dropped to a bench to figure out what the heck was poking me and what to do next.

The backpack contained a ton of pockets. In the largest one, I found only the "new" clothes I'd bought, none of them with tags, sharp angles, or anything in the pockets. I turned my attention to the other zippers. The front pouch was empty. Behind it, I found another zippered compartment. Squeezing the bag, I felt something hard and square near the bottom. No, rectangular. This had to be whatever I kept feeling when the bag jostled.

The zipper stuck at first, but I eventually coaxed it open enough to stick my fingers inside. They closed against something smooth and hard. Slowly, I pulled the item out until I held a Canadian passport in my hand.

The book looked brand-new, although it was issued in 1998. The only stamp marring the perfect pages showed the day this person—Christina McCall—entered the U.S., more than a year ago. I wondered what happened to her. If she ditched the bag and the passport on purpose.

On the main page, Christina stared out at me with dark, serious eyes and lips thinly pressed together. She hadn't smiled for this photograph. Her hair was about the same color as mine, her skin a few shades lighter. There must not be much sun in her part of Canada. The book said she'd been born in Saskatchewan. I didn't have a clue where that was.

Trees rustled in the breeze, pulling my attention away from

the book in my hands. White clouds drifted across the sky. Birds twittered in the trees. It was a perfect day to lose yourself. Maybe that's what this Christina did. Lost herself in the city, changed her name, ditched her passport to become someone new. Having never met this woman, I identified strongly with her fictitious desire to start over.

Across the park, a guy about my age sat on a blanket, reading. I approached, hoping he'd be able to direct me back toward downtown. Nearly all of my belongings rested on my back, but I wanted to retrieve a picture of Jess left next to the nightstand in the hotel and catch another night of sleep. Figuring out where to go would be a bonus, but whatever. One thing at a time.

When he told me where we were, I just blinked at him. I'd come further than I thought in my daze. Maybe the long walk back would clear my thoughts.

Then I spotted something resting against a nearby tree. Something to help me get out of town much faster.

"Thanks for the directions," I said. "I'll give you fifty bucks for your bike."

He clapped my back with one hand. "My friend, you've got yourself a deal."

CHAPTER THREE

Up, down. Up, down. The next morning, the road disappeared beneath the wheels of the bike. The wind rushed past my face, a sensation I hadn't experienced in years. Another equally-foreign emotion made me want to laugh out loud and sing with the birds. I'd peddled for miles before I recognized it for what it was: relief.

With no particular destination in mind, I followed my instincts, turning north and west, always moving away from Boston. As my legs worked the pedals, my mind was free to explore the possibilities. Brett Cooper died, I was reborn. Who was I? I could be anyone I wanted.

While I rode, I thought about the first time I met Jess. It was the week before my freshman year at Lancaster High. Buses in town were slow, unreliable. Not as unreliable as my older brother, Brad, though. After I stupidly wheedled him into giving me a ride, Brad got distracted talking to a couple of pretty girls at the gas station. Next thing I knew, I was late for my first day of football practice. Of course.

Not the best way to make a good impression on my new teammates. Being a freshman was hard enough without earning a nickname like "Belated Brett" from some asshole. Luckily, most of the fourteen-year-old football players didn't have a word like "belated" in their vocabulary yet.

The second the rusty old Pontiac Bonneville slowed to a halt, I threw the door open and dashed across the lot, not even bothering to close the door behind me. Brad yelled from the driver's seat, but I didn't catch what he was saying.

I was too busy getting the breath knocked out of me by a blond tornado. A *cute* blond tornado. She slammed into me so hard, she fell backward and landed on her ass.

"Oh, shit!" I said. "I'm so sorry!"

It wasn't my fault, but when a cute girl falls at your feet, it's okay to take the blame to get her to talk to you. Brad would've been proud of me taking control of the situation.

For reasons I never quite fathomed, she smiled up at me from the ground. "S'okay. I should've been paying attention to where I was going instead of to my friends over there."

I reached one hand down to pull her up. "You a cheerleader?"

"Yeah. I'm Jess."

When she stepped on her left foot, she winced.

"Are you okay?" I asked.

"I'll be fine," she lied. Jess took another step, but her ankle buckled.

I caught her around the waist and pulled her toward me. Her blue eyes matched the sky. I swallowed, trying to ignore the feeling of her body against mine and instead focus on the situation. Last thing I needed was to show up at football practice with a boner—and late. Was "Boner Brett" a better nickname than "Belated Brett?"

No. No way.

"Here. Let me help you across the field," I said. "I'm Brett."

When we got closer to the field, Coach turned and hollered at us. "Cooper! Stop hitting on the pretty—What's this?"

He trotted over, muttering under his breath. The cheerleading coach spotted us at the same instant and broke into a run. She fussed over Jess for a moment before picking her up and carrying her toward the bleachers, calling for someone to get her ice. I didn't see who she was yelling at, but I watched them go, wishing I had the strength—and the guts—to sweep her up like that. That really would've made Brad proud.

Once they were gone, Coach smacked my shoulder. "If you're done savings damsels in distress, Cooper, are you ready to play some football? Five laps for tardiness. But first, drop and give me twenty."

In between push-ups, I glanced at Jess, now with an ice pack on her ankle. She winked and waved, as if she wasn't hurt at all. I congratulated myself. If you have to accidentally mow someone down on your first day, might as well pick the prettiest girl in school. At least she'd remember my name.

She certainly did remember my name. Would never forget it now. And if she knew where I was, what I was doing, she'd curse that name until the day I died for real. I deserved her fury, but Jess shouldn't have to live with that pain.

I rode and rode, stopping only when my legs threatened to give out, sleeping at rest stops or the occasional motel that accepted cash and didn't require ID. After about a week, I crossed the state line into Vermont. Despite having lived in New England my whole life, I'd never set foot in Vermont. I didn't know a soul there, which made it perfect.

Days on the road took their toll on my body. Before my "rebirth", I hadn't been in the best shape. The loathing directed toward my body had nothing to do with size or shape. Attaching large biceps or chiseled abs to a frame I hated, making my body manlier, made little sense to me. As a result, my clothes now hung from my frame. I needed a place to stop, rest for a few days, and come up with a plan. Riding a bike until I ran out of money or winter came and I froze to death wasn't a plan. Not a good one, anyway.

Another ten miles up the road, I found what I needed. A

crooked sign hanging on the battered wooden fence welcomed me to the "Tranquility Cooperative Bed and Breakfast."

A long, partially overgrown gravel driveway led up the hill to a ramshackle old house. Pits in the gravel would be hell on a car. For safety, I wheeled my bike up the drive while I further examined the place. Several worn spots on the roof where shingles should have been. A crumbling chimney on one side. Several of the windows on the upper floor were missing screens. When I climbed onto the porch, stepping over a missing slat in the steps, something brushed my face. At first I thought it was a fly strip, but then I realized it was a curl of paint dangling from the ceiling. Part of me worried the whole thing would give way beneath me.

I didn't have the slightest idea what made a B&B cooperative. This place looked more like a hostel than a fancy bed and breakfast. But I needed a place to stay, the cash in my wallet was dwindling, and a place this rundown couldn't cost much.

Before I'd convinced myself to go in, the front door opened. A short, smiling black woman with chin-length grey curls and breasts hanging down to her knees enveloped me in a hug. Not knowing what else to do, I patted her back awkwardly. "Hello?"

She pulled back. "Hello, hello! Welcome to the Tranquility Cooperative B&B! Come in, come in. I'm Henny, and my partner Val's around here somewhere. What's your name, dear?"

I paused, unsure. Brett was dead, after all. My whole reason for being here was to start a new life. But I'd yet to stop and think of a name. I thought of the passport hidden in my backpack, of the person who'd left it behind. Had she once stood in a place like this, given a similar fake name? I couldn't be this Christina, but I could borrow her name for a few days.

"Chris," I said. "Nice to meet you."

Henny offered to take my backpack, but I waved her away. She bustled me through the front door into the building. The lobby gleamed in stark contrast to the exterior of the house. Polished wood floors glowed in the sunlight: not a speck of dust hovered anywhere, and none of the furniture appeared about to rot out from under the unsuspecting sitter. For the first time in days, the knot in my stomach started to loosen.

"Now, this is a cooperative bed and breakfast," Henny said. "That means you work for your keep. As long as you help out with chores, you can stay as long as you like, no charge. There's always something that needs to be done."

Some quick mental calculations told me that, if I stayed until the outside became as welcoming as the inside, I'd be here long after Henny died of old age. But I had nothing to do and nowhere else to go. "I'm not afraid to get my hands dirty."

"Excellent! Then just sign your name in this book here, and I'll take you upstairs to your room." She chatted as we headed up a staircase as well-maintained as the rest of the interior. "Val does most of the cooking, so you don't have to worry about that. But there are weeds to be pulled, gardening to do, fences to be mended. We even have a maple grove out back. In the spring, someone's got to collect the sap, empty the buckets, and make syrup. We always have plenty of work to go around."

At the top of the stairs, Henny ducked under a beam, then headed down a long hallway. Only a square of light through an open doorway on the right provided illumination. She never paused to take a breath. "This place was built in the late 1600s, so some of the ceilings are a bit low. Watch your head. Now, the door at the end, that's me and Val. This open door here is the bathroom, we all share, and we all take turns cleaning it—even if you're doing other work."

"Understood," I said. Having gone from my mother's house to the dorms to my place with Jess, I'd never cleaned a bathroom in my life, but I'd figure it out. How hard could it be?

"Excellent! We've got a few other guests at the moment. A lot of people stay one night, do some dishes, gather eggs, and move on. There's a girl who checked in earlier, she'll probably be one of those. Two others have been here for a bit. One of them is a few years older than you, quiet, keeps to herself mostly. Val and I think she's hiding from a bad husband. She may take some time to warm up, but don't worry. It's not you. The other is about your age. She's... pretty much the opposite of her in every way. You'll see." Henny paused at a door on the left, just past the bathroom. She opened it with a flourish. "And here's your room!"

Light filtered in through dirt caked on the window, but the flick of a switch beside the door turned on a bare bulb swinging in the middle of the room. The tiny rectangular room resembled a college dorm, with its twin bed perched atop wooden drawers. Not fancy, but after sleeping on the ground for the past few nights, the thin mattress looked like heaven.

A narrow closet occupied the wall next to the window, so shallow, I marveled at how small early Americans must have been. Luckily, none of my new clothes required hanging. Henny hovered in the doorway, her fleshy face nearly swallowing her brown eyes.

"This looks great, Henny. Thanks."

"Wonderful!" She clapped her hands together twice. "It's just past three-thirty now. Dinner's served promptly at six. I'd stay out of the kitchen until then if I were you—Val rules with an iron fist, and she won't let you anywhere near her domain until she gets to know you."

I nodded. After days on the road, what I wanted more than anything was to take a shower and then sleep until morning. But this was a cooperative bed and breakfast, and I might as well start earning my keep now so I could go to bed early. "What can I help with?"

"Almost anything." She laughed. "There's so much to do around here. The front lawn needs to be mowed. We've only got a push mower, but do as much as you can. Val says we need to make this place more welcoming."

"I can do that. Want me to pull the weeds, too? Cut back around the path a little?"

She chuckled. "Sweetheart, I'm joking. You look like you're

about to keel over from exhaustion. Why don't you take a nap, sleep for a couple of hours, then clean up and join us for dinner? I'll wheel your bike around the back into the barn in case it rains."

It was official: I loved her.

∞ ♡ ∞

WHAT THE HELL was I doing? It wasn't too late to turn around, call Jess, and tell her everything. She'd be pissed, sure, especially when I told her that I couldn't stay married to her anymore. But she'd also be relieved I was alive. Maybe one day she'd understand that I couldn't be myself and be her husband at the same time.

These thoughts circled in my head all night: Call Jess, forget Jess, be myself, be Brett Cooper, run away, start a new life. Finally, when the sun peeked over the horizon, I gave up and went to have a smoke. These things would kill me, but a plane already took care of that.

Early mornings in Vermont carried a bite in the air, especially in mid-September. I dug in my backpack until I found a hooded sweatshirt before grabbing the crumpled pack and padding downstairs.

"Oh, good! Another early bird! Hold the door!"

A tall, curvy brunette hurried toward me, cradling a basket of eggs under one arm and carrying a pail of milk in the other. She wore a pink T-shirt with "Tranquility" on the front in white script and gray sweatpants that had seen better days. A lot of better days.

I groaned. The last thing I wanted was to swap stories with another traveler. I'd missed meeting everyone the night before by oversleeping dinner, then chopping wood until well after the sun went down. Henny had served me reheated casserole when I finally stumbled back into the house, exhausted and bleary-eyed. I never even saw her partner. The longer I could avoid other people, the better.

"You must be Chris," she said when she reached me. "I'm Val."

The cook and co-owner. I dredged up a smile for the person who was partially responsible for giving me a place to stay. "Chris, yeah. Nice to meet you. I was—"

She thrust the basket into my arms and headed toward the kitchen, giving me no choice but to follow. "Give me a hand putting this stuff away. I'm sure glad to see someone else up to help me out in the mornings. You're built like an old farm boy, Chris. Do you know how to milk a cow? Of course you do. Anyone can milk a cow. It's just like squeezing a tit, and Lord knows, we're all born knowing how to do that. I bet you're a natural. Gee, you're a quiet one, aren't you?"

My head spun at the direction the conversation had taken, but we had finally reached the kitchen. I set the eggs where she pointed. "Sorry. Not much of a morning person. I talk better after coffee."

Under Val's direction, I sliced bread, cracked eggs, and set water to boil for coffee. She kept up a steady stream of orders between chatter, hopping from one topic to the next so fast I didn't try to keep up.

A bleary-eyed girl with long blond curls stumbled in, making a beeline for the coffee pot on the stove. Val slapped her hand. "Not so fast. You can't drink it until it's finished brewing or the whole pot's ruined."

"But, Val—"

"Bat those big blue eyes somewhere else, sister. You can have the coffee when it's ready. Meanwhile, make yourself useful. Go set the table."

She grumbled before turning toward me. She did have big blue eyes, a couple of shades darker than Jess's. Her stringy blonde hair hadn't seen soap in at least a week. She wore a long gray T-shirt that didn't quite cover the dark blue lace of her panties, which peeked out from underneath the hem.

"Why, hello, there. I'm Julie." She tossed her hair over one shoulder, sending a wave of patchouli toward me. "About time we got some testosterone in this henhouse."

My spine straightened at her words. For a heartbeat, I wanted to give her a woman's name, just to see her reaction. Before I could respond, she continued, "You're Chris, right?"

She misinterpreted my confusion. "Henny told me to come into the kitchen and find Chris. You're the only person here besides Val."

"Yeah," I said. No need to say more.

When she put out one hand to shake, I thrust a stack of plates into it. Behind me, Val chuckled. Not fazed in the slightest, Julie grabbed a handful of silverware and spun toward the dining room. "When I get back, there better be coffee," she called over one shoulder.

By the time the table was set, the coffee bubbled on the stove. Val poured the steaming liquid into assorted heavy, ceramic mugs. No two matched each other or the plates.

When we got married, Jess spent three weeks picking out the perfect china, making sure it matched the silverware, the glasses, the informal everyday dishes, and even the tablecloth. It took for-freaking-ever. She would've raised an eyebrow at the mish-mash, but seeing handmade pottery decorate the roughly hewn wooden table somehow gave the place a homey feel.

I needed to stop thinking about Jess. Even without anywhere else to go, I couldn't turn around and go home. That ship sailed when I didn't call her the moment the second plane hit the Twin Towers.

Until I figured things out, Tranquility was my new home.

CHAPTER FOUR

People came and went at Tranquility. One girl took off the afternoon I arrived, having never spoken to me. A forty-something guy arrived on a Harley a few days later; he and Julie rode off into the sunset together shortly thereafter. Others came and went, many giving names as fake as my own. It didn't matter. We all pitched in to keep the place running. Val and Henny never turned anyone away. Even when we filled up around Halloween, our hostesses slept on cots in the living room, giving their own bed to a young mother wearing a hijab and her three-year-old daughter. Everyone was welcome at Tranquility.

Most of the guests kept to themselves, like I did. Even when we worked on two-person tasks like pulling up stumps, I kept my head down and spoke only when spoken to. For those first few weeks, I could count on one hand the number of times I voluntarily entered a conversation or offered up information about myself—none of it true, anyway. Physical labor helped me think, and I couldn't think if I was chitchatting.

About a month after I first showed up on the doorstep, I knelt in the side yard, pulling weeds, when an engine roared at the end of the driveway. Tires squealed, and the sound died. I barely had time to wonder about the new arrival before feet pounded up the steps. Moments later, a voice traveled through the open window above my head.

"Hello?"

A new visitor, apparently. Val was out back feeding the chickens, and Henny had gone into town to pick up a few things we couldn't make or trade to get. I headed into the main room, pulling off my gloves and wiping them across my forehead. The grungy bandana that held my now longish hair out of my eyes while I worked got stuffed into a back pocket.

"Excuse me? Anyone here?" *Ding, ding, ding.*

An extraordinarily tall woman towered over the desk, in a skintight red mini-dress that matched her lipstick and hair exactly. She looked like a firework. On taking another look, I realized that she wore the highest heels I'd ever seen in my life. Once she removed them, she'd likely be about my height. Her frown remained as I appraised her.

"What you looking at?" She demanded. "Ain't you never seen a drag queen before?"

"Sorry, ma'am. I was looking at your shoes." Her face softened. "They're amazing."

"They are pretty sweet, aren't they? Anyway, I need a room."

"I can help you with that." I summarized the rules and handed her the guest book when she nodded agreement. "Welcome to Tranquility. Are you working nearby?"

"Girl, you think there's an audience for a Chinese drag queen named Nina Wun-Wun these days?" She pronounced "Nina" with the long "i" sound. "I wear all red and walk around screaming things like 'Help! Emergency!' Shoot, I'm lucky no one used pitchforks when they ran me out of Buffalo. Second generation in America, I'm a citizen, but do they care? Of course they don't care. Everyone walking around with non-lily-white skin these days is a terrorist. You spend a bit more time out in the sun, you might be in trouble, too."

She didn't need to know how much trouble I was already in,

so I raised my eyebrows at one tanned arm and kept my mouth shut.

Nina kept up her monologue as she headed up the stairs. I grabbed her bags and followed. "Anyway, girl, I need a whole new act. New clothes, new make-up, a new name. I'm here until I figure my shit out. Meanwhile, you can call me Bo."

"Bo?"

We'd reached the room, so I opened the door and carried her bags into the hallway. My friend took off her red wig, revealing close-cropped black hair. "Sure, honey. You don't think I walk around like a lady man all the time, do you? Oh, hell no! I'm out of costume ninety-nine percent of the time. Bo is fine. And who the hell are you?"

The change of subject was so abrupt, it took me a minute to remember the fake identity I'd been using for weeks. This was by far the most interesting person I'd ever met, and I had a million questions. But for now, he tapped one high-heeled foot, waiting for my answer. "Chris."

"You need to answer quicker, or people know it's a lie." Bo removed earrings and wiped off lipstick, transforming from red-headed bombshell to rather ordinary-looking black-haired, brown-eyed man in a matter of seconds. His eyes narrowed as he skimmed me from head to toe. "Oh, honey, you're lucky you met me. You look lost, and helping people find themselves is my specialty."

A FEW DAYS LATER, I found myself in the barn, listening to the sweet rhythm of milk pinging into our metal buckets. Bo sat beside me, making small talk about the weather, the inn, the cows. When he paused for a minute, I seized the opportunity to ask a question that had been on my mind from the moment we met.

"How long have you been doing drag?" I asked.

"Feels like forever now," he said. "I started dressing up like a girl for Halloween when I was a kid. My junior year of high school, I expanded into weekends. Then, when I turned eighteen and moved out of my parents' house, I got a job at a local club."

"How did you get into it?"

It took all my courage to work up the nerve to ask him about this. But I couldn't live in a cooperative bed and breakfast in Vermont forever, so I needed to figure my shit out. Everything inside me told me that I didn't want to be a guy anymore. Drag wasn't the same as allowing myself to be a woman all the time, I knew that. Still, of everyone in my newly tiny social circle, he seemed the most likely to understand how I felt, trapped by my own skin.

Bo leaned around the edge of the stall to meet my eyes. "Why? You looking for a new job?"

I focused on the teat in front of me, on the stream of milk swishing into the bucket between my feet. "Just curious."

"Uh-huh. Like you were just curious about my bras and make-up? Yeah, I seen the way you eye my things." His face vanished behind the partition, and a moment later, sounds of milk hitting the bucket reached me from the other side. "You don't have to be embarrassed, you know. A man who puts on women's clothes and dances around in front of people for a living ain't in no position to judge anyone else."

I didn't know how to express what I was thinking, so I focused on the task at hand. Milk neared the top of the bucket before I spoke again. "Sometimes, I wonder what it would be like."

"To wear women's clothes?"

"To...be...a woman."

These were words I'd never even allowed myself to think, much less say out loud. Not really. Maybe it was the illusion of isolation, each of us sitting in a separate stall. Maybe it was Bo, who had never been anything but open and honest with me. Or maybe it was that I felt like I was talking to Bessie, who cared not at all about my words or my gender, as long as I scratched behind her ears before leaving.

"Well, the shoes are better, the pay is worse, and you'll never be able to piss in public without standing in line for half an hour first."

I hung my head. I should've known he'd treat the whole thing as a joke. I was a joke. This wasn't going to work out.

His head appeared over the partition. "Hey, I'm sorry. My natural instinct is to go for the cheap laugh first. You shouldn't be afraid to be who you are. I'm a boy who dresses in women's clothes for a living, and that's okay. If you're a woman trapped in a man's body, that's okay, too. Really."

"Do you think that's what's wrong with me?"

"I'm no therapist. I'm the last person to tell anyone there's something 'wrong' with them or what it is." I smiled at him. "But maybe there's a reason you're feeling so disconnected, and I can help you figure that out. Let's go out tonight. See for yourself what it's like."

My heart leaped at the thought, but fear made me shake my head.

He continued, "Honey, you're hiding in a cooperative bed and breakfast in the middle of nowhere. You don't have any friends or family, right? What could you possibly have to lose?"

He was right. I had no friends outside this property, no family who knew I was alive. If I put on the clothes and felt ridiculous, I could take them off, and no one ever had to know. I could write the whole thing off as youthful experimentation and move on with my life.

If it felt right, maybe I'd waited long enough to find that out. Twenty-two years was a long time to live a lie.

Still, this conversation put me miles outside of my comfort zone. "All those people looking at me? I don't know."

"They won't be looking at you. They'll be looking at me. You think I'm going to make you up better than me? C'mon. I know how to do the natural look. We'll find you something to wear. I'll do your makeup. Your hair's long enough now, you don't even need a wig if you don't want one. I can flat-iron it for you, maybe trim the ends a bit so it doesn't look so scraggly."

Self-consciously, I touched my dark locks. They had grown a lot since I arrived. I like the way my hair looked a bit longer. "Where should we go?"

"Does it matter? Any place you really want to go—or avoid?"

Trying to hide a smile, I picked up my buckets. Bo had a keen eye for reading people, so no need to mention I'd prefer to avoid everyone I'd ever met. We weren't likely to run into anyone up here, anyway. I scratched Bessie's ears and followed Bo back to the house. "I guess it doesn't matter where we go."

"There's a college town about half an hour away," he said. "We can drive to a bar if you want. Or maybe we should start out small. We'll go to a movie theater, you can dress like a lady, sit in the dark, and realize there ain't nobody out there who cares what you look like. We're all the same sitting in a dark room, staring at that screen. Save the bar for next week."

The more he talked, the more excited I grew. It couldn't hurt, just once, to try it. To see if dressing as someone else made me feel more like myself.

By the time we handed the buckets over to Val back at the kitchen, I felt a million times lighter. I could do this. One night, go out, see what it's like. Excitement filled me for the first time in as long as I could remember.

CHAPTER FIVE

Hours later, Bo led me into his room and shut the door firmly behind us. "Before we start, take off your shirt."

"What? Why?"

"Because it is my job to make you look like a woman, and if you've got chest hair peeking out the top of my favorite bustier, it's going to ruin the illusion."

More things I'd never thought about. Watching Jess get ready thousands of times, I'd focused on the movements of her fingertips, the lowered lashes when she applied mascara, the puckering of her lips, the smoothness of her skin. Not her lack of chest hair. It hadn't occurred to me how much work it would take to make my outsides match my insides. I started to worry I'd bitten off more than I could chew. Or Bo had, anyway.

"Stop thinking, start moving," he said. "I've done this before, this is what you've been wanting to try your whole life, and I'm not about to let you talk yourself into chickening out at the last second. Shirt. OFF."

I pulled the T-shirt over my head and tossed it on the floor. My new friend appraised me for a minute before handing me a razor.

"That's what I thought," he said. "You need to go into the

shower, shave your face, your chest, and your armpits, and come back here. Shave your balls, too."

"Why?"

"Don't ask any questions. You'll thank me later. And don't take too long, or I'll come in and finish the job myself. I'll be here, finding something for you to wear."

As I exited the door, razor in hand, he muttered behind me. "At least there's no back hair."

Roughly half an hour later, I returned after removing quite a bit of hair, most of the skin off my testicles, and at least three quarts of my blood. A volcano of clothing erupted inside the room while I was gone. Skirts, dresses, pantyhose, belts, bras, and things I couldn't even identify lay strewn across every surface.

I offered Bo his razor, but he chucked it at the trash can in the corner. Probably a good idea, considering how much of my skin now coated the blade.

"You're a sadist," I said. "Most painful half-hour of my life."

"Beauty is pain, darling. Learn it, live it, love it."

He directed me to sit at a stool in front of mirror draped with a towel and ordered me not to peek until he finished. I considered protesting, but my interest lay more in the final transformation than in how we achieved it. I could figure out all that other stuff later, once I saw if this "costume" felt more natural than the skin I wore every day

Besides, after the horror he'd already caused me to inflict on myself, I feared what would happen if I ignored his warning.

"Yes, sir."

"Now, shut your eyes."

I obeyed. A moment later, a stabbing pain hit me in the forehead. "Ow! What's that for? I wasn't looking!"

Bo blew on the top of my eye socket. Unless he was trying to piss me off, whatever he was doing didn't work. I raised one hand to push him back, but he slapped my hand away.

"I'm plucking your eyebrows. Now sit still, princess. Didn't you say you used to play football? I thought you'd be able to take a little prick here and there."

"Being tackled is nothing compared to this," I grumbled.

I'd watched Jess pluck her eyebrows a dozen times, and she never screamed or jerked. All her nerve endings must have fallen out after years of abuse. What kind of asshole did this to themselves on purpose?

Bo chuckled and raised the tweezers. I gritted my teeth but said nothing.

His face hovered inches from mine as he plucked, dabbed, swept, blotted, and blew stray hairs off my face. When he finally finished, he wiped lotion across my brow. It felt so soothing, I could've kissed him.

"Is that it?"

"Are you kidding? We're just getting started."

Bo picked up what looked like concealer and a large brush and went to work, the tip of his tongue clamped between his front teeth. A few times, he gave me directions to open or close something, but the room was otherwise silent. The air grew heavy with anticipation. The longer he took, the more I fretted that perhaps this was all a big mistake. Surely, if I was meant to look like this, it wouldn't take so much time and effort, right? Maybe I looked even more wrong as a woman, and he couldn't make me right?

What if I was just losing my mind, and the whole thing was in my head? I'd been born a boy. In church, they said God didn't make mistakes. Maybe it was time to go home, beg Jess's forgiveness, and strive to be a better man. I could go to a thera-pist and learn to love myself. Then Jess and I might even start a family. That's what people expected, right? Brett Cooper excelled at doing what other people told him.

These and other doubts raced through my head in an endless loop as Bo continued his ministrations.

Finally, he set down his brushes and stepped back. "Beautiful!"

"Can I look?"

"Nope. We have to do a couple more things." He picked up the concealer that had been cast aside what felt like about three hours earlier.

"Can you conceal after you put on everything else?" I asked.

"This isn't for your face, honey. It's for your breasts."

"My what?"

"Your breasts. Those beautiful, bouncy balls of flesh us womenfolk have sitting on our chests that we like to put on display when we're in public? You know what those are?"

"Yes, I'm familiar with the concept." I gestured at the mountain of clothing on the bed. "Can't I just wear a good push-up bra?"

"You can, and you will. But sometimes nature still needs a little help. That's where I come in. Now sit back and shut up while I give you some cleavage."

I couldn't begin to see what he was going to accomplish with a brush and some makeup, but I'd already promised to give myself over to this process, so I leaned back and shut up.

A few minutes later, Bo stopped back a second time, walking around and scrutinizing me from all angles.

"I changed my mind. You need a wig," he said. "I'm not sure I have time to trim you after all, and your hair's not quite long enough to pull back to hide the split ends."

"Do you have more than one wig?"

"Do I have more than one wig? What kind of drag queen do you think I am?" Bo pulled a trunk out from under the tiny bed and flung the top open. "Now, Nina Wun-Wun is dead, but I do love her red wigs, so I'm going to wear that one until I can figure out my new character. But you can be blond, brunette, have striking raven-colored locks... There's even a rainbow wig in here for Pride, once you can handle it."

I grinned, considering the possibilities. The chestnut color of my own hair was fine, if not terribly exciting, but the point of this experiment was to become someone else. "Give me the one on the right. We'll see if blondes really do have more fun."

"Excellent choice!"

Bo showed me how to brush the wig, which probably wasn't necessary when he was doing all the work. Still, the knowledge could come in handy while I waited for my hair to grow. Then he arranged the blond locks on my head, fogged me with a hair spray bomb that made my eyes water, and declared the deed done before I even stopped coughing.

"Are you ready?"

Equal parts excitement and terror filled me. What if I still hated what I saw? My palms started sweating. But after all the time and effort Bo put into helping me, there was only one thing I could say. I'd spent years learning to "man up" at my brother's insistence; maybe now was a good time to "woman up" and go out into the world with my head high. I could do this.

"I'm ready."

"Okay. Ta-da!" With a flourish, he removed the towel from the mirror and stepped out of the way so I could see myself.

My jaw dropped. A total stranger looked back at me. A totally strange, gorgeous *woman*. "Wow."

This—this—was me. The me I always knew lived somewhere inside. My heart pounded at the way dark green shadow outlined my brown eyes brought out gold flecks I'd never notice. Forest green eyeliner made my eyes larger, set further apart than I'd ever noticed them. The blonde wig looked more natural than I'd feared after seeing how Bo teased his own locks.

For the first time in my life, I had cheekbones. My lips were full, red, luscious, stretched into the biggest grin I'd ever worn. Womanly. Concealer softened the angles of my face, covered the five o'clock shadow that never went away entirely, and created the illusion of soft skin. The longer I looked, the more alive I felt.

"You couldn't fix my nose?" My fingers reached toward the bump, a souvenir from the time Brad and I were wrestling in the living room. I was winning until he knocked a lamp off the side table onto my face.

Bo slapped my hand away. "Don't you dare touch my masterpiece. Besides, I like your nose. Gives you character. If there's one thing we could all use, it's more character. Don't you dare ever change it."

"I'm just kidding," I said. "I never dreamed I could look like this. I love everything about it. You're a miracle worker."

"Not really." He winked at me. "Just showing you what you could look like every day, if you wanted."

"Thank you." Tears welled in my eyes. This was it. This was who I was supposed to be. "Thank you so much."

"None of that," Bo said. "You cry, and you'll mess everything up. Quick, think of something funny. Or gross. Like that episode of Seinfeld where George has a tiny cock after he went swimming."

I chuckled at the memory, which allowed me to dab at the corners of my eyes a bit and force the tears to stay in. Everything was going to be okay. For the first time in my life, I felt like everything was going to be okay.

"But you haven't said a word about the *piece dé resistance*! How do you like your cleavage?"

My gaze hadn't even gotten that far yet, so amazed by the rightness of the face looking out at me. When I finally noticed the area below my neck, a gasp escaped me. Without using any stuffing or padding at all, Bo had somehow given me supermodel boobs. Jess had the most perfect breasts I'd ever seen in my life, but these beat hers by a mile, from the front, anyway—and it was all done with just makeup. She'd never believe it. Too bad I could never tell her.

"How on earth did you do that?" I asked.

"I told you, girl! The magic of makeup!" Bo held up his hand for a high five, and I slapped it, chasing away the memory of the wife I no longer had. "You don't need to spend hundreds of dollars on breast plates or miraculous bras when you've got some good highlighter!"

"Wow. This is amazing." I wanted to touch one, but I was afraid to mess up his hard work.

"Don't get me wrong. You need to get yourself a bra or two for everyday wear. But for a night out on the town, showcase that cleavage. All it takes is a good bronzer and a little high-lighter. Next time, I'll show you how. When we go out, all the boys'll be staring. I promise."

My blood ran cold. "I don't want… I mean… What if…?"

His tone softened. "You worried someone's going to look at you and think you're a boy in woman's clothes?"

Wordlessly, I nodded.

Bo's hand connected with the back of my skull. "Who cares what those assholes think? I've turned you into a beautiful woman, and that's the only thing people are going to see when they look at you. A beautiful woman with spectacular cleavage. Just don't let anyone get close enough to touch. You may be boobalicious from ten feet away, but no one's going to be fooled by the illusion after placing a hand on your flat chest."

More things I'd never thought about. Men finding me attrac-tive. Wanting to touch me. If I wanted that. It all seemed so fast. My head swam.

His eyes watched my expression. "Do you like men? I'm sorry, I shouldn't have assumed."

I shook my head. "Never thought about it. The only person I've been with is my wife, and we've known each other since we were kids. We were teenagers; I could've rubbed up against a tree and gotten off."

"Hold up. You're married?"

"Not really. Not anymore. Long story." The last thing I wanted was to ruin this evening by talking about my abandoned marriage, my failure to be the man Jess deserved, and, oh yeah, by the way, I legally died last month. I changed the subject. "How did you learn all this?"

"When I was growing up, other boys played with Star Wars toys and Legos. I played with my sister's makeup. I liked pretending to be other people." Bo looked like he had more to say, but maybe he figured we'd pushed my boundaries enough for one day. "Let's see if we can find you something to wear."

Much of Nina's wardrobe was too flamboyant for my tastes, but we managed to find a tasteful gray skirt—once I closed the slit with a row of safety pins. Bo showed me how to tuck my testicles up inside my body and pull my penis back toward my ass, giving the front a smooth look. It wasn't as easy as he made it sound. I spent a good ten minutes twisting and tugging at my junk, which made the eyebrow plucking feel like a loving massage by comparison.

By the time I finished, my friend had transformed into Nina, fully ready and tapping one red vinyl platform boot.

"It takes some practice," she said, giving me the once over. "Here, put on a second pair of pantyhose to hold everything in place. You should be fine."

Finally, I was dressed. The navy blue bustier showed off my now-narrow waist, slimmed by months of eating only what we grew and working hard. My cosmetically-enhanced cleavage winked at me. My heart sang at the image. I refused to move from the mirror until Nina tugged my hand, reminding me that the movie theater wasn't open all night.

She happily offered me any pair from her collection of five-to-eight-inch platform heels, guaranteed to break my ankles—or worse. When we discovered that our feet weren't the same size, I feigned disappointment.

"But you can't go out barefoot!" Nina said. "It'll ruin all my hard work. Hold on. We'll see if someone else left anything we can use."

When Nina first suggested dressing me up, the thought of going out, talking to people, let them see me like this terrified me. But now, after seeing what I could be—who, I could be—the thought of hiding from them seemed scarier than going out and talking to Val and Henny, who knew what we were doing. They waited at the front desk.

My heart beat a thousand times a minute on the way down the stairs. Had I moved any slower, I might have been going backward. However, Nina stood behind me, making sure I kept going. When I stopped and gripped the railing, trying not to hyperventilate, she cupped my chin. "You can do this. You're not some boy who doesn't know his own self anymore. You're a strong, powerful woman. Who is not afraid of a little thing like showing off her new look."

Her words oddly reminded me of my own brother, telling me over and over to be a man. *Be a woman,* I told myself. *Grow some ovaries.*

Standing here all day wouldn't make it any better. I took another deep breath, smiled a thank you to Nina, and held my head high as I finished the trip to the lobby.

When Henny saw me, a smile split her face in two. She clapped with delight. Val never wore her emotions on her sleeve the way Henny did, but it was clear she approved as she swept her eyes up and down my body.

"You clean up real nice, kid," she said.

Blushing, I thanked them while Nina explained our mission to find footwear.

Lost and Found contained only an old pair of fifty-inch-waist jeans, a condom that expired in 1996, three mismatched socks, and a hijab. No women's shoes. We were about to stuff the toe of Nina's heels with tissue when Val offered to loan me a pair from her closet.

Nina gave her the once over and snorted. "Girl, Chris is not putting those nasty orthopedic things on. We'll come up with something."

"Will these work?" Henny stepped forward, holding out a pair of silver glittery shoes with a two-inch stacked heel and straps around the ankle. Not quite as big as Nina's, they should fit. They were the most beautiful shoes I'd ever seen. They reminded me of the pair Jess when we got married.

"Oh, Henny!" Val said. "Not your wedding shoes."

"If the day ever comes when we can marry, I'll get a new pair," she said. "But I trust Chris to take care of these for me. Glad these canoe feet the Lord gave me can finally serve a purpose."

"I'll take care of them," I promised. "And I'll buy you any shoes you want when you get married."

Val set them on the floor. I approached, almost reverently, before bending down to remove one sock, then the other. With great care, I slid my right foot into the first shoe and bent down to buckle the strap.

Instantly, my ankle appeared slimmer. My entire foot became more delicate. I stepped into the second, fastened it, and stood. They fit perfectly. I wobbled but held myself upright.

"See if you can walk in them," Nina said.

The only time I'd dared to try on Jess's shoes, I'd quickly discovered that my feet were much larger than hers, and I couldn't walk for fear of stretching them out. Now, I wasn't quite sure what to do. I slithered one toe forward along the floor, not trusting myself to put any weight on this beautiful contraption attached to my foot.

"Not like that," Nina said. "Walk. Put one foot in front of the other. The heels aren't that high. You'll be fine."

Like a toddler finding her footing for the first time, I finally took one step, then brought my feet together. When I didn't fall, I beamed at my friends. "I did it!"

"You took one step," Val pointed out. "Try another. It's at least fifteen feet to the car."

Under their direction, I walked the length of the room, turned, and walked back. On the third pass, they started correcting my posture and stride. After the fifth turn, they pronounced me ready.

"You look great," Val said. "But how do you feel?"

Biting my lip, I thought before I answered. It would be easy to make a joke, to say something flippant, but this moment felt more powerful than that.

"I feel like I've finally found my truth," I said finally. "For all these years, I've felt wrong, and now I feel *right*."

"Then you are right, honey child," Henny said. "You can't be wrong as long as you're being true to yourself."

On the way out the door, I pulled them both into a bear hug. "Thank you so much for everything, both of you."

"You're welcome, Chris," Henny said. "Good luck out there."

Behind me, Nina spoke up. "Girl, you're not going by 'Chris' after I spent all that time to make you so gorgeous. You need a name that stands out, that grabs attention. Who are you tonight?"

In all the flurry of activity surrounding the night out, I'd never stopped to think about using a female name. Jess was out, for obvious reasons. All the other names that sprang to mind were people I knew: Val, Henny, Julie. But I'd chosen to go by Chris for a reason—the female passport in the bag, a woman about my age with not entirely dissimilar features. And it could help me one day to have an ID I could use, just in case. It was like added insurance.

There were lots of forms of Christina I could use, including the full name. But one diminutive fit me so much better than the others. Fit the person I wanted to be. The answer came easily to my lips.

"Call me Christa."

CHAPTER SIX

Nothing earth-shattering or terrifying happened at the movie theater, so Bo and I made similar little trips. Some people looked at us, but no one pointed or laughed or approached. Vermont was a pretty open-minded place, and most people took no interest in us. When I was Christa, the world made more sense.

A few weeks after our first night out, I finally felt ready to try a real outing. Vermont unfortunately wasn't exactly a haven of gay activity, and while we weren't too far from New York City, I wasn't ready for the big time. The nearest large city was over a hundred miles away. However, we were living in probably the most liberal state in the U.S., so we decided to give the only bar in town a shot. We didn't have to stay long.

Low light and a smoky haze filled the room. The place was a dive, with a jukebox in the back corner blaring songs old enough to drink, a pool table near the middle of the room, and over-flowing ashtrays on each table.

Nina led the way to the bar, hips sashaying to *Let's Get It On*. Trying not to meet anyone's gaze, I followed. The shoes still wobbled a bit. A few steps from the door, I slipped on the sticky floor, catching myself on the edge of a table. The top slammed into my side, thankfully missing my hipbone. I winced but kept walking in hopes no one else noticed.

The battered bar, like the rest of the place, had seen better days. Tranquility sat ten miles outside the nearest town, which mostly served the local college. We didn't exactly have loads of entertainment options at hand. Just going to the movie theater meant driving almost an hour each way.

At least thanks to the cluster of guys in the corner wearing khakis and dark blue button-down shirts and guzzling beer, Nina and I didn't appear to be the youngest people in the bar. We were probably the youngest people who were actually over the drinking age, but that wasn't my problem.

The bartender approached, wiping down the counter in front of us with a grayish towel. "What'll it be, ladies?"

"Sex on the beach for me, baby," Nina said. "And an orgasm for my good friend here. She needs one."

The bartender winked, then vanished.

"Did it hurt?" A voice at my left elbow drew my attention.

One of the college guys must've peeled himself from his identically-dressed friends. He stood behind a few inches behind me, invading my personal bubble.

The bar was deafening. I cupped one hand over my ear and tilted my head with a questioning look.

He stepped closer and repeated his question. "Did it hurt?"

So much for hoping no one witnessed my stumble. I shook my head, hoping he didn't notice I inched toward Nina. "Thanks, but no. Won't even bruise."

Confusion crossed the young man's face. "No, I mean. Did it hurt? When you fell from heaven?"

Beside me, Nina was quicker on the uptake. She slid one hand across the bar and grasped the young man's hand. "Thanks, doll, but we're not looking to be picked up tonight."

That was a pick-up line? Really?

Every single time Jess's friends complained about guys in bars suddenly made sense if "Did it hurt?" was the best thing this dude could come up with to show interest. Here I'd always hugged Jess and thanked her for being less picky than her sorority sisters.

Now a wave of shame washed over me, as I realized what a jerk I'd been. If only I weren't dead, I'd have called them and apologized.

"Who asked you?" the guy said to Nina.

I smiled up at him. When Nina and Christa ventured out of the inn the first few times, we visited movie theaters, a coffee shop, a restaurant. I rarely spoke more than a few words at a time, and never above a whisper. To be heard in this place, I'd have to shout. No matter what my friends said, I worried that my deep voice gave me away. I didn't feel like an imposter dressed this way; far from it. But I was still self-conscious about my voice. Plus, this guy didn't look like he was the most accepting of people who weren't like him.

Before I thought of what to say or how to say it, Nina come to the rescue. "My friend's mute. And she's *not* interested, are you, Christa?"

The guy scowled at her obvious lie. I looked down and shook my head.

The bartender returned with our drinks, so we threw down ten bucks and headed toward a table on the far side of the room. We'd made it only a few steps when one of the guy's friends stepped in front of us. Other than the fact that he had thick, wavy dark hair instead of his friend's buzz cut, they could've been twins. Inwardly, I groaned.

Maybe I hadn't fully thought through what it meant to be a woman inside *and* out. But I needed to know now, so I could make a fully informed decision before I started taking hormones or bought a whole new wardrobe and changed my name. The type of life changes I was contemplating weren't something to enter into lightly. This wasn't a lark, a game. My entire body would turn into something I didn't recognize. People would treat me differently. A lot of people wouldn't understand my decision, and they'd think I was some kind of freak.

He squinted at me, then glanced at Nina, and back. "Dude, Trent! Your *girlfriend* here's got an Adam's apple! So does her friend! You're hitting on a couple of *homos*!"

My fists clenched reflexively, and my first instinct was to punch this guy for talking about my friend like that. Before I could step closer and teach him some manners, Nina grabbed my arm and started toward the restroom. I staggered but managed to keep up, making it to the door without incident. My drink wasn't so lucky; half of the liquid sloshed onto the ground in my wake.

As the door swung shut behind us, a voice rang out. "Hey, queers, you're using the wrong bathroom! That one's for *ladies*."

Thankfully, no one else stood in the restroom to overhear the comment. I leaned back against the counter, gasping for air.

Humiliation flooded me. I squeezed my eyes shut until cool hands touched my face.

"Hey, girl," Nina said. "Look at me. Look at Nina."

I shook my head miserably. Maybe this had been a horrible mistake. So what if I finally felt like myself? The rest of the world saw me as a joke.

"What was I thinking?" I moaned.

"You were thinking you can't live your whole life based on other people's prejudices. You did that for twenty-something years, right? It's time to live for *you*. Not the rest of the world. And you are a beautiful, strong woman, inside and out. You can handle this, and you can handle all the obstacles on the road ahead."

I forced a weak smile to my lips. "Thanks."

Finally, she managed to talk me into leaving the bathroom so we could head out. The night had been a bust, but there was no need to make it worse by hiding in a dingy bathroom. I held open the door for her.

"No way." Nina shook her head. "You first. That way, I can put my foot up your ass if you try to run back in here and hide."

"Ok, fine." I threw back the rest of my drink, then grabbed hers. "Liquid courage, right?"

When she continued to glare at me, finally I moved back into the bar, head down.

Dynamite exploded across my cheek, igniting a fire behind my eye socket. In my surprise, the empty glass still in my hand crashed to the ground. Pain stabbed my calf as a shard bounced off the floor, into my leg. Less than a second later, a fist rammed my stomach, knocking the breath out of me. The asshole caught me off guard instead of just walking up and hitting me like a decent person. He reeled back, preparing to deliver another blow. Just in time, I ducked and side-stepped. My left arm swung upward toward the space where he'd stood.

Not only was this guy a piece of shit, he was overconfident. Wearing women's clothing didn't mean I'd never been in a fight. I grew up with an older brother, played football in high school. I knew how to hit and be hit. Working at Tranquility had made me strong. My fist connected squarely with my attacker's jaw, sending him reeling into the bar.

"Hey, hey! That's enough!" The bartender rang a triangle over the bar repeatedly. "No fights in my bar. All of you, out of here, before I call the cops."

To the left of the bathroom door, I spotted Nina, lying on the ground, holding one hand to her bleeding lip. I went to her and crouched on the sticky, peanut-covered floor. "Are you okay?"

"Fine. Just help me up so we can get the fuck out of here."

"Ladies! Out!" The bartender said behind me.

"We're going!" I yelled, before muttering, "Asshole."

Nina was taller than me, but thin. She didn't weigh much. I wrapped one arm around her back and another under her knees, cradling her to my chest. No one offered to help.

We left a silent room in our wake. A drop of moisture flowed down the outside of my lips. Until the copper taste hit my tongue, I hadn't realized I was bleeding.

Once we made it outside, I stopped. The rain hadn't let up since we entered, and our umbrella now sat on a table on the other side of at least half a dozen hostile Vermonsters.

"Can you walk?" I asked Nina.

"I think so. Dropped my lipstick when I fell, but I'm okay. Put me down."

With Nina's right arm draped across my shoulder, and my left arm wrapped around her waist, we limped toward the waiting car. We'd made it exactly four steps before something slammed into the small of my back. I stumbled, dropping Nina a split second before my knees cracked onto the ground.

"Get up, faggot!"

I didn't know if the unseen attacker spoke to me or Nina, but it didn't matter. I turned and lunged, silently thanking my parents for pushing me toward football for the first time in my life. Even in a dress, I knew how to tackle. My arms wrapped around the guy's shins, and he toppled. It was the guy from inside. Trent, someone had called him. He swore, and I rammed my fist into his perfect face, feeling his teeth smash.

Beside me, Nina pushed herself to her feet. The lights from the bar showed a shadow moving up behind her.

"Nina, look out!"

If she heard me, she didn't have time to react. She hadn't managed to turn around before the long-haired one punched her in the kidneys. She stumbled forward.

A fist impacted with my head, taking my attention away from my friend. The world faded away until Nina's screams cut through the grunting and flying fists. A burst of anger gave me the strength to shove Trent off me. I rolled to my feet, squinting through the downpour until I spotted my friend.

She lay face down on the ground, several feet away. Long Hair straddled her, one hand pushing her head into the ground while the other moved to raise her skirt. Beneath him, Nina twisted, rolled, kicked, and clawed at the slick pavement, trying anything to get away.

"Stop fighting!" Long Hair yelled. "You wanted to be a woman, right? This is what it means to be a woman."

His fingers gripped her wig, pulled back, and slammed her face into the ground. Nina's nose hit the ground with a sickening crack. When her attacker released his hand, her head lolled to one side.

CHAPTER SEVEN

"No!" The sound escaping me was less a scream, more the sound of agony personified. "Nina!"

With the superhuman strength that allows mothers to move cars off children, I shoved my attacker, sending him stumbling back toward the dumpster. I ran toward Nina. She hadn't moved since her nose crunched into the pavement.

Sirens interrupted the silence.

"Man, let's go. Let's go!" One of the guys said. Trent, maybe. The other kicked me, and I moaned. "Chet, police! LET'S GO."

Chet must be Long Hair. He stopped, foot poised to kick again, as he finally noticed the approaching sirens. Then he rolled Nina onto her back. "Oh, fuck. I think he's dead."

The words sliced into my heart. Not Nina. She couldn't be… She was so vibrant, so full of life. The wind rushed out of me as if they'd kicked me in the gut. I couldn't breathe.

I fell to the ground with a wail, not caring if they killed me, too. A wad of spittle landed on my face; I didn't see who sent it. It didn't matter. The rain washed it away in a heartbeat. Just like my best friend's life. Footsteps receded across the parking lot. An engine roared, tires squealed, and they were gone.

Nina lay a few feet away. I scrambled to her on my knees,

needing to see for myself if what they said was true. Her eyes were shut, but a pulse beat in her neck. Her breathing was slow, yet steady. Not dead, just knocked out. Thank all the gods that ever walked this earth. Not knowing what else to do, I sat back and held her hand. The sirens grew louder.

The fall had mussed her wig. I adjusted the red locks, ignoring the pain that exploded in my chest when I moved my arms. My fingers combined through the strands, arranging them around her face. She looked like an angel. An angel with smudged lipstick. I didn't have a purse, so I dug in hers until I found a bright red tube. Fire engine red, for Nina Wun-Wun. One last emergency before she retired the look.

With my thumb, I removed the streak across her chin. Then I dabbed the tube against her lips, stroking back and forth until she looked as beautiful as when we left home.

There, perfect. My perfect friend. What if she never woke up? The world around me blurred, faded away. I collapsed against Nina's chest, tears and rain mingling until it was impossible to know where one began and the other ended.

A police car stopped on the pavement nearby. I didn't look up. A second later, flashing lights entered my peripheral vision. An ambulance screeched to a halt. Doors slammed.

"Are you hurt, ma'am?" A man's voice spoke at my ear. A paramedic crouched beside us.

Wordlessly, I nodded. I didn't move.

"We need to look at your friend. We can't do that unless you stand up. Can you do that, or should I get someone to carry you?"

My legs wouldn't hold me. I managed to crawl a few feet away and sit, legs splayed, watching rain patter into a nearby puddle. Beside the puddle stood a red six-inch platform heel filling with water. The sight startled me out of my reverie, and I grabbed it.

"Wait!"

Two police officers and three paramedics looked up from

where they were loading Nina's stretcher into the back of the ambulance. The flurry of activity and my limited knowledge of medical television shows told me they were stabilizing her. I prayed it wasn't too late.

One bare foot poked through the open back door, reminding me what I held in one hand. When Nina woke up, she'd be pissed if to find one of her favorite heels missing.

"She lost her shoe. She needs her shoe."

One of them patted my arm. "I don't think she needs shoes right now, sweetheart. You can bring them to the hospital to her later."

"NO! She needs her shoe. Nina never goes anywhere without her shoes. Make sure—" A sob cut off my words. My shoulders heaved.

One of the female paramedics wrapped an arm around my back. "Hey, it's okay. We'll make sure your friend gets her shoe back." She took it from me, handed the heel to one of the policemen. "Now, let's go get you checked out, okay? You're pretty banged up, too."

Unable to speak, I nodded.

"Where does it hurt?"

Vaguely, I gestured up and down my entire body. My knees gave way, but another paramedic appeared at my other side, and the two of them held me upright. Seconds later, a stretcher appeared behind me. They helped me sit, then lie back.

The moment my head touched the pillow, I closed my eyes and willed the whole world to fade away.

When I came to in the hospital, two police officers asked me questions while a couple of doctors poked and prodded at me. I answered woodenly, the questions barely penetrating the fog of my brain. I couldn't begin to guess whether they got anything useful, but they eventually left.

The driver's license bearing the name Brett Cooper lay in the Charles River, never to be seen again. The wig I'd borrowed from Nina got lost somewhere between the first punch and the hospital. I couldn't remember the last time I had it. Plus, the doctors had probably checked me thoroughly enough to discover my junk. Instead of telling them my name was Christa, which seemed like a bad idea under the circumstances, I went with Chris.

"Do you have ID, Chris?" A police officer stood on one side, a nurse on the other. I didn't see which of them asked the question.

I shook my head. "The bar didn't ask for ID."

The officer wrote that down. I wondered if the bartender would get in trouble. Not that it mattered.

"Do you live around here?" the nurse asked.

"I'm staying at the Tranquility Cooperative Bed and Breakfast. Just passing through the area." I gave the address, but failed to mention that I'd 'passed through' weeks earlier and had no idea where to go next. Before Nina hit the ground, I hadn't been planning to move on until my hair grew out and we figured out how to grow some all-natural female hormone supplements. But I wasn't safe here anymore. Neither was Bo.

The doctors wouldn't tell me much about Bo since I wasn't family, but he still lived and breathed. They didn't know how long, and they wouldn't let me see him for at least a few days without consent from a family member. Considering what Bo had said about his parents, they wouldn't be happy to see me when they arrived. It was better for everyone if I made myself scarce. After speaking with the doctor again, I checked myself out of the hospital. I'd gotten a bit banged up, but I'd be fine.

Not knowing what else to do, I called Henny from the pay phone in the lobby. Then I sat inside the doors, shivering but not from the cold, trying not to think about Nina. Tears ran down my face. She was going to be okay. She had to be okay. A nurse sat beside me, holding my hand for as long as she could, but eventually went back to work. I didn't mind. Being alone suited my dark mood.

The Tranquility van arrived ten minutes later, screeching to a halt at the red curb that was supposed to be reserved for emergency vehicles. Henny tumbled out the front passenger door before Val even turned off the engine. I went through the doors and fell into her arms without a sound.

"Oh, honey," she said, wrapping her arms around me. "I'm so sorry. She's going to get better. Don't you fret."

Val looked as shell-shocked as I felt. She went through the motions as if she knew she'd break down the moment she stopped. I found it strangely comforting the way she checked me over as if the doctors might have missed something, bundled me into the car, and took off within seconds after pulling up.

Once we were moving, I buried my head in my hands and sobbed. I hadn't said a word since they arrived. Dimly, I felt the car turn out of the parking lot, heard Val tell me we were going home, but I didn't care where we went. I couldn't care about anything anymore. My home wasn't safe, and my best friend in the world was dying.

It was all my fault. We never would've gone to the bar if she hadn't been helping me live as a woman, to find out if that was what I wanted.

Then I sat up straight, realizing another reason I wasn't safe going home. "I can't go back to Tranquility. Police. Reporters. Big news. I can't."

"It'll be fine," Henny said. "You'll do a couple of news stories..." Val shot her a look across the front seat, and she stopped talking.

"I can't go on the news. No one can see me." Silently, I begged them not to ask questions. I couldn't tell them who I was, what circumstances brought me to Vermont. Couldn't risk them turning me in after everything. Faking your own death seemed like one of those things that was probably illegal, but I didn't want to find out.

Val said, "No problem. We see a lot of people around these parts who prefer to keep to themselves. Our job is to help them on their way to their final destinations. We've learned not to pry. Your business is your business."

Henny twisted around in her seat. "We hate to see you go. You're one of our best workers. You're part of the family now. But we understand. Tranquility will be a hive of activity until something else interesting happens around here."

My brain still wasn't working right. Thoughts tumbled around like socks in a dryer. "Where? How?"

Val said, "There's a ton of makeup still in Bo's room, and lots of wigs. I'm sure he'd understand if you take a couple of things to get yourself started. Send us your address when you get settled, and you can pay him back."

I nodded. It seemed wrong to take my friend's things while he was unconscious, not knowing if he'd ever wake up. At the same time, I couldn't stay here another minute. Val and Henny would keep me posted about his condition. There wasn't any other way, not right now.

"Henny will teach you how to put your face on. No one will recognize you when we're finished."

"Thanks," I said.

Losing at least twenty pounds since 9/11, getting a tan, and shaving my beard did wonders to change my appearance, too, but a little insurance never hurt. Learning to put on makeup was more than that, though. If I didn't continue down the path I started, if I put aside the wigs and the makeup and the clothes and went back to being "Chris" or worse, Brett, then all of the pain I caused my family was for nothing.

"You can take Bo's car, too," Henny said. "Drive into New York, then take I-87 up toward Canada. Leave the car in a rest stop this side of the border with the keys under the front seat, and we'll go pick it up in a couple of days if he's not awake yet."

I gulped. In the hospital, I overheard a nurse say that if he didn't wake up in a few days, he probably wouldn't. But then the rest of her statement sunk in.

"The border?"

"Yeah. Canada," she repeated. "Start over where no one knows you. We'll stock you up on herbal supplements and estrogen pills before you go. People are always leaving pills behind. We've got a drawer full of birth control in our bedroom. You can find a doctor in Montreal."

My hopes rose when I told them about the passport in my bag, then plummeted. "I have no keys for the car, no money, and no other way to get to Canada without hitchhiking."

"Did she leave the keys on the rear tire before going into the bar?" Henny asked.

When we first got out of the car, Nina had bent down for a minute to adjust her shoe. She did that a lot, but I never thought much about it. Shoes needed adjusting, right? But maybe she had a hiding spot. There certainly hadn't been any place to store keys in the dress she'd been wearing.

"Maybe. I'll have to check."

"For now, let's assume you'll have the keys," Val said.

"Am I really going to try to cross the border using someone else's passport? Isn't that illegal?"

Henny reached back, squeezed my hand where it rested on the seat. "Desperate times call for desperate measures. Crossing the border won't be a problem. You're white, you're young, and you're headed into Canada, so no one will look too closely. I'll do what I can to help you look more like the photograph, and we'll get you some jewelry and sunglasses to complete the look. You'll be fine."

Just like that, I had my new life all planned out.

My PLANS TO disappear immediately evaporated when police tape and media vans prevented us from getting into the bar parking lot to retrieve Bo's car. After I hid in my room at Tranquility pretending not to exist for a few days, the reporters moved on to a bigger story. Once my taped ribs didn't ache so much, I returned to the bar in the light of day. If possible, it looked even more run-down, less inviting than it had before. A lump rose in my throat, and I refused to let myself look at the stains on the sidewalk near the door. Bo still hadn't woken up. I hated this place with every fiber of my being, and every second spent thinking about why just meant being here longer. It was time to get going.

Bo's battered Hyundai remained untouched in the parking lot where we'd left it. Police didn't know who it belonged to, maybe, or they didn't care. Either way, I was glad the bar owner hadn't towed it before Henny drove me back to pick it up. We hadn't made a back-up plan, and I didn't much want to ride my bike all the way north across Vermont as autumn turned to winter.

Before I got out of the car, I leaned in for one final Henny hug. "Thank you so much. For everything. I'm really going to miss you."

She adjusted my wig. "Long good-byes will only turn us into a giant two-headed, blubbering mess. Chris was a nice guy, but I hope Christa stays in touch. If you ever need anything, let me know. Val and I have both grown to love you."

"I love you, too. You guys saved me."

"We did no such thing. You're stronger than you think. Now go, before you make this old woman cry. With a bit of luck, we'll see each other again someday. The goddess go with you."

With a final hug and a kiss on the cheek, I steeled myself and opened the door. I don't know what I was expecting, but nothing happened, other than cold air entering the car. Henny shivered, and I slammed the door shut.

Afraid someone might try to stop me, I approached the other vehicle quickly. I found the key on the wheel well of the back tire, just where Henny said it would be. Then I moved to the driver's side door, which was already unlocked.

Locking the doors of a convertible is just asking to have to fork over a thousand bucks to replace the cover, Bo once explained to me. *A person who wants to break in isn't going to be stopped by a top made of fabric flimsier than one of my bustiers. Better to let the bastards in and not bother upgrading the stereo.*

A wave of sadness hit me, but I forced it down. Henny waited in the parking lot to make sure I got off okay, and I didn't want her to see me break down. There would be plenty of time to be sad later. After all, I had the rest of my life in front of me, nowhere to go, nothing to do, and no one to turn to. For now, I had to believe that he was going to be okay, or I'd never be able to move on.

My only regret was never getting to see those fuckers who did this brought to justice. Plenty of people had been at the bar that night, though. When Bo woke up, he would testify as to exactly what happened. The D.A. could get a conviction without my help. I wouldn't have to go on TV and risk being spotted.

The morning after I left the hospital, the local newspaper had reported that both men sat in jail awaiting their arraignment. I hoped they sat there, without bail, until they rotted. For a moment, I prayed Vermont had the death penalty for attempted murder.

Taking a deep breath, I banished those thoughts with a turn of the car key. The engine roared smoothly to life, and I flashed Henny the thumbs up before shifting into first gear. Moments later, I turned west, toward the New York border. Behind me, Henny's battered old truck turned to the east, back toward Tranquility. I wholeheartedly wished I could go with her, but it wasn't safe anymore. A couple of reporters had already been sniffing around. If what happened to Bo made national news, a swarm would descend. I didn't want Jess to find out about me like that. Or my mom, or anyone.

It killed me to know they were hurting, that I'd caused them pain. But at the same time, I needed to take care of myself before I could deal with righting that wrong.

Approximately two minutes passed before the next wave of sadness overwhelmed me. Maybe it was the scent of CK One still lingering in the air. Or the cassette in the old stereo flipping over, filling the car with Madonna's sultry voice. The road before me blurred, and I pulled over.

Henny and Val were like the parents I'd always wanted, but Bo was my only real friend. The person who gave me the courage to be who I was born to be. My confidant, my guide. Maybe he didn't understand my need to live as a woman, but he certainly understood enough about being different to help and support me. The reality of driving his car, headed toward a new life, while he lay in a coma, possibly never to recover, punched me in the gut and left me gasping for breath.

For a long time I sat, sobbing into the steering wheel. What if I just stayed here, engine running, until the carbon monoxide penetrated the floorboards?

Maybe it was like those movies: When you defeat death, it comes after you again. Maybe I was supposed to die on September 11, and when I didn't, death created other circumstances to take my life. Or maybe I cheated death, and Bo was the price I had to pay for my new life. I'd thought Brett needed to die before Christa could be reborn, but what did I know?

My parents raised me Catholic, but I hadn't thought much about Jesus, or the afterlife, or anything. At least not since I graduated the eighth grade and no longer served as an altar boy. But now I wondered.

After what felt like hours, Bo's voice rang in my head, as clear as if he sat next to me. *Girlfriend, what the fuck are you doing? Put the car in gear and go. You didn't escape the worst terrorist attack in American history to go hide on a farm for a couple of months and then freeze to death by the side of the road. You've spent your entire life doing what other people expected of you. It's time to start living your life for you. Be who you were meant to be.*

He was right. Or more accurately, I was right, and my subconscious borrowed a familiar voice to tell me what, deep down, I already knew.

With a final sniffle, I sat up, wiped my eyes, and drove back onto the road. I cranked up the radio and blasted Madonna, belting out the lyrics Jess made me listen to a thousand times when we were kids while I pretended to hate it. The miles melted beneath the tires as I left New England and my old life behind. It was the furthest west I'd ever been. By the time I reached the New York border, I felt almost like a human being. When I neared Canada, I thought perhaps I could act normal enough not to freak out everyone I encountered.

I parked at the far end of the rest stop for Bo to retrieve the car when he woke up. I headed into the women's room to splash water on my face, steeling myself for the task ahead.

The first three drivers I approached for a ride sidled away, eyes planted on the ground, and made vague excuses. I'd have felt safer with a family, but most families had so much junk stuffed in their backseat between their kids, there was no room for me. Then a big rig with Quebec license plates pulled into the lot. Truck drivers were lonely, right? Maybe this guy could use someone to talk to.

I waited near the picnic tables until he exited the restroom, then approached. "Excuse me, sir?" I kept my eyes down, my voice low. A demure woman.

"Yes, ma'am?"

"My car broke down a ways back." I pointed down the road. "It can be fixed, but not until Monday. I have relatives near Montreal. I was wondering if you could be so kind as to carry me over the border?"

His gaze traveled up and down my body. Suspicious, not leering. "You got a passport? I'm not smuggling anyone across the border."

"Yes, sir." No need to mention that the passport was stolen.

After all, I had one. "I'm not asking to hide in the back of the truck. Front seat, seat belt, and everything."

"Why can't your relatives come get you here? Montreal's not so far." He chewed thoughtfully.

My mind raced. "They keep their passports in a safe deposit box, sir. House kept getting broken into. They can't get to the bank to retrieve them until Monday. I'd rather not to have to sit here for two days."

"Don't call me sir. Doesn't sit right. Name's Pat." He turned his head away from me. A stream of tobacco juice flew from his mouth, landing near the wall of the restroom. A moment later, he put out one beefy hand.

"Nice to meet you, Pat." His palm warmed mine. "I'm Christa." The more I used the name on the passport, the more it grew on me.

He jerked a thumb over his shoulder. "That's my truck there. I'm going to grab something from the vending machines. Want a snack?"

I shook my head, but my traitorous stomach rumbled, giving me away.

He laughed. "What can I get you?"

"Anything's fine," I said. "Except white chocolate. It's not real chocolate."

"No problem. I'll be right back."

We climbed into the cab in companionable silence. My heart fluttered wildly as I tried to think calming thoughts. *Almost there, almost there. He doesn't know I have a penis. It's going to be okay. Just a couple more hours, and I'll be safe.*

I cast a final glance at Bo's car, blinking back tears. *Goodbye, friend. I hope to see you again someday.*

The rest stop sat only a few miles from the border. One last chance to get out and pee on American soil, I guessed. Before I knew it, the truck rolled to a stop before the gate. Pat rolled down his window and handed our passports through. My heart pounded so loudly in my ears, I feared the customs agent might hear it. He examined Pat's passport, asked a few questions I barely heard over my beating heart, then picked up my booklet.

Wiping my palms against my skirt, I leaned forward. Here goes nothing. My tongue filled my entire mouth. How did it get so large?

The officer glanced from the passport to my face and back. "Canadian, eh?"

Too terrified to speak, I nodded.

"Welcome home, Ms. McCall."

The arm of the gate lifted, Pat restarted the engine, and a moment later we were through, heading down a road where signs displayed warnings in French in English, and the speed limits were expressed in kilometers.

A whole new world unfolded before me.

PART 2

―――――

JESS

Those who are easily shocked should be shocked more often.

— Mae West

CHAPTER EIGHT

September 2001

No one needed to tell me my husband was dead. After dropping Brett off at the airport, I wasn't feeling well, so I drove home, made tea, laid down on the living room couch, and turned on the Today show. When NBC cut away from an interview with some guy who wrote a book about Howard Hughes to say we were going to a breaking story at the World Trade Center, I got up to go to the bathroom. Matt Lauer was so calm, the upcoming story seemed about as exciting as watching paint dry. I never could've dreamed what I was about to witness, not in a hundred years.

When the second plane flew into the south tower, my heart stopped. I couldn't breathe. The idea that I'd just watched thousands of people die tore me apart. At that moment, I'd yet to realize that I witnessed my own husband's murder.

Like millions of Americans, I spent the morning glued to my television. I picked up the phone and called Brett, despite knowing his plane wouldn't have landed yet, that he couldn't answer while in flight. Shaking fingers dropped the phone twice. The FAA cancelled all flights, so I assumed (prayed) Brett's flight would be making an emergency landing somewhere. Planes were still unaccounted for. He could be on any of them, headed anywhere.

Every time the footage paused or went to commercial, even for a second, I skipped frantically around other stations, hoping for more information. Someone reported that fifty planes were missing, thought to be aiming for the fifty state capitals.

My heart beat a million times a second. I gasped for air, but nothing happened. Finally, I managed to find my husband's name in the call history of my phone and press the button. The sound of his voice calmed me almost a fraction before I recognized what he was saying.

"Hi, this is Brett. You know what to do. If this is Jess, I love you."

The message usually made me smile, but today I wondered if I'd ever hear him say those words again. I left a voice mail, begging Brett to call me the second he landed, anywhere, for any reason.

Seconds after I pressed "end call," they reported that a third plane had flown into the Pentagon. My fast breathing escalated into a full-blown panic attack. Part of me considered calling for help, a friend, my mother, anyone—but my fingers fell open. The phone dropped to the floor. I couldn't think, couldn't move. I sat, feet rooted to the floor, butt glued to the couch.

Finally, feeling like a zombie, I forced myself to get up, wash my empty mug, put on make-up, and start my day. The doctor's office expected me to arrive when they opened after lunch, so I needed to get my shit together. I was going through the motions, mechanically applying mascara when one of the newscasters started talking about the planes. An American Airlines jet, en route from Boston. I breathed a sigh of relief. We never flew American. Still, a close call. Whoever thought people would hijack planes in Boston of all places. What if Brett had bought a ticket for that flight instead?

When the doctor's office called to reschedule my appointment, I felt a mixture of relief and disappointment. As much as I needed to know what was going on, part of me thought the best way to ensure Brett would be okay meant going about my day as usual.

The receptionist and I spent more time than we should on the phone, sharing our horror. Having anyone else to talk to, even a stranger, comforted me. I didn't mention Brett's flight. If I talked about it, the danger would be real. He'd call me any minute to let me know he was safe. Cell towers everywhere must be jammed. As soon as he got to a landline, a call would beep through on the other line.

The newscaster's voice penetrated my thoughts as I settled our cordless phone onto the base to charge. "United Airlines."

What was that? No. It couldn't be. My concerns were making me hear things.

"…deeply concerned about Flight 175, headed from Boston to Los Angeles," he said.

I raced to the table, scrambling through my purse for Brett's flight information, even though I remembered yelling it through the car window at his back. Maybe if I took the time to find the paper printout, it would magically have changed.

The growing sense of dread in my chest told me everything. There was no need to wait for final confirmation. The airlines knew where their planes were supposed to be, the timing of the crash fit when Brett's plane would have flown by New York City, and I still hadn't heard from my husband, whose plane should have been on the ground by now. All the airports were closed; his flight never would have been allowed to continue to Los Angeles after the attacks.

He had to have been on that plane.

Dead.

Gone forever.

The last words I'd ever speak to my husband were screamed through a car window at his back. At that realization, the numbness dissipated, and I broke.

∞ ♡ ∞

THE WEEKS FOLLOWING Brett's death passed in a haze. When my mother finally dragged me out of bed and forced me to rejoin the living, I remembered nothing about those first days.

Unfortunately, I couldn't forget that he was gone. That I would never look into his warm brown eyes again, never kiss his soft lips. Never hold him or laugh with him or watch bad reality TV with him again.

Having a funeral without a body was weird. We didn't even have ashes sitting in a pretty box or anything. Nope, no remains, period. Just a picture. My husband's body was spread somewhere around the ruins of 1–2 World Trade Center. Or maybe the wind carried him around the city a bit. Took him down to Battery Park. Hopefully not toward Yankee Stadium. Brett hated the Yankees. He wouldn't want to spend eternity on that field.

Before 9/11, I never thought of myself as a black humor kind of person. Now morbid thoughts wouldn't leave me alone.

It took time to have Brett officially declared dead, which didn't make sense. Anyone with two brain cells to rub together could guess that when a plane slams into the seventy-eighth floor of a building, the people inside don't have the best chance of survival. But I wasn't in any condition to deal with that stuff, so I waited. When my parents and Brett's parents started to push, I finally went through the motions of putting together a ceremony. Like I cared which hymns were sung, what Bible readings we gave. Brett wouldn't have wanted any of that. A religious funeral would make him roll over in his grave. Except he didn't even get a grave.

A voice jarred me out of these thoughts. "What about this one, dear?"

Mom and I sat on the living room floor, surrounded by pictures of me and Brett. There must've been hundreds. That's what happens when you start sharing your life with someone at fourteen. School pictures, yearbook shots, prom pictures, lots of formal posed photos. Not a single candid shot—Brett always preferred to be the one behind the camera. There were about a thousand images of me with my friends, but he wasn't in any of them. Instead, the only recent photographs were wedding pictures. That was all I had left. Our wedding album, and the memories.

That had been the happiest day of my life. On that day, I never dreamed that "'Til death do us part" would come so soon… that a few short months later, I'd be more miserable than I ever knew I could be.

A tear dropped onto the pictures in my lap. Mom reached for them, presumably to blot the moisture away.

"It's fine," I said without looking. "I don't care."

"This is a lovely picture," she said. "I'm glad the photographer caught the moment Brett spotted you walking down the aisle."

I'd been glad at the time. Now, seeing the love shine out of his eyes stabbed me in the gut. That love was gone forever. Our love, our dreams, everything.

Again, I said, "Use whatever you like."

Mom sighed, clucked her tongue, but didn't bitch about how detached I was from this process. How could I be interested in something like this? How did anyone distill someone's entire life into a one-hour service? An afternoon with finger sandwiches and cookies?

"Have you thought about Bible verses?" Mom asked. "There are some lovely Psalms."

"Go with Leviticus 26:29," I said. "That was Brett's favorite."

Unlike our parents, neither of us were religious. But we'd both gotten a kick out of the website that went through the darker parts of the Bible, and Brett found "Thou shalt eat your babies" to be particularly funny. He'd love to know we read it at his funeral. Except for the part where he was dead.

Mom sighed heavily. "I know this is hard for you, Jess..."

"Do you? How many times did your husband die?" She flinched, and I sorta recognized that I should feel bad. But worrying about how my grief affected people around me just wasn't going to happen. I didn't know how to act, what to do. No one prepared you for this. Especially not at twenty-two. I wasn't ready to be an adult yet.

When Mom spoke again, her voice was softer. "I can do this on my own if you want."

"Sure," I said. "It doesn't matter."

Nothing mattered.

A FEW MONTHS AGO, when I'd stepped into this church for our wedding, I assumed it be the last time, at least until one of my parents died. I wouldn't miss the red walls, the hard pews, the kneelers that dug into my knees week after week growing up. Never did I think I'd be back in this church so soon, for this reason. The stained-glass windows were beautiful, and as a child, I'd loved to watch the colors play across the congregation, but today, I hated them for reminding me of the beautiful, sunny world outside.

Acquaintances flocked to the church. When we got married, perhaps a hundred people scattered throughout the building, and we'd invited half our graduating high school class. Today, at least a thousand mourners crammed themselves into the rows. Everyone I'd ever met, everyone Brett had ever met, neighbors, every teacher, everyone who'd been at school with us or Brad. Everyone who'd played football against us or cheered for the opposing school. Not just from Lancaster, but the neighboring towns, too. Apparently, being murdered by terrorists brings everyone you ever knew—and plenty of people you didn't—out of the woodwork to mourn your passing. To be glad it wasn't them; their brothers, their sons, their cousins, classmates, friends. I hated them all for coming. I'd have traded all of them to get Brett back.

The thought of having to talk to all of those near-strangers made me hyperventilate. I couldn't do this. But the time for socializing was after, and I already had a plan for escape, so I bit the inside of my lip, squeezed Mom's hand, and lowered my head to at least pretend to listen.

At the front of the church, Father Thomas droned. "We gather today to honor the memory of Brett Cooper, a man taken from this world much too soon."

The sermon nauseated me. Or maybe it was the nasty coffee Mom tried to make me drink before we started. Either way, I felt like shit. Delaying the ceremony two months didn't make me feel any better when we finally held it.

As the priest spoke, I tried not to listen, to focus on other things, anything to keep from having a breakdown in the first row. I imagined Mom's reaction if I'd managed to talk the priest into using some bizarre Bible reading instead of the usual "better place" crap. How was Brett in a better place? What place was better than here, with me? With his family and friends? What place was worse than being obliterated into a billion subatomic particles?

For some reason, they put a coffin at the front of the room, draped with the American flag. I didn't know if my mom or Brett's mom asked for it, and I didn't care. A "Never forget" banner hung on the back wall. I wanted to scream and rip it down. That's the stupidest fucking slogan I've ever heard. No one with a soul was ever going to forget the day more than two thousand innocent lives were taken by terrorists.

Brett's parents sat in the pew across the aisle. His mother

sobbed into a handkerchief, loud gulping weeps that would've been comical if not for the fact that she was crying over the murder of my husband. I wanted to wail with her, but I was all cried out.

Father Thomas finished his sermon and asked if anyone wanted to come up and share their memories of Brett. Mom and I had talked about this; no way in hell could I stand up in front of two hundred people and talk about how this felt. Anyone who couldn't imagine what I was feeling right now could fuck off. I didn't want to tell them, I wanted to go home.

But my mom stood up, walked to the front, head held high. "I've known Brett for eight years, and I loved him like my own son. From the day they met, he and my Jess were inseparable. I still remember the first time he came over, when they were only fourteen years old. He dropped by to ask if Jess was home, but she was at Bible study, wouldn't be home for a couple of hours. He asked if there was anything he could do around the house to help out while he waited." She paused, smiled at the memory, and continued. "I told him that I was making Jess's confirmation dress. At the time, he and Jess were about the same height. That boy, bless his heart, stood there and wore that dress while I sewed the hem all around him. Didn't complain or anything. Just quietly waited for Jess to come home so he could see her. I knew then, he was a keeper."

A chuckle went through the crowd. Brett always hung out with my mom, helping her sew or cook or whatever she was doing. At first, I thought he was just sucking up to her so we could hang out without a chaperone, but I realized after a few months that he really enjoyed their time together. It wasn't uncommon for me to leave Brett chopping vegetables while I quizzed him on French words or read to him from our English assignments.

When we got married, I'd dreamt that one day, our children would help him in the kitchen the same way he helped my mom.

Stupid dreams. Just like my husband, they were gone in an instant.

Brett would never teach our child to cook, never change a diaper, never grow old with me. Never learn my mother's top-secret cake recipe that she always promised to teach him when he was older (the "magic" ingredient was probably butter), never start a 401(k), never hold my hand again, never kiss me. And there was nothing I could do to make any of it right again.

Forgetting about everyone else in the church, finally, I lowered my head and let the tears flow.

CHAPTER NINE

September 2019

Eighteen years ago today, my husband died.

Everyone said, "But you're so young to be a widow!" as if tragedy only happens to the elderly. As if the fact that we were newlyweds meant Brett couldn't be dead, that my loss never happened. Like I'd imagined it.

If only that were true. That Brett could've been instantly restored to me because I was too young to have lost my husband, we were too newly married.

I wasn't the only person who lost a loved one that day, not even close. That stupid mantra, "never forget," plastered everywhere like that helped. I hated seeing those reminders even more now than I did in 2001. The phrase was such an obvious overstatement that it had no meaning to me at all.

Of course we'll never forget. What are we, robots? Even after almost twenty years, I thought about Brett every day. Especially on the anniversary.

When I got in my car and pressed the ignition button, pop music blared, making me jump. I turned it down and flipped the dial, glad to get to pick my own music for once. The radio turned to an "oldies" station (how could my high school days be "oldies?"), and a familiar song filled the car.

As I drove, I tapped my fingers on the wheel, matching the music's rhythm, automatically singing along. "I'm too sexy for my shirt…" A song I hadn't listened to in years, probably because it was the song playing on the football field when Brett and I met for the first time.

I'd been headed to my first cheerleading practice, weeks before my freshman year. I hadn't really been all that excited about being a cheerleader, but I liked handstands and cartwheels, and my friends talked me into the rest.

"It'll be fun," they said. "Something we can all do together!"

Personally, I thought going to classes and studying and watching *Swan's Crossing* tapes on the VCR was something we could all do together, but my mom swore high school was about pushing your boundaries and trying new things or whatever.

Going to a high school three times the size of my junior high was scary enough; I didn't want to imagine what it would be like if all my friends made the squad and I didn't. So, I tried out. I was both surprised and relieved when they announced the results.

That day, the other girls were meeting half an hour before practice to watch the football players warm up. I'd dragged my feet as much as I could, but there was no use in stalling. I'd made my bed, and it was time to lie in it. So, I got out of Mom's car when she dropped me off and squinted into the sun. Across the field, my friends were already lined up along the bleachers in their shorts and sports bras peeking out from under their tank tops. The boom box beside them blared, blasting Right Said Fred across the field. I didn't see the fourteen-year-old future quarterback trotting toward me.

He slammed into me with a crunch. The impact sent me teetering. I tried to catch myself, rolled my ankle, and landed on my ass.

Awesome. Way to be coordinated, Jess. You'll make a terrific cheerleader.

"Oh, shit!" the guy said. "I'm so sorry!"

Shading my eyes with one hand, I peered up at him. Dark hair, cut short on the sides, a little longer on top. Brown eyes. Perfect straight nose, not like my stupid snub nose. No freckles, also unlike me. He was cute. Very cute. Much too cute to want to talk to me once he finished apologizing. At least he could be bothered to say sorry, not like some of the jerks at my old school.

My butt hurt from slamming into the ground, but I smiled at him, anyway. "S'okay. I should've been looking where I was going instead of at my friends over there."

He reached one hand down to pull me up. "You a cheerleader?"

"Yeah."

When I stepped on my left foot, a flare of pain shot up my leg. I tried to cover it up, but I'm not that great an actress.

"Are you okay?"

"I'll be fine," I lied. I took another step, but my ankle buckled, and I instinctively reached out for support.

He caught me around the waist and pulled me toward him. He felt solid. If you have to get mowed down by some guy before the first day of school, it's wise to run into one who's strong enough to carry you.

"Here. Let me help you across the field," he said.

When we got closer to the field, the football coach spotted us and yelled. "Cooper! Nice of you to—What's this?"

Coach Wall spotted us at the same time. She fussed over me for a moment before picking me up and trotting toward the bleachers, muttering about ice. I looked back at Brett over my shoulder, thinking that this moment would be a zillion times better if he'd been the one to lift me into his arms.

Then I shook my head, cursing myself for being such a hopeless romantic. High school wasn't really like *Say Anything* or *Sixteen Candles*. This wasn't the '80s.

When you're fourteen, you never really know how good-looking you are. When Brett approached me for the second time, I assumed he wanted to talk to my friend Sue. After all, she was tiny. Short, adorable, great at tumbling. Or maybe he wanted to apologize again. I had no idea he'd be into me. I'd gone from gangly to pretty practically overnight, and the change in how boys reacted took me by surprise.

From early on, we were inseparable. We both had overbearing parents who put a lot of pressure on us to be who they thought we should be. We both dreamed of leaving our small town and moving to the big city, both loved *Seinfeld* and *My So-Called Life*, and were fascinated by the human body. He even watched *Swan's Crossing* with me. In ninth grade, that's more than enough to form a lasting bond.

Until the day he died, I never dated anyone else. When I was fourteen, Brett gave me my first kiss. We were each other's first loves, the golden couple, crowned Prom Queen and King. When we announced our engagement after college, people were surprised we'd waited so long.

Some days, I still couldn't believe he was gone. In the back of my mind, part of me always expected to run into him, everywhere I went. Even when I started dating again, I waited for Brett to show up and ask me what the heck I was doing. And on the rare occasions I allowed myself to ponder the afterlife, I expected to see my husband there, waiting for me at the pearly gates, holding one hand out to me.

For the most part, I didn't believe in Heaven, but losing Brett made me want it to exist with a desperate need.

The song's chorus brought me back to reality, and with a shake of my head, I switched the radio off. The nineties music I'd once enjoyed brought me no pleasure anymore. And on this day of all days, listening to the news was out of the question.

So much time had passed, most of my employees didn't even know about Brett. I'd taken the day off after bin Laden was killed, unable to explain to everyone why that news didn't make me happy. Of course it didn't. More death wasn't better. Killing the enemy didn't bring my husband back.

If it stopped more killing, great, but it didn't fill the void inside me.

Even after all this time, I couldn't face going to work on this day. Listening to the news on the TVs in the waiting room all day. I never planned to take the day off, but when the sun rose on September 11, I always found myself making the same call.

"Quincy Orthopedics," a man said.

"Hey," I said. "It's me. I'm taking a vacation day."

Teddy's voice exhibited zero surprise. "Of course you are. Take care of yourself, Jess. Do what you need to do. Are you taking Ethan out of school?"

"No. It's just another day for him. The school won't make a big deal out of it."

"In that case, you should call my friend Steve and see if he wants to spend the day with you," Teddy said. "It would do you both some good."

Not for the first time, I mentally shook my head at my partner's interest in my personal life. I pictured Steve's friendly smile, neatly trimmed goatee, and kind eyes. The image raised no emotions within me whatsoever. A nice enough guy, but not for me. "No. I don't think that's going to work out after all."

Teddy clucked his tongue into the phone. "You've got to put yourself out there. It's been, what, ten years since you last had a serious relationship?"

Eighteen, but who was counting? Other than my mother, my friends...I'd been on a few dates here and there, but Teddy's quiet gasp on the other end of the phone told me he realized his faux pas. "I'm sorry, Jess. I didn't mean..."

"I know," I said. "It's okay. You know I like to take things slow. Running a practice and raising a child by myself doesn't leave a lot of time for making friends. This isn't the right time for me to get involved with someone. It'll happen."

"What will be the right time?" he asked softly.

"Once Ethan leaves for college?"

Teddy sighed. "Okay, I see your point. I'm sorry."

"Anyway, I'm headed to a resort in the mountains outside Montreal. It's too early for snow, but I can hike and practice my college French and go to a spa and not worry that I'll burst into tears while explaining to a patient how to take care of himself after we repair his rotator cuff."

"I approve," Teddy said. "You haven't taken a vacation day in almost a year. Take as long as you need. I don't want to see you back here for at least two weeks."

"But what about—?"

"There are plenty of doctors here. We'll reschedule. Your patients will manage. Doctor, heal thyself."

"Fine," I grumbled. But when I put the phone down, I was smiling.

Maybe if I took some time off to clear my head, I'd be ready to give dating more of a shot when I got back. Steve wasn't too bad, even if he spit whenever he said the letter S. An unfortunate name, really. Too bad his parents couldn't have known before they named him Steven Samuel Schmidt II. Poor guy. And yes, that was an immature reason for not going out with him. The fact that I was looking for stupid reasons to reject poor Steve spoke volumes about my interest level.

Maybe when I got back I'd meet someone that gave me butterflies in my stomach, would make me stop rolling my eyes at the romantic comedies offered on Netflix. Someone I couldn't wait to bring home to meet my friends and family. One day, I might even be able to watch a Nicholas Sparks movie without throwing pillows at the TV.

An hour after hanging up the phone, I was on my way, headed west on the Mass Pike in my Nissan crossover SUV. In early September, the leaves weren't yet turning colors. The lush green landscape promised a new life. Or else I was trying way too hard to be optimistic about sitting in a hotel room by myself, mourning the husband I'd never be able to replace.

No matter how many online profiles I read, how many blind dates people arranged for me, no one else seemed good enough for me. After all, Brett and I built up a lifetime of memories before we even became adults. No one else knew all my little quirks and secrets, got jokes that stemmed from watching the same TV shows over and over, could read my moods and my silences.

Mom's voice echoed in my ear. "Replacing Brett in your life doesn't mean replacing him in your heart. There's always room inside a person for more love."

She was probably right, but what did she know? She stayed with my father for thirty-five years, letting him tell her how to act, who to be friends with, what to wear, what to believe, how to think. Since he died of cancer, she'd finally found herself, blossoming into a new person. No one had been surprised when she started dating a couple of weeks after the service.

How sad that my sixty-year-old mother had a more exciting sex life than I did.

Only seven more hours until I could get to the resort, pour a glass of wine, and lose myself in a long, hot bath before starting a reality show marathon. I'd make a quick call to check in, and then I was on my own to grieve in silence. My family mourned Brett, too, but it wasn't the same. For one day each year, I needed to be alone to deal with the feelings inside me.

Or maybe what I needed was to go to the hotel bar and find a man to spend a few hours with. With a wry smile, I shook my head. That was Teddy's voice in my ear, not mine. One-night stands weren't my style; not even anonymous one-night stands in the middle of nowhere with a man I was guaranteed to never see again. I'd tried to force myself to feel attraction to strangers, and it never seemed to work out. It was difficult to even understand when people talked about instant lust, because I'd never experienced it. And I had other things on my mind than sex.

Taking my time, driving slow, and stopping whenever I wanted, I reached the resort around four o'clock.

Red and light green turrets topped the exterior of the hotel, which resembled a Swiss chalet. A mountain dotted with trees soared into the clouds, reminding me how insignificant my problems were in the grand scheme of things. I wanted to stand on top of that mountain, breathe in clean, fresh air, and remind myself of all the things in my life I had to be grateful for. But first, the whirlpool tubs from the pictures on the website called my name.

A valet took my car with a promise that it would be available any time I needed it. I had no intention of going anywhere outside of walking distance, and I told him so. Before entering, I stopped to enjoy the view.

As I approached the front door, I tapped out a message to my mom on my phone, letting her know I arrived okay. Intent on the device, I didn't notice when the front door opened, and I walked right into the woman exiting.

CHAPTER TEN

"I'm sorry, ma'am. Excuse me," the woman said.

In my shock at recognizing the voice I never expected to hear again, I stopped dead in the doorway. The timbre was higher, more feminine, but still—I knew that voice. I knew that face, too. The cheeks were smoother, make-up changing some of the contours, but that thick, dark hair hadn't changed—it was longer, sure, but still had the silky texture I'd envied as a teenager. The slightly crooked nose was the same, a bump from where his older brother broke it when he was sixteen. And the eyes. A person could change their entire appearance, but always kept their eyes. Those were Brett's eyes.

My heart stopped. How was this possible? What was going on? Why?

In my shock, words escaped me without my meaning to speak. "Holy shit. Is that really you?"

My suitcase continued to roll forward, the back hitting my knees. Stumbling, I stepped forward, putting one hand out to steady myself. The woman before me—impossibly, my dead husband—stepped back, shaking her head.

For a split second, I thought the long drive went to my head. The thoughts in my head couldn't possibly be true. I tried to laugh off my faux pas. "I'm sorry," I said. "You have a very strong resemblance to my husband. I don't know what came over me—"

I broke off because she was still shaking her head, one hand over her mouth. And as her brown eyes filled with tears, I knew with one hundred percent certainty that I hadn't made a mistake. How or why the late Brett Cooper came to be standing in front of me, in this Canadian hotel, wearing a dress, was a mystery, but all the same, there was no doubt.

It was him.

Clothes and makeup could hide a lot, but they couldn't hide the bump on his nose I'd kissed a thousand times. I knew the look of mortification in his eyes, I knew the set of his shoulders, the curves of his lips, and the unique scent of him, beneath the lilac perfume. It startled me to realize she'd chosen a scent so similar to the one I used to wear. These days, I smelled more like hand sanitizer and coffee than flowers. Of course, Brett wouldn't know that.

Before I could say anything, she turned and sprinted back into the hotel. If that hadn't happened, perhaps I could've written the whole thing off. Fatigue gives people delusions, right? A physical manifestation of my sadness? Or the stress of it being the anniversary of Brett's death, combined with several hours on the road listening to a book about magic? But if I'd made a mistake, the woman I'd just walked into wouldn't have run away from me.

Dropping the handle of my bag, I sprinted after her. When we were kids, Brett won every time we raced, having the benefit of longer legs. I'd have expected the high heels to slow him down, but apparently not. As a doctor, used to jumping whenever the phone rings, I should've had the advantage, but the time it took to overcome my shock meant he got a head start.

"Stop!" I called, as if it were a magic word. If my quarry heard me, I couldn't tell.

My mind whirled as we raced across the lobby and out a side

door. A ghost? Witness protection? Some kind of horrible prank? World's worst reality show? Long-lost twin, separated at birth?

Before I could make any sense of anything, a young child stepped into the path several yards ahead of us. A little girl, perhaps three years old, tow-headed and blissfully unaware of the danger stampeding toward her.

"Watch out," I yelled, not sure if I was yelling at the toddler, her parents, or my husband. Hopefully someone within the sound of my voice spoke English because I couldn't remember the warning in French.

Brett leapt over the child, brilliantly avoiding a collision. When he landed, one ankle turned. He yelled and tried to keep walking, but his knee buckled, and he fell to the ground not far from the child. The girl's parents jerked her from the road and down the sidewalk, threw an apology toward Brett, and dragged her through the open door of one of the shops lining the road. The little girl seemed unharmed, so I ignored them.

Slowing, I continued heading for Brett, until he stood and began limping away. I hadn't won this race yet. With a burst of speed, I moved ahead and planted myself in the path in front of him.

"Stop."

He stared at the ground, and I grabbed her arm. "Brett. Stop."

Finally, he met my eyes. "You can't call me that. Please, Jess. I'm not Brett anymore. No one here knows that name."

The words were a punch to my gut. I knew, but I didn't really *know* until he admitted it. Even while running down the street, part of me never expected to hear this woman say my name. There was no way she could've known me. Unless she was Brett.

My mind whirled. I couldn't begin to understand how to process all of this. Not today, of all days. The day my husband died. Also, apparently, the day he came back. Why was he dressed like a woman?

At the look on her face, the pleading in her voice, long buried memories rushed to the forefront of my mind, hitting me like a ton of bricks. My razor, duller than I thought it should be after only a couple of uses. Old lingerie unworn for months, pushed to the front of the drawer. Hour after hour of Lifetime Original Movies, watched without complaint. Brett's fascination with looking at my body, even when he didn't want to touch it. The fact that he always used private browser windows, swearing it was a good habit to get into for privacy. I'd wondered if he was having an online affair, but I'd never considered this, whatever *this* was.

Before I could begin to think of what to say or do, he—she—took another step, and her ankle twisted again. I shoved aside the myriad emotions roiling within me and reached out without thinking. "Let me help you."

"I'm fine."

"No, you're not," I said. "And I can help you. I'm a doctor."

"Really?" The pride in her voice upon hearing those words was unmistakable.

"Yes, really. A lot's happened in the past eighteen years. You'd know that if you'd been around." I didn't hide the note of bitterness that snuck into my voice. Part of me wanted to walk away, leave this person on the side of the road with a possibly broken foot. If this was Brett, he didn't deserve my compassion.

Except we don't give compassion because it's *deserved*, and if this was my Brett, I needed to know what happened to him. I'd loved him too much to walk away, even if he'd abandoned me.

Tears filled her eyes. "Yeah. I'm sorry. What are you doing here?"

My hands went to my hips. "You're asking me that? What are you doing not dead?"

Her face turned bright red. "I'm sorry. You're right. I have no right to ask you anything."

"No, you don't. But I drove up from Boston to spend some time alone because today is the anniversary of my husband's death."

At my words, she flinched. Pain flashed through her eyes, but I didn't feel terribly inclined to make her feel better.

"You still live in Boston? I would've thought you moved to Los Angeles, like you dreamed."

"Yeah, well, a lot of things changed for me that day. I imagine you have a few things to tell me, too." I hesitated. "You said no one knows Brett. What do I call you?"

She flinched at the sound of her own name. "My name is Christa McCall. Brett died years ago."

This was insanity. Less than half an hour ago, I was a grieving widow who'd waited much too long to move on. And now, the universe was punishing me somehow by sending some woman into my life who thought she was my dead husband.

Except, that wasn't what was happening at all. My head spun. I didn't know what to say, what to do, where to even start. I needed to lie down. Or get out of there. Something.

"Christa," I repeated mechanically. "I always liked that name."

A chill hit me, and I shivered, rubbing my arms. The temperature must've dropped ten degrees since I'd left my car, unthinkingly leaving my coat draped across the passenger seat. Going to get it would give me an escape. But if I walked away, would I find her again? Did I even want to?

What the hell was going on? Why was this happening to me?

"I'm sorry. I can't. This is…no."

"I know," she whispered, looking at a group of people who'd exited the hotel and started walking toward us. "We need to talk. I'll come to your room, and I'll explain everything. Later."

Letting her out of my sight before getting an explanation seemed like the dumbest thing I could possibly do, but we couldn't stand there forever. Maybe if I walked away, I'd wake up and find out this was all a bad dream. Or if she vanished, I could forget this ever happened and resume my life as Jess Cooper, tragic 9/11 widow.

I hated that life.

No. I loved my life now. Loved my job, my family. I hated being a statistic.

My heart pounded. None of the thoughts swirling around inside me made any sense. Numbness crept through my veins; I watched a stranger moving and talking in my body. Clearly, I was in shock. I only knew how to treat other people for shock. In that moment, all I could think was what a funny word it was: Shock. SHOCK! Shock. Say a word enough, it starts to become meaningless. I needed to sit down before I fell.

Christa cleared her throat, and I realized that I was just standing there, holding her in place, staring blankly down the street. I didn't even remember what she'd said to me.

"Huh?"

"Can I come to your room to talk about this in about half an hour?"

Now knowing what else to do, I nodded, finally releasing her arm. "I'm going to go check in. I don't know my room number yet, but we can meet in the bar and talk there."

She shook her head. "I work at the hotel. I'll look up the room number."

If she worked at the hotel, that at least meant she might not disappear again.

"Fine. I need to unpack, have a drink, take a bath. Come by in an hour."

ALONE IN MY ROOM, I paced. Thinking, seething, wondering. Why had Brett abandoned me? Why had he missed his flight? The thought that he'd somehow managed to live and escape after his plane hit the World Trade Center with no memory of his former life was ridiculous. I didn't allow myself to consider that possibility for a second.

Since he couldn't have survived the crash, that meant Brett must've intentionally walked out of my life. He didn't die. He left me. Dying isn't a choice, but abandonment is. That knowledge tarnished every memory I had of him, of our relationship. Every kiss, every caress, every declaration of love had been a lie. A man who loved his wife didn't leave her a couple of months after their wedding.

Emotions flashed and raged before I managed to get a firm grip on any of them. Elation that my best friend and lover hadn't died after all. Fury that he'd left me. Confusion at seeing him dressed as a woman. Sadness that I'd lost the past eighteen years with him. Rage that my son grew up without a father. Astonishment at everything. My surprise pushed most of the other emotions aside. I had no idea what to do after I was done crying and pacing and raging and hitting pillows.

I needed to call Ethan, to let him know. No, I couldn't. None of this made sense. What would I even say? Where to start?

Only one person could help me sort through everything, and that person was both the only and last person I wanted to see. It took two bottles from the mini-bar to give me the courage to fix my destroyed makeup and hair so I'd look presentable when she showed up.

By the time a knock sounded on the other door, a thousand questions swarmed around in my brain. But when the door opened and I saw her standing there, all other thoughts were crushed by the swell of rage that rushed through me.

"Hey," she said, stepping past me into the room.

"What the fuck do you think you're doing? Who are you? Why are you here?" I slammed the door shut behind her and Brett—Christa—my husband? wife? stepped into the room.

It was hard to think of the feminine person standing before me as the man I once slept beside every night. The form was unmistakably female. Not even knowing which pronouns to use only made the mix of emotions swirling within me more power-ful. This was the man who promised to love, honor, and cherish me. The man I mourned for more than a decade. And he was alive and he was a she. That bastard.

The rage was so strong. I wasn't Jess anymore. Someone I didn't even know had control of my body when I stepped toward Christa and slapped her across the face. Twice. Again.

She grabbed my hands, and my sobs turned into screams. I struggled, but her grip held firm. When I realized that I couldn't get loose, my knees buckled. Christa led me to the bed. I didn't want this person to comfort me—all I wanted was to run out of the room, drive home, and forget any of this ever happened. But I was crying too hard to stand.

Long arms wrapped around me, somehow both alien and familiar. This wasn't my Brett, didn't smell like Axe body wash and Suave shampoo. This Brett smelled like a bouquet. Like a woman. The voice that murmured meaningless plati-tudes in my ear wasn't as rough, as husky as it used to be. It was womanly, a voice I'd never have expected to hear from my husband's mouth. But the touch, the words, reminded me that I was sitting on the bed with my best friend. With the person I grew up with, expected to grow old with. The person I'd lost. Finding him again was a miracle.

Even if he looked like a woman, and I didn't understand why. I didn't understand any of this.

When the tears wouldn't stop, I stopped fighting them. Instead, I leaned into the warm body and let myself sob.

A long time passed before I composed myself enough to carry on a conversation. Brett/Christa handed me a tissue, which I gratefully accepted.

"I'm so sorry," I said. "I don't know what came over me."

"I do," she said. "You've had one hell of a shock. I'd say your reaction was better than I expected."

"You thought about this moment?" I sure hadn't. All the

times I'd allowed myself to dream of Brett being alive, this never occurred to me.

"Of course I did. At first, I dreaded it. But then I started to wonder. Late at night, I'd let my mind wander, think about what if. I've missed you, Jess. I've wondered what you're doing now, who you turned into, whether you found love…" She trailed off, looking at her fingernails.

I swallowed. "I did find love. I married my best friend three weeks after I graduated college. Remember?"

The words sounded bitter even to my own ears. I may have spent the better part of two decades dealing with the death of my husband, but I'd only had a couple of hours to adjust to him being alive. Her being alive. This was all so confusing. My head hurt. "Maybe I should go."

When I stood, Christa grabbed my hand. "Please stay. I'd like to talk to you. I'm so sorry."

My head and my heart pulled me in different directions. My brain screamed that this was not a good situation, that I should run. My heart told me that Brett had clearly been through a lot, that he was once my best friend and lover, and that I should hear her out, just for a bit.

I reached for another tissue and wiped my eyes. "I don't even know what to call you. Brett/Christa. He/she. Him/her. Husband/wife. Dead/alive. Who are you?"

"I'm Christa. I've been living and working as Christa for eighteen years, since I moved to Canada." She cleared her throat. "I know this must be hard for you—"

My laugh cut her off. "I… God. Yeah. I don't even know what to say. Christa. I'm so confused right now. This is all so…What the hell is this? Are you in some kind of reality show? Witness protection?"

"No, I'm just me. Christa. A woman living in Canada, trying to lead a good life."

"Why didn't you just tell me?" Maybe that was what hurt

most of all. Once, I'd have sworn on my life that we told each other everything. Clearly, I'd have been wrong.

"Tell you what, exactly? That I'm a woman?"

I nodded.

She twirled a lock of hair around one finger as she searched for the right words. Brett used to do that, when his hair grew too long. Seeing it somehow made my heart ache both more and less. "I didn't even know myself, not really. Besides, what would you have done?"

"Freaked out, probably. Called your parents." A realization hit me. "Oh, God. Your parents. Your family."

"I don't have a family," she said quietly. "I gave all that up years ago. Brett Cooper died on September 11, 2001. Christa doesn't have a family."

A pang hit me. She must've been so lonely. All by herself in a foreign county. No family. Probably too afraid of being found out to make real friends, at least in the beginning.

And yet, it was her own fucking fault. How could she do this to me? My best friend, my lover, the person I promised to spend the rest of my life with. Not knowing what else to do, I perched on the edge of the bed, putting my head between my knees.

Christa rubbed my back. For a moment, I let her, but it was all too much. I couldn't stay in this room. The walls were closing in on me. With a cry, I jumped to my feet. "I'm sorry, I can't."

I rushed for the door. Behind me, Christa called my name, but I didn't stop. There was too much to deal with, and I couldn't work out how I felt while she watched me. I raced to the end of the hall, down the stairs to the ground floor, and out. I didn't know where I was going, and I didn't care.

CHAPTER ELEVEN

Halfway across the hotel lobby, I realized I'd just fled my own room with nowhere to go like a dumbass. Not knowing what else to do, I wandered into the bar and ordered a shot of whiskey. Liquid courage. I waited for the welcome numbness of the alcohol to hit me. It didn't come; I hadn't felt anything since my eyes locked with Brett's. Christa's. Dammit. There was no need to drink away my feelings: the shock was doing an excellent job of that. I couldn't think, could only react, try to appear normal.

Still, the alcohol couldn't hurt. After downing a second shot, I forced my feet to carry me back to the room. Maybe I'd get lucky, and Christa would have left.

No such luck. When the door swung open, she sat on the bed, right where I left her.

"You knew I'd be back?"

"I hoped so."

"You know me so well," I grumbled. "I don't know you anymore at all."

"Then let's go somewhere you can get to know me. Some place where you can walk out if you need to. I'm pretty open.

And, God, Jess, it's good to see you. I never let myself think about how much I miss you. I'm so sorry I had to leave."

I wanted to believe her. Brett had always been a terrible liar, or so I'd thought. Like the time he told me he hadn't jumbled all my shoes in the closet, that a panther had broken into our house. He'd never been able to hold my gaze, though, which made it easy. Christa stared at me, meeting my eyes steadily. Had she gotten better at lying? Or did she mean the words?

After a moment's hesitation, I nodded. It was easier to go along with her than to argue, and my brain still wasn't working properly. Without speaking, I grabbed my jacket off the chair it had landed on when I entered. The two of us headed silently down the hall toward the elevators. She was probably at as much of a loss for words as I was.

When we got outside, away from the hotel, I finally found my voice. "How did this...? When? Why?" My face burned, and I couldn't finish the sentence. "I'm so sorry. It's none of my business."

"No, it's fine," Christa said. "I know you must have a million questions. I had all those questions too, and more. It's not like I woke up one day and said, 'You know, I think I'd like to try looking like a woman.' That's not how it works. At least, that's not how it was for me."

"How does it work?" Science. Focus on the science, don't think about the emotions. That was something I could do. Knowledge could help me understand one day. Maybe.

Her words came out woodenly, as if this was a speech she'd practiced or maybe recited over and over. She must be exhausted from having to explain her life choices. For a minute, I wanted to withdraw the question. But having more information would help me process, to start feeling normally.

"It's a long process," she said. "For me, the decision came after decades of feeling like something was wrong, months and years of agonizing over how to make things better. Not all trans people go through that. There was a lot of soul-searching, confusion, self-loathing, and therapy for me, before and after I got to Canada. It took time to learn to accept why I felt the way I did, and then longer to decide how to make things right. Some people never start, or never complete, the physical changes, some do them in stages. Some people have the full surgery all at once."

It felt like she was talking about someone else, a stranger. Not like my husband saying these things to me. A horrible, dark feeling rose in my chest. Quickly, I asked another question to distract myself from the feelings.

"What about you?"

"For years, I felt off. My body wasn't right. You remember how we used to pore over those biology and anatomy books in high school?" I nodded, and she continued, "You always wanted to be a doctor, so of course it made sense. But I was just fascinated with the bodies. I know you thought it was all about sex, or that I was helping you, but that wasn't it. The female bodies were so beautiful, and my body felt *wrong*. I don't know how else to say it. On the inside, I've always been a woman. It took a long time for me to come to terms with why I felt the way I did, and even then, I needed to gather the courage to live my truth."

"Is this why you never came home?" My voice cracked, but I didn't try to hide the tears forming in my eyes. "Why you left me?"

The sadness in her eyes made the jumble of emotions inside me whirl even more. She didn't get to be sad about leaving me. And behind the sadness, a hint of pity made me want to smack her. She didn't get to feel sorry for me. Not after everything she did.

"I never planned to leave you. I didn't want the job, didn't want to move to Los Angeles, and the thought of getting on a plane terrified me. While I was waiting, I had a panic attack, and when the flight started boarding, I gave my boarding pass to this guy in the waiting area. Dan. He was there saying good-bye to his kids because he couldn't afford to go with them. He got on the plane instead of me." Her voice cracked. "I live with his death on my conscience every day.

"I know what you think, how you must feel. But my leaving wasn't about you."

My heart broke at the words. Running out on me wasn't about me. Abandoning me wasn't about me. *Faking his own death to get out of being married to me* wasn't about me. I just shook my head, not even knowing how to react to that. Obviously, Brett had gone through something huge, but hearing him say that the decision to walk away had nothing to do with me stabbed me in the gut. How horribly dismissive.

"I guess I thought I meant more to you than that."

Her eyes widened. "Oh, Jess. That's not what I meant at all. Of course, you meant something to me. You meant everything to me. I thought you deserved better. You remember how miserable I was?"

When someone you love dies, it's easy to push aside all the bad, to remember only the good. After years of practice, it took me a minute to recall those last few days. "I remember how freaked out you were. How you were so quiet for days before the flight, and you kept trying to think up excuses to stay home."

Now that she mentioned it, I also remembered the fighting, the tears, the frustration, but now wasn't the time to mention those things.

"Yeah. I wanted to go, for you, but in the end, I couldn't. I wandered around, trying to figure out how to tell you what I'd done, when I saw the first plane crash on the TV. And when I realized that it was *my* plane that hit the second tower...I know I've never really believed in religion or anything, but on that day, it felt like God had finally freed me. Like He made things right by leading me to decide not to board. I guess, I had to feel like I was given a second chance, like there was some greater purpose, or the guy who took my boarding pass died for nothing."

"I'm very glad you didn't die that day. What if I hadn't made you accept an interview for a job you never wanted in a city you didn't want to live in? Would this still have happened?"

Christa squeezed my hand, sending a wave of warmth through me. This was so alien, yet also weirdly familiar. "Probably. I wasn't happy with who I was. In the end, I'd have come to the same conclusions. The only difference is if I hadn't been on that plane, I'd have spent God knows how long hiding it, hurting you, and you'd have started to resent me."

"No, I…" Whatever words I might have used to finish that sentence would have been a lie, so I didn't.

She continued as if I hadn't spoken. "We'd probably have moved to Los Angeles, where I'd have been miserable while you went to medical school. How did you even pay for it on your own?"

The blood drained from my face. "I used the life insurance money. Your insurance."

"See? We couldn't afford the schools you wanted. You wouldn't have gotten the life insurance, which means you would never have been able to go."

"You think I care about that?" I stopped dead in the middle of the cobbled street, not caring that other tourists had to move around us. My heart pounded with fury. "You think I would've chosen to trade my husband, the only man I ever loved, for a medical license?"

"Of course not, but your career is the silver lining. I never would've been the husband you deserved. I woke up every day hating myself. I resented you for being so good, so happy with being you; something I never thought I could be. The plane crash saved me, Jess. Before September 11, all I did was wonder how much longer I had to go through the motions, whether I'd be able to find a way out or whether I'd get so desperate I had no choice but to end my life."

My blood ran cold. All those years, living beside him, and I'd had no idea. He'd hinted at it once, one day when we were in high school, but not a peep since. I'd thought it was just a bad day, that he'd gotten over it. How could I have been so self-absorbed? How did I miss emotions that ran so deep?

"That day was tragic for everyone, including me. I sat in a state of shock, just like everyone else. But then I had a revelation. All of a sudden, I didn't have to worry about facing you, of putting you through fights and therapy. Brett Cooper was dead, and Jess Cooper was free to start her life over with a husband who appreciated her."

"So glad the terrorists could help you out by killing thousands of people," I said bitterly.

She flinched. "You know it's not like that. It was a horrible day for everyone. But if even a tiny light can be borne out of that type of darkness, Christa is that light. And I'm proud to be Christa.

"I can't say I'm not glad I didn't get on that plane. That doesn't mean I wouldn't go back and stop the attacks if I had the chance. I'm not trading my life for all the others—that was never a decision I got to make. It's not the choice I would've made, if I'd known."

On the surface, her words didn't make much sense, but the more I thought about it, the more I sort of got what she was trying to say. "Yeah. I'm sorry."

"No, Jess, I'm sorry for hurting you. I really am. But I'm not sorry for who I've become or for being happy with myself now." Again, she met my eyes steadily. Her pupils nearly swallowed the brown. Not a hint that she was lying. Maybe I was fooling myself, but she seemed sincere.

"Or for having better legs than me?" I grumbled.

She smiled. "Longer legs, maybe. Never better."

"Still. Unfair."

Our walk brought us to a small poutinerie located at the base of the mountain. My stomach growled, reminding me that I'd meant to eat dinner at least an hour ago. After we ordered and sat, Christa asked if I had more questions for her.

I glanced around. "Is this the place? Is it okay to talk here?"

"Absolutely. It's so crowded, no one will overhear anything."

"Okay." My head was so full of questions, it was impossible to know where to start. "What is the preferred term? What do I call you?"

"Call me Christa," she said. "My pronouns are she and her, just like yours. Honestly, I prefer that you call me a woman, because that's what I am. But transwoman is fine too."

I leaned in and lowered my voice. "Do you have a vagina?"

Her jaw ticked, reminding me how Brett used to bite his tongue when he was angry. Shit. That was a horribly insensitive thing to say. "I mean..."

She swallowed, and when she spoke, her voice had gone up three octaves. "Why? Do you want to see it?"

Our eyes met, and I realized she was joking to hide her discomfort. My cheeks flamed at my faux pas. "Oh, God. I'm so sorry. I shouldn't have asked that."

"No, you absolutely shouldn't. If anyone else asked, I'd walk away. But under the circumstances, I'll let it go this once."

I started to apologize again, but she cut me off.

"No, really, it's fine." She took a bite of her pulled pork and bacon-covered poutine and chewed it thoroughly before answering. "I started living as a woman a few months after 9/11. My friend Bo helped me get started. He did drag, and his confidence inspired me to explore myself. I had to learn not to be afraid." She paused, blinking rapidly. I wanted to ask more, but waited patiently for her to continue.

"After I moved to Quebec, I started seeing a psychiatrist who had worked with people with gender dysphoria. It wasn't a specialty back then. My doctor started me on female hormones and had me live as a woman, as Christa McCall for a few years. The estrogen raised my voice a bit, but I trained to make it even higher, more feminine."

That was the difference I'd noticed when she first spoke, the one thing that might have made me think this was all a fluke, if

Christa hadn't recognized me. Brett's voice had been rough. Christa's voice was softer. I told her that.

"I was too surprised to pretend not to recognize you. That would've required quick thinking. And I've never been able to lie to you."

I snorted and swept my gaze from head to toe. "Oh, really?"

She flushed. "That's not the same. I wasn't lying. I didn't know who I was, not when we were kids. Part of me can't believe you recognized me. I've had a ton of work done: my brow's been softened, my nose shaved, and I got cheek implants."

"I'd know you anywhere. Besides, your eyes haven't changed at all. It's like my soul recognized yours. We always had that special connection." Even with her looking the way she did, sitting here with my Brett seemed so comfortable, so natural. Just another layer to add to my intense confusion.

"Yeah, we really have." She squeezed my hand, looking down and blinking rapidly before she continued. "Anyway, to answer your original question, I did have a couple of operations. I couldn't go through the system, because my identifying documents said I was already a female. So, I talked to the friends who helped me get across the border. They know a lot of people, made some calls for me, and found a doctor who'd accept cash and wouldn't ask questions. That doctor gave me breasts in 2006. I kept saving, and five years later, I had the money to complete gender reassignment."

"Was it weird?" My breasts were such an integral part of my identity, waking up without them seemed like as much a loss as if I woke up without a nose or my left arm.

"No." She smiled at me. "That's the difference. I felt like, finally, my body was right. I'd been fixed. Waking up after the surgery felt like coming home. For the first time, I wasn't at war with my own body."

"Then I'm glad you did it," I said. "I just wish you'd been

secure enough in me, in our relationship, to tell me what was going on. Maybe I could've helped you."

"Maybe, but I couldn't worry about how other people would feel or think, or whether my actions might hurt you. Sometimes in life, a person has to put themselves first. I didn't have a choice. I was drowning, and you couldn't save me." She took a deep breath. "But I'm glad to see you again. I always hated having to hide part of myself from you, and I hated not being able to tell you I was alive and well." She took a deep breath. "And I'll understand if you tell me to go to hell and never talk to me again."

My eyes met hers. Christa wasn't the only one carrying a big secret. I could've nodded, walked away, checked into a different hotel, and never spoken to her again. But that wouldn't have been fair to anyone. I didn't know what I thought, how I felt about any of this. Couldn't know, until I got a lot of time to myself to process. But there was one thing I did know, and that one truth propelled my next words.

"From the day I met you, I wanted you in my life," I began. "I fell in love with the person that you were then. I don't know who you are now, but I owe it to myself to find out."

She smiled and opened her mouth, but I raised one hand to quiet her.

"Because," I said, "if I walk out that door and never speak to you again, it wouldn't be fair to our son."

CHAPTER TWELVE

A million emotions washed over Christa's face. Her mouth opened and closed, but no sound came out. I waited, watching her over my water glass, not sure whether to say anything else. Maybe there was a better way to tell her. Maybe there was a better way for her to tell me she'd faked her own death. Or any way, other than waiting for me to literally run into her. Too late now.

Finally, she eked out a noise that nearly resembled a word. "Wh-ow?"

My lips curled upward, but there was no humor in my smile. I downed the glass and folded my arms on the tabletop. "Before you left, remember I wasn't feeling great? Lethargic, not really hungry? I wasn't sick in the mornings, not then, but I didn't feel right."

For a split second, a huge smile split her face. Then, slowly, her smile dropped. I didn't know if she was sad to find out she had a child, sad that she missed out on almost eighteen years of his life, or worried that he wouldn't want to meet her. Possibly all of the above.

She'd get around to telling me how she felt eventually. But first, I had a lot to share with her. "I scheduled a doctor's appointment after you bought your plane ticket. My period had been late before, so I wasn't sure, but I suspected. That was actually why I had my wedding dress out to make you the square in the first place. I had christening gowns on the brain. I didn't want to mention it until I knew for sure. But then I never got a chance to tell you."

What if I'd told Brett before he left? Would he have gotten on the plane and died in the attack? Or would he have still had a panic attack and come home, grateful for a second chance at life, excited to start a family with me?

Christa wore the same question on her face, but I wasn't about to ask. Maybe knowing about the child would've convinced Brett to make a commitment to his family, but maybe that would have killed him. Besides, I couldn't go back and change anything, even if I wanted to. The train of thought starting with "what if…?" led straight off a cliff.

Her question interrupted my thoughts. "What's his name?"

My gaze dropped to the table. I'd spent a lot of time debating the best name, almost choosing "Brett" before I decided it would simply be too painful. "Ethan. After his grandfather."

"That's a lovely name. Ethan Cooper, II."

"Thank you. I always thought his father would have appreciated the gesture."

"I do, Jess. Really." Our eyes finally met. The storminess in Christa's brown eyes mirrored my own inner turmoil. "Is he here?"

I shook my head. "I left him with my mother for a few days. I always take September 11 off work, but this year, I needed to get away. Most of the time, I bury my pain, but on anniversaries, everything comes rushing back."

She reached toward me, but I pulled away. Maybe we were talking, but I wasn't ready for hand-holding. Part of me still wanted to run away and forget all of this ever happened.

"I'm so sorry to have put you through this," she said. "I

never meant to hurt you. But it would mean the world to me if I could meet him, even once."

"I know, I guess. I'm still processing." I cleared my throat. "I'll think about it. This is a lot to take in, and I don't want to make any rash decisions. I mean, I know, legally. . . Give me time. Ethan's almost eighteen now. I'll have to talk to him about it."

A hurt look crossed her face. After all she put me through, it was petty, but part of me was glad to see that she even had feelings.

"Sure. Take all the time you need," she said.

A thought hit me, and a slight smile tugged at the corners of my lips. "If you come to Boston, I can't wait to see the look on my mother's face."

Christa chuckled. "She hasn't changed?"

"Oh, she's mellowed a lot since my father died. But she might see your resurrection as proof of the grace of God and go back to trying to make me and Ethan join her at church every Sunday."

"Tell me more about him. His birthday, anything."

Brett should've been there with me. Should have been my birth partner, gone to Lamaze classes, brought me kale and peanut butter or whatever to satisfy cravings. He should have held my hand during the birth, smoothed my hair back, brought me ice chips. Should have held his baby in his arms, signed the birth certificate himself. If he hadn't left us, he'd know everything already.

Part of me felt like he didn't deserve to know anything, that he'd forfeited that right by walking away. But that wasn't fair. He didn't intend to leave me with a baby. And it was impossible for me to understand what he was going through when he left.

"He was born a week early, in April 2002. Maybe he sensed how lost I was, I don't know, but he was a perfect angel. Slept, ate, hardly ever cried. I had the life insurance money, so I didn't bother looking for work right away. I'd already been accepted to medical school, so there was no point. That fall, Ma moved in with us and I started classes."

"I'm so sorry you were alone for all that."

"Me, too." I glared at her for a minute. "Don't think for a second that you're forgiven. But I think I kinda get that you were going through something huge. You were scared. My upbringing suggested I wouldn't understand, and who knows? Maybe I wouldn't have. The world has changed a lot in the past eighteen years. Transpeople made enormous strides in the past few years...at least among younger people and liberals."

"We made progress, and then we lost it after the 2016 election."

I heaved a big sigh. I couldn't begin to figure out how to feel about anything anymore. "Maybe you did the right thing. If you'd told me what you were going through back then, we still would've lost each other. Maybe I'd have tried to stop you from knowing Ethan, just because I didn't understand. I don't know."

"Thank you."

"I'm still furious with you, of course. But, maybe one day, if you win Ethan over, we can be friends again."

She grinned. "I can't wait to meet him."

A rush of college students entered the tiny eatery, bringing bursts of noise and gusts of cool air that would turn frigid in another couple of months. It wasn't worth trying to talk until they left, so instead I stood. Christa stood as well, offering me her hand, and I put my empty tray in it. That probably wasn't what she was going for, but whatever.

At least I didn't dump poutine in her hair. I still wanted to.

We walked back toward the hotel in silence, lost in our own thoughts. Tourists milled around the shops; children ran in the streets and played nearby. I wondered what it would've been like to come to Mount Tremblant as a family. Me, Brett, and our son.

Would Ethan grow to love Christa? Or would he resent her for not being around while he was growing up? What if our son hated her for being different? Would he one day be okay calling her Mom? Did I mind sharing that title? Would Christa object to being called Dad? Was I more OK with that?

When we reach the hotel lobby, I finally spoke. "Did you ever think about coming back? As the world got more progressive?"

"No. You and Ethan would be much better off if I'd stayed dead."

WHEN I GOT BACK to the room, Christa's words still ran through my head. The idea that she'd think she was better off dead than in my life tore at my heart. I thought of all the things she'd missed after she left, moments that could never be recaptured. If only Brett had told me what he was thinking, maybe I could have helped somehow. But that wasn't true. This wasn't my experience, was miles outside my comfort zone. What could I have possibly done?

How could I have missed something so huge going on inside the person I was supposed to know better than anyone else in the world? How had he hidden this from me?

I shook those thoughts away. It was impossible for me to understand what had been going through Brett's mind when he chose not to get on that plane. Impossible to understand how it felt for him to be at war with his own body. The only thing I understood was that I may have stumbled into the one thing I'd never been able to provide for my son: his father.

My first inclination was to call Ethan and tell him what happened. But somehow, "Hey sweetie, guess what? Your father is alive!" didn't seem like the best conversation to have over video chat at eleven o'clock on a school night. Especially when the explanation involved gender reassignment surgery, and the boy was going to be alone with my deeply conservative, everyone-who-isn't-just-like-me-is-a-whackjob-or-a-deadbeat mother for the next few days.

Ethan was a smart young man, but I couldn't risk him giving in to the temptation to ask his grandmother for advice. Worse, if she caught him looking at websites on being transgender—and he would definitely look—she'd make his life miserable until I got back. She'd probably force-feed him testosterone supplements while he read the Bible or make him beg Jesus for salvation while doing push-ups or something.

This trip was supposed to clear my head, help me cope with my loss finally so I could move on with my life. It wasn't supposed to set my whole world spinning.

I chuckled bitterly to myself. At least I didn't feel sad about my husband dying anymore. Instead, I was sad about many, many other things. Confused. Was I even legally married? Brett's death was recorded and a certificate issued in October 2001. Brett Cooper, as such, no longer existed. Was I now married to Christa McCall?

A full night's miserable tossing and turning gave me no real answers, but at least I made one decision in the wee hours. When dawn peeked through the slit in the curtains, I rose, throwing the few items I'd used back into my suitcase. Christa would have to understand if I took off, after all; she was in no position to bitch about it.

We'd been best friends once. Brett was the person I cared about more than anything in the world. When he died on that plane, part of me went with him. I couldn't just walk away.

After much debate, I dropped a letter at the front desk for her. It would've served her right to vanish without a trace, but I owed our son more than that. He had a right to know his father, if and when he was ready. Maybe I also owed the relationship we once had a chance, I didn't know. I owed it to myself to leave the door open to get closure.

Dear Christa,

I know things seemed okay when we parted last night, but my senses are still reeling. Having never run into a deceased loved one before, I don't know how to feel about any of this. Of course, I'm glad you weren't murdered by terrorists, but there are so, so many more emotions beneath that.

I'm checking out early and heading back to Boston. All things considered, I can only assume you'll forgive me for leaving like this. If you need to contact me, I've enclosed a business card.

But I'd prefer that you don't reach out to me. I'll call you at the hotel when I'm ready. There's a lot to work out, and I need to figure out what to tell our son. Thank you for understanding.

Best,

Jess

IT SEEMED A LITTLE FORMAL, but what level of familiarity was best for these situations? I was on the road before four o'clock in the morning with a paper cup of hotel lobby coffee in one hand and a sworn promise to myself that I'd stop at the first open Tim Horton's I passed.

Adrenaline and whirling thoughts fueled me throughout the long drive. I'd expected to pull into a rest stop to sleep for a couple of hours once I crossed into the United States, but there was no need. After a couple more coffee breaks on the MassPike, I arrived in Boston early enough to be grateful I hadn't passed through any speed traps.

Not wanting to go home yet, I instead turned the car toward downtown Quincy, where Teddy and I kept our office.

When I finally pulled into my parking space, the dam I'd been holding back for the past several hours burst. Tears streamed down my face. Time stopped as all the anger and shock and frustration and fear poured out of me.

Finally, I managed to pull myself together enough to wipe my eyes, blow my nose, and stagger through the back door into our break room.

Once I saw the box of donuts sitting on the table, a bone-deep weariness hit me. I'd been awake for more than twenty-four hours. In that time, I'd had the shock of my life, driven hundreds of miles (kilometers?), and consumed nothing but coffee and a few bites of poutine. Still, the sweet smell of the doughnuts turned my stomach. I never wanted to eat again.

Not knowing what else to do, I sank into a chair, rested my head on the table, and closed my eyes, just for a minute.

"No, no, no," a voice said some time later. "You're supposed to be living it up at a fabulous resort, getting massages, climbing mountains. You can't be here. Jess, you're fired."

It took me a minute to even realize where I was, how I'd gotten there, and who spoke to me.

"You can't fire me, Teddy," I mumbled through the mass of hair covering my face. "We're partners, remember?"

When I lifted my head to meet his eyes, the snappy comeback on my best friend's face faded away. "Oh, shit. Who died?"

The question led to another round of tears, just when I thought I was all cried out. I couldn't answer. Teddy quickly pulled over a chair and sat, putting one arm around me. Leaning into him, I sobbed, grateful to have someone to lean on. Coming here had been the right decision.

"I'm so sorry. I didn't mean it. Seriously, did someone die? Is it your mom? Is Ethan okay? What are you doing here? Why did you come back so early?"

Behind me, the break room door opened. Teddy shook his head at whoever entered, and the door closed again. I didn't know how long we sat there before the tears subsided enough to let me speak.

"Br...Alive," I croaked out through a wad of napkins.

"Bra Live? What's that? some kind of fancy new undergarment that makes your breasts sing and dance?"

A snort of laughter sent me choking into the snotty mess in my hands. When I finally got myself under control, I said, "It's Brett. He's alive."

"Brett Who?" My eyes met his, and realization slowly dawned. "Wait. You don't mean your husband?"

I nodded.

"The one who was on United Flight 175?"

I nodded again.

"Your dead husband." It was a statement, not a question, so I didn't answer. Teddy took a deep breath, blinked repeatedly, then ran one hand through his hair. "What the fuck?"

"My thoughts exactly."

He stood with a glance at the clock. "Hold on. I'm going to cancel my one o'clock, and then we're going to find a bar with a lunch menu, and then we're going to have a long, private chat, okay?"

This wasn't the place for all the things I had to say, and knowing I had someone to listen made me feel better already. "Sounds good. Thanks."

Twenty minutes later, we settled into a booth in a dark corner of a nearby pub. Teddy ordered two pumpkin beers and two shots of vanilla vodka from the hostess as she sat us and tapped his foot under the table when she walked away.

"Okay, spill. Let's start with—what the fuck?"

The entire story tumbled out, from the moment I saw Christa's face, to the jolt of recognition that hit me, to telling her about Ethan, and slinking out in the middle of the night like a coward. I didn't even pause when the waitress brought our drinks. Neither of us opened our menus.

When I finished, Teddy stared at me, the drinks untouched in front of him. Before he spoke, he downed the vodka. Then he picked up a beer and swallowed three-quarters of the glass in one gulp.

"Congratulations," he finally said. "You've always wanted to be the star of your very own Lifetime Original Movie."

"Gee, thanks, *Téodoro.*" He winced at my use of his full name. "I'm so glad I came to see you instead of a therapist."

A plate of French fries appeared on the table, although I

didn't remember either of us ordering it. My stomach growled, reminding me that most people ate at regular intervals. Now that I'd unburdened my soul, the aroma tantalized me. I ordered a bacon cheeseburger with the works, which I never let myself eat, and Teddy asked for the same. There were times to worry about health, and times to eat garbage while you marveled over the shitshow your life had turned into.

"Honestly, honey, you're going to need a therapist. Ethan will, anyway." He pulled out his phone and started tapping the screen. "Here. My ex does child psychology. And while he's completely incapable of figuring out how to keep his dick in his pants, he's brilliant. He's got a few patients with transgender parents, and he counsels transgender teens. I'm texting you his number, and I'm texting him a note to expect your call. He owes me, so he'll see you and Ethan as soon as you're ready."

"He owes you an emergency psychology session because he cheated on you?"

"No, he owes me because I made three house calls to his mother when I was a resident trying out oncology for a few months, and her 'eye tumor' turned out to be a spot on the contact lenses she hadn't removed or cleaned in over a year. He'll make time for you."

A thousand-pound weight lifted off my shoulders. Just knowing someone else had my back made this whole thing easier. Having a plan to hold onto felt like solid ground beneath my feet. Finally, my world stopped teetering.

A few minutes later, my phone beeped inside my purse. A quick glance confirmed that Teddy's ex had already sent me an email introducing himself and offering to arrange a phone call before meeting with Ethan.

I reached across the table to squeeze Teddy's hand. "Thanks. You're a lifesaver."

CHAPTER THIRTEEN

Teddy's "beach house" was amazing, a three-thousand-square-foot Cape Cod with a sweeping wraparound porch, heated floors throughout, floor-to-ceiling windows facing the ocean, and a master bathroom the size of my kitchen at home. He'd gotten extremely lucky buying a rundown foreclosure when the housing market crashed and did most of the restoration himself on the weekends. The realtor living next door estimated that it was worth about four times what he'd paid for it. If a person needed to hide and decompress, doing it in style sure beat sleeping in the break room of a medical office. I wasn't ready to go home yet.

For about twenty minutes after I arrived, I sat on the back porch, sipping a glass of red wine and looking out over the water, waiting. Seeing my dead husband again only raised about four billion questions, so I pulled up Google and got to work, looking for as much information as I could: what it was like to be transgender, the process of transitioning from male to female, what gender reassignment surgery entailed, how a person is declared UN-dead, what happens to life insurance proceeds if the insured turns up alive.

My head spun with the potential ramifications. Was it legal to fake your own death? Had Brett unknowingly made me an accessory to felony theft when I accepted a two-hundred-fifty-thousand-dollar life insurance payout? What about the money from the government? I needed a lawyer.

With a start, I realized that I knew a lawyer. We'd gone on dates. Two dates, at least. He hadn't made my heart go pitter-pat, but Steve was a nice enough guy, he seemed smart, and maybe he could answer some of my questions. I slugged back the rest of my wine and picked up the phone to call him before I lost my nerve.

When he answered the phone, I told him I was staying at Teddy's place on the water for a few days, that a legal problem had arisen, and asked if he'd made plans for dinner. He volunteered to pick up takeout on his way. Half an hour later, white lights swept across the backyard as a car turned into the driveway. I barely had time to put a dent in my second glass of wine.

Suddenly realizing how awful I must look, I used the selfie camera on my phone to check my appearance before getting up to answer the door. Ugh. Blond curls sticking out in all directions, bags under my bloodshot eyes. I'd gotten so caught up in my research that I'd forgotten to even brush my hair or change out of the clothes I'd been wearing for more than twenty-four hours.

If I'd ever looked worse, I couldn't remember. Maybe in the days after 9/11, which my subconscious mercifully blocked as soon as my pregnancy made itself known and I had to start acting like a human being for the sake of the baby.

Oh, well. If asking for legal help didn't make it clear this wasn't a booty call, my appearance definitely would. As long as Steve didn't take one look at me and run away, everything would be fine.

When I opened the door, Teddy's friend held a bag of takeout in one hand and a bottle of wine in the other. He wore black slacks, a long-sleeved blue dress shirt, and a five-hundred-dollar tie. I strongly suspected he had a suit coat in his car and hoped he'd dressed up for court earlier, not for me. Maybe he had canceled other plans to be here.

His eyes widened when he took in my disheveled appearance. "What happened to you?" I stepped back to let him in, and he put one hand over my mouth. "Actually, don't answer that yet. I'm not your lawyer, you're not my client, and that means nothing you say to me is confidential. I'm going to need you to pay me $1 to retain my services before we can talk. And if you killed anyone, I don't want to know."

The way he took charge of the situation made me wish I'd been more attracted to this guy. "I didn't kill anyone. There's a hundred bucks on the counter to cover the food and your time."

"My firm charges four hundred dollars an hour for my time."

My stomach growled as if objecting to that exorbitant rate. "Well, then, I'll write you a check. But first, grab a plate and I'll tell you what happened. I'm starved."

Over a plate of pad thai, I filled him in on Brett's death. Steve knew I was a widow, of course, and that I had a teenager, but I hadn't been ready to share the circumstances of Brett's death with him the couple of times we went out. Apparently Teddy hadn't told him, either. He expressed sympathy when I went over the details, but could tell he had no idea why I'd invited him over or what type of problem I was about to present.

When I mentioned that I'd run into a very-much-alive Brett, he choked on his wine. "Okay, *now* I get why you called me."

"Yeah." So much to say, so little clue where to start. "And I received the payout on a two-hundred-fifty-thousand-dollar life insurance policy after he died, plus a settlement from the September 11 Victim Compensation Fund."

We sat for a beat while he let that sink in.

"If you'd known about this when you applied for those benefits, that would be a federal offense."

"The comp fund money was only a few hundred dollars," I said. "I'm happy to give it back. But I had no idea."

"Are you also happy to repay the life insurance company?

Because they'll probably want their quarter of a million dollars back."

The thought had crossed my mind, and I'd been pondering it for much of the afternoon. My gut reaction was, "Hell no, I'm not giving the money back!" But I suspected it wasn't that simple. How could I in good conscience keep money I never should've had in the first place? What message would that send to Ethan?

Quincy Orthopedics did well. I wouldn't be delighted to turn over a quarter of a million dollars to an insurance company, but it wasn't impossible. And I could always take out a mortgage on the house and pay the debt off over time. Still, that sucked. What if I didn't have the money? Or didn't particularly feel like using it for that purpose?

"Can I make Christa pay it?" Suing wasn't ideal, and it would probably wind up putting us both on the news, but it still beat turning over that kind of money.

"You could, but there are a couple of problems. For one, he doesn't have any assets in the United States, so you'd have to sue in Canada, which means you'd need to consult with a Canadian lawyer. But also—Brett Cooper didn't spend that money. Neither did Christa McCall. Jess Cooper is the named beneficiary of the life insurance policy, she's the one who benefited from her husband's death, and she's the one who, it now turns out, wasn't entitled to that money. You're lucky they can't take back your medical degree."

A sound of frustration escaped me, but I knew when I'd been beaten. If I had to pay it back, there was nothing I could do. Wasn't I always talking to Ethan about accepting his responsibilities and doing the right thing? It wouldn't be right to keep that money. Even if none of this was my fault. Damn it.

My shoulders sagged and I drained my glass, then refilled it. "I'll call them as soon as Brett's declared alive again. But I don't even know where to start. How do you undo a death certificate? Are we still married?"

"As long as Brett Cooper is dead, you're legally a widow. So, the first step is to file with the probate courts to have the death certificate set aside. That's not terribly complicated, but the judge is going to need to see DNA. If Christa won't cooperate, you need a court order. But as soon as he's alive, you're still married. You'll have to get a divorce. This type of case could get expensive."

It didn't escape my notice that Steve kept saying "he" when referring to Christa, even though I'd made a point to use "she."

"I don't think Christa will fight a divorce. After all, she doesn't benefit from a long-distance marriage to a woman in the U.S., either."

"It will reduce costs significantly if he agrees," Steve said. "But what if he doesn't? What if he claims that he's entitled to half of everything you've earned while he was dead? Are you willing to hand it over to him?"

Once upon a time, I'd have given Brett every penny I had if he asked. But now? I didn't even know Christa, not really. Nor did I want to know the type of person who would abandon a spouse then ask for half the money they earned during the resulting separation.

"No fucking way," I said grimly. "Especially not if I have to fork over money to the insurance company because of her."

"So that could make things more complicated," he said. "The other issue is, because of our personal history, I don't think I'm the best person to represent you here. I'm happy to refer you to a friend, and we can talk more about the general legalities of your case, but I shouldn't represent a woman I've dated, however casually, in a divorce against her husband. Especially because I'm a contracts attorney."

I smiled at him. "I completely forgot about that. I guess it's like how people hear I'm a doctor, and they'll randomly open their shirts to show me a mole or something. And I'm like '… not an oncologist, but thanks for the peek at your tits.'"

Steve chuckled. "Your occupational hazard sounds more interesting than mine."

"Maybe, but it's also super awkward."

"This may not be the most sensitive question," he said, "but I'm not sure how else to put it. Before you get into this, before you revoke the death certificate and repay the money and notify the insurance company: are you absolutely, one hundred percent beyond all shadow of a doubt positive that the person you encountered is really Brett Cooper and not some scam artist taking advantage of the fact that there's a resemblance? Do you know that this person used to be a man?"

"She didn't exactly seek me out. I don't know any way she could have planned that meeting," I said.

"If I were the type of person who would pull this kind of scam, I could arrange an accidental encounter. For all you know, this woman was waiting around for hours for the opportunity to run into you."

"I don't think so," I said slowly. "The look of shock in her eyes when I recognized her seemed genuine. Besides, the voice, the mannerisms, the eyes… it was Brett. I know it sounds insane, but Christa is my husband. I felt it in my bones."

"As a lawyer, I'd strongly advise you to get a DNA test or otherwise seek confirmation. I know you feel like you've rediscovered your dead husband, but imagine the consequences if you're wrong. And as a fellow parent, I'd suggest getting that confirmation before you tell Ethan. Imagine the psychological harm you could do if you tell him that his father is alive and well, living as a woman in Canada, and it turns out to be a scam."

Yikes. I hadn't even thought of that. Christa was Brett. Or was she? Would someone go to all this trouble to scam me? She hadn't asked for anything, other than the chance to meet Ethan, who she didn't know about until I mentioned him. Unless that's what she wanted me to believe.

I didn't even know how to confirm her identity. Ask her for a DNA sample? I didn't want to offend her, but Steve had a point.

"That's a good idea. Thanks."

"Speaking of psychological damage," he said. "How do you feel about all of this? What's it like to know that the person you pledged to spend the rest of your life with not only betrayed your life and your trust, but was hiding this huge secret?"

Something in his tone grated at me, but I took another sip of wine and reminded myself how pissed I was to find out my husband faked his death. It was only normal for other people to be curious. "Honestly... I think I'm still in shock. I'm pissed, I'm confused, I'm frustrated, I'm angry, I'm sad that he didn't trust me enough to tell me he'd decided to run away, I'm sad that my son never got to meet his father—"

"Not to mention, it's fucked up to find out that the person you thought you knew was a total fucking weirdo," Steve said.

I froze, my wine glass halfway to my mouth. "I wouldn't use that phrase."

"Why not? I mean, I didn't go to medical school, but it always seemed to me that feeling like your whole body was against you was some kind of mental problem. That the solution wasn't painful and expensive surgery, but a psychiatrist and lots of therapy." With every word he spoke, my opinion of him dropped further. "Personally, I think you should take Ethan to get checked out. If all this is true, then you want to make sure Brett didn't pass this nuttiness onto his kid."

I set my wine glass down and rose to my feet, rage simmering in my veins. Where had Teddy found this guy? Did he know what a bigot he was? "Thanks for coming by, Steve, but I'm afraid it's been a long and draining day. I'm going to have to ask you to leave."

The words were pleasant enough, but the smile on his face dropped at the look on my face. "Hey, I'm sorry. I didn't mean to offend you..."

"How could I *possibly* be offended by the insinuation that there's something wrong with being transgender? That my best friend and first love is somehow broken, in addition to my son? By your intentional misgendering of Christa since you arrived? And by the outdated and offensive language you used to convey both?"

Steve's reaction wasn't rare, by any means. But I'd been right not to get involved with this guy, not to let him get to know my child and share his narrow-minded ideas. He wasn't someone I wanted in my life, spreading that poison. Sure, I was pissed that Brett left me, but that didn't make him a weirdo or a freak or anything. A bad husband? Yes. A bad person? No fucking way.

"Hey, Jess, I just meant that any guy would have to be nuts to let you go." Steve reached for me, but I stepped back.

"Are you fucking serious right now? You insult me, and the man I loved, then you hit on me? Get out before I throw you out."

Steve started to say something else, then wisely thought better of it. I stood my ground, practically shaking with rage, glaring until he turned and walked out of the house.

"Thanks for dinner," he said. "I'll email you a few names tomorrow."

"Don't bother," I said. "I can find a lawyer on my own."

He didn't answer.

A moment later, the front door closed. I didn't move until a car door slammed, the engine roared to life, and headlights moved across the yard as the car backed down the driveway. My blood boiled, pounding through my veins until I worried I might explode.

For what felt like hours, I sat, seething, rage billowing out of my pores. Finally, I felt like I might only scream for a long time rather than forever. I picked up the phone, prepared to chew Teddy out for introducing me to Steve in the first place until he hung up on me, but something stopped me. Teddy wasn't the bad guy here. He wasn't the one I was mad at. Steve was a convenient target for my rage, but he also wasn't the reason I still needed to sort through my feelings. And my momentary anger at Steve's narrow-mindedness was nothing compared to the tornado of emotions I'd been through in the past thirty-six hours.

Instead, I took a deep breath, drained my glass yet again, and sent a message to Christa. Steve might be an ass, but he wasn't stupid, and one thing he'd said resonated with me. I needed to pursue it.

Do you have time to chat?

CHAPTER FOURTEEN

As soon as I sent the message, my computer started ringing. Christa's face filled the video screen so fast, she must've been waiting by her phone, hoping for a text.

"I'm so glad you messaged me," she said. "I thought it would be a lot longer before I heard from you."

"Don't count your chickens. I haven't forgiven you yet," I said.

"That's reasonable. So what's up?"

"This has been a huge shock," I began.

"I know."

"Shhh. Let me say what I need to say."

"Okay, sorry." The long "o" in the word made me smile. My Brett, turned into a Canadian. I wonder if he even noticed the accent. She.

"Anyway, I have a son to think about. The father he's always known is dead, so before I bring someone new into his life, I need to be really, really sure. I know you could file for custody or visitation, but that means coming to America and outing yourself, and I think we can work things out before it gets that far."

"I'd never try to take him away from you like that."

The Brett I knew certainly wouldn't have, but who was this person, anyway?

"That's good, because I'd drag things out until Ethan turned eighteen, wasting your time and money."

Her face fell. I hadn't meant to be quite so confrontational. I forced myself to soften my voice as I said, "What I'm trying to say is, I need proof. I could get a paternity test, but that also takes time. Tell me something only Brett and I would know. Tell me a story about us. Even though I feel in my bones that you used to be my Brett… I need to know it in my brain. I'm a scientist, and I need evidence. Tell me a story."

Part of me worried that she'd get insulted, hang up, and I'd never hear from her again. But if that was the case, then this could just be some bizarre fluke. I could spend tomorrow on the beach, mourning my husband, convince myself today was a dream or something, and go back to work the next day like none of this ever happened.

She tapped one long red fingernail against her mouth before she started to speak. "I'm happy to reminisce with you all day long, but first, can I tell you another story from when we were kids? Something I never told you?"

It seemed like an odd request, since it wouldn't really prove that she was who she claimed to be. "Why?"

"Trust me."

If she was who she said she was, the story would reveal something important, or she wouldn't be telling it. If she wasn't Brett, I'd only waste another five minutes of my life before terminating the call and blocking her number. There wasn't much to lose.

"Sure," I said.

"As a kid, Brad was always after me to 'be a man,' which is funny, all things considered. Maybe on some level, he sensed how I really felt. I don't know."

I smiled at her. "Really?"

"Yeah, there was this one day, I was standing in my room in

front of the mirror, looking at my body. I was thinking about how we'd just had sex for the first time, about how that was supposed to make me feel like more of a man, but I really didn't. How your dad would cut my balls off if he knew."

"Yeah," I said. "Guess he could've saved you some money in the long run, huh?"

She rolled her eyes, and immediately I regretted my insensitive comment. "Anyway, I stood there, looking at my naked body. My football player's build, my tapered waist, narrow hips. Thinking about how much you envied those things, even though you had the perfect body, with your curvy hips and full breasts."

Self-consciously, I looked down. After giving birth, my already-large breasts had never returned to their original size. After long days on my feet, my lower back throbbed with the intensity of a thousand drums. I'd trade these boobs in a heartbeat for a solid B cup. "I guess we always want what we can't have."

"The grass is always greener." Christa agreed. "So I was standing there, cock pushed back between my legs, glaring at my chest hair, wondering if I could rip it all out. And in comes Brad, bursting through the door to tell me dinner's ready."

I chuckled, imaging Brad's reaction to something like that. "Oh no! What happened?"

"First, he was like 'Are you checking yourself out like that dude in *Silence of the Lambs*?' Which of course I hadn't seen yet, but it made sense later. Anyway, I told him to get the fuck out, and he gave me this speech instead. I still remember it. 'You want to know what you'd look like as a girl, whatever. That's cool, I guess. But you gotta keep that shit to yourself. Guys get beat up for wearing chicks' clothes. They get killed.'"

Tears filled her eyes, and she looked down, away from the camera. There was much more to this story, but it wasn't relevant to verifying her identity, and it was up to Christa to decide if she wanted to tell me. I waited, sipping my wine while she composed herself.

She cleared her throat and shook her head. "Anyway, he gave me this whole speech about banging as many chicks as possible, which I found completely appalling. I told him that I loved you, and he said that you'd be ashamed to see me pretending to be a girl."

My heart broke for the boy I thought she'd been and the woman she'd become. "I'm not ashamed, Christa. I'm confused and incredibly angry, but I'm not ashamed. For you or for me. Neither of us asked for this."

"I know. But he went on and on about what a small town we lived in, how I'd be begging for trouble, and I needed to just be a man. I repeated his words to myself over and over, for weeks. *Eat pussy, be a man. Don't get your ass kicked. Be a man. Be a man, Brett.*"

"Why are you telling me all this?" The story rang true, based on my interactions with Brad, but it wasn't something Brett had ever shared with me. It didn't tell me that the person peering at me through the screen was my once-dead spouse.

"I just want you to understand that I tried. How much I loved you, and that I wanted to be the best man I could for you."

FOR THE NEXT WEEK, Christa and I talked every night after Ethan went to bed. I wasn't ready to break the news to him yet. One day, probably soon, I'd have to tell my son that his father was alive. And I no longer had any doubts that the person on the other end of the phone was my Brett. Not after everything we shared.

We talked about the time our sophomore year he beat up one of the other guys in the locker room for implying that I was easy.

That memory made me laugh: I'd long forgotten how pissed I

was when I found out, how I railed at Brett for defending my honor, and how I went and socked that stupid Aaron Porter in the face when I heard what he did.

The principal suspended me, of course, when I wouldn't tell him why I did it. Brett and I spent the next three days at the new movie theater in Hartford, watching R-rated movies my mom would never let me see. Even today, as a grown woman, she disapproved of me watching movies with swearing, sex, or violence. She'd have had a heart attack if she'd known Brett and I went to see *Pulp Fiction* and *Exit to Eden* together—instead of being at school. Sex, drugs, violence, BDSM, and truancy all in one go. What a great week for us.

We talked about how he only understood freshman biology when I explained it to him, how I'd never have passed freshman year English without him explaining what the hell Dickens was talking about. Reading was great, sure, but the title of *Great Expectations* really had me expecting an interesting book, not something that put me to sleep when I tried to read it. Or listened to the tapes I found at a second-hand bookstore. We relived our first kiss, the first time we had sex on my sixteenth birthday.

She not only remembered everything I brought up, she reminded me of things I hadn't thought about in years.

"I still can't believe your dad gave you that creepy locket for your birthday." Christa laughed. "What did he say? 'By wearing this necklace, you promise to save your virtue until you're married. I'll hold the key until your wedding night, and then I'll give it to your husband.'"

I shuddered at the memory. "If only he'd realized that his words were the push I needed to lose my virginity in the boys' bathroom at the skating rink while all our friends watched Clara Chen skate the routine that almost got her into the Olympics. He was standing less than a hundred feet away."

"Maybe he'd forgotten how fast teenage boys could have sex if they had the chance."

That made me chuckle. "What's even creepier is that he gave you the key the night before we got married."

"That was so bizarre," Christa said. "At the time, I figured it was the most awkward conversation anyone could ever have with another adult."

We both paused for a minute, me drinking a glass of wine, Christa going to refill her water glass. The conversation moved easily between us, but I still wasn't sure what to do next. It might be time to give Teddy's therapist friend a call.

Christa sat down and cleared her throat. "Do you remember when we were seniors, when we ditched school and drove to Massachusetts?"

I closed my eyes for a minute, searching for the day she referred to. It didn't take long. We'd spent days dreading the trip.

Brett had driven in silence, white knuckles gripping the steering wheel. I peered intently out the passenger window, twisting my fingers in my lap. For the first time, I understood how death row prisoners might feel being led to the electric chair. I'd focused on minute details through the window, biting my lip, to avoid a conversation I didn't want to have. I didn't have the energy to carry on a conversation, and I didn't want to think about where we were going, what we were about to do.

Welcome to Massachusetts, the sign read. Thousands of people drove by it every day, if not more. How many of them felt the same way we did?

Brett focused on the road, the dotted white lines disappearing one at a time beneath the front of the car. What if I grabbed the wheel, swerved the car into oncoming traffic? That might solve our problems, but I could never hurt Brett like that. This wasn't his fault. Not entirely.

He pulled into the parking lot, shifted into park. I opened the door and slid off the seat like butter melting before he could reach for the ignition key.

"You don't have to come in with me." I didn't stick around to hear his reply.

Behind me, one car door slammed, then the other. His footsteps pounded on the pavement behind me, but I was way ahead of him. Clouds filled the sky, throwing a bleak pallor over the entire outing. Fitting.

I didn't pause or look around until I was safely inside the building, the door shut behind me, and only then, enough to find the front desk. Despite the thousand-pound weights attached to each foot, I approached, feeling the eyes of the others in the waiting room. They judged me, just as my parents would judge me if they knew. But my father would also lock me away in a room forever, and I couldn't have that. Worse, I couldn't stand hurting my mother, making her feel like she failed as a parent, when that couldn't be further from the truth. My mistake wasn't her failure.

When I reached the desk, the front door closed behind me. Brett. Of course, he wouldn't stay in the car. The woman behind the desk possessed twinkling blue eyes and a gray bun that seemed more fitting to Mrs. Claus than anyone found here.

"Hi," the receptionist had said. "Can I help you?"

"I'm here for an abortion," I whispered, biting my lip. A coppery taste filled my mouth.

The word ricocheted around the room. I flinched, having never spoken it aloud before, not even when they talked about coming here. Abortion was a sin. So was suicide, and if I told my parents about any of this, they'd kill me and Brett. I didn't want to end my life before it ever started. Having a child wasn't an option for us, and I couldn't face adoption if it meant telling my parents what we did.

I'd known in my heart that I had no other choice, unless I wanted to run away to Florida, to beg Aunt Mary Anne to take me in. She hated my dad, always had, so I might have an ally in Ma's sister. But I couldn't risk her telling my mother. So, this was it. I knew it.

Still, I hated myself for what I was about to do.

"Okay, dear. Do you have an appointment?"

I shook my head.

"It could be a bit of a wait. Just give me a name, and we'll be with you as soon as we can. Would you also like to talk to someone about birth control before you leave?"

I nodded vigorously. Until the woman spoke, I'd thought these places only did abortion. If I'd known we could get birth control, Brett would've driven me here months ago. We wouldn't be here today.

Too late for that now.

A hand fell on my shoulder, and I started out of nervousness. As soon as I realized who stood behind me, I relaxed. Brett, of course. The receptionist eyed us through bulletproof glass.

"Is everything okay? Should I call security?"

"It's fine. I'm just jumpy today."

The woman clucked her tongue. "Everything will be okay, dear. Just fill out these forms, and someone will be with you shortly."

A few others scattered around the stark waiting room, sitting in uncomfortable, hard-backed chairs. A guy I recognized from the football games against Hartford High sat alone, holding *The Catcher in the Rye* open near the middle. His eyes didn't move. He hadn't turned a page since they entered. A purse sat on the empty seat beside him. A woman about my mom's age sat near the door in cheap, well-worn clothing.

Brett followed me to two seats in the corner. His mouth tightened the way it did when he wanted to say something but didn't know what. He was extra fidgety, but silent. I appreciated that. I didn't really want his help, but he knew I couldn't do it alone. With nothing else to do but wait, my eyes traced the pamphlets sitting on the table beside them: Birth control, herpes, HIV, adoption. Adoption, HIV, herpes, birth control.

Silently, Brett took the forms from me and started filling them out.

I put one hand on his knee. "Do you have to put my real name?" I mouthed the words, afraid of making a sound.

He shrugged. Then he scribbled a note on his hand. *We're paying cash.* I nodded, and he returned to the forms without responding.

Name: Tori Spelling

Address: 301 Cobblestone Way, Bedrock

Phone Number: 860-867-5309

Brett nudged me. "You need a real phone number. What if they have to reach us?"

"They can't call my house!"

He pointed to the form. "Look. They'll use a fake name if they have to call to talk to you. It's okay. I'll put my number and tell them to ask for Brett."

"Are you going to keep speaking to me after this? I thought…" Even in a whisper, my voice trembled.

Brett put his arms around me. My body relaxed against him, seeking his warmth. That was how we got into this mess in the first place, but I didn't pull away. My stomach churned.

"Shh. Everything is going to be okay," he said.

"But, don't most couples break up because of this kind of thing?"

"I love you. You're my best friend. Nothing's going to split us up."

When the nurse beckoned, I insisted on going in alone. Behind me, Brett sat, staring at his hands, avoiding making eye contact with the linebacker who'd yet to turn a single page in his book.

Less than fifteen minutes later I was back, feeling like a million bucks. Brett looked surprised to see me but shot to his feet instantly.

In a hushed tone, he asked, "Is everything okay?"

"I'm not pregnant!" I wouldn't have believed it, but speaking those words to him made me feel a thousand times better than when I spotted the blood in my underwear.

My words echoed around the room, and I flushed, clapping my hands over my mouth. Grinning, Brett gave me a chaste kiss, and we hurried outside.

"Right after I went in there, I started my period," I said. "I'm so sorry. It's been six weeks and I'm always so regular and…"

"Shh." He kissed my forehead, smoothing back my hair. "It doesn't matter. All that matters is that you're okay and we're going to get through this."

"That's not *all* that matters."

"I know. We need to make sure this doesn't happen again. Do you want to maybe… wait? Not have sex again?"

I wondered if this was the first time any sixteen-year-old boy spoke those words, and the thought made me want to burst out laughing. But he seemed so sweet, so earnest, that I hugged him instead. In my right hand, I carried a bag given to me by the nurse. Now, I waved it around.

"Nope! They gave me the Pill. We should wait a couple of weeks, just in case, but then we're good. I just need to find a place to hide them from my parents."

He wrapped his arms around me, cradling my head against his shoulder. "I love you." He'd said it a million times, but something felt different now. As if we shared a deeper connection now.

"I love you, too. Let's go home," I'd said.

After we finished the story, I remained silent, wondering why Christa would choose that particular memory over all the others. It hadn't been a happy day for either of us. On the other hand, I'd never told another soul, and I suspected she hadn't, either. The only people who knew we'd been there were the nurse and the couple from Hartford High—and they certainly weren't sharing.

"I've thought about that day a lot over the last eighteen years," Christa said, swallowing. "Even though you turned out not to be pregnant, I still felt like I missed out. Like I'd never get my chance to have a child." Tears brimmed in her eyes, tugging at my heartstrings.

I looked down, trying to stop the sympathy tears that hit me. After a moment, I regained my composure and cleared my throat. "You want to meet Ethan."

"Please, Jess." Her voice trembled. "He's the only child I'll ever have. I've been giving you time to get used to this, and you can have more, but I really need to know that someday, I'll get to talk to my son, to hug him. Be part of his life, even if it's a small part."

"Then maybe you shouldn't have walked out on him." The words were cold, and I knew it. I felt bad, but at the same time, I didn't. She couldn't expect me to get over this huge lie in just a couple of weeks, even after everything we'd been through. It took time to rebuild trust, to decide whether you're even willing to reopen your life to someone.

At the end of the day, if she pushed things, I wouldn't have a choice. In court, I probably didn't have any basis for denying her access to our child. But if this Christa was the same Brett I knew, she wouldn't push. She'd let me come to the right decision on my own.

"That's not fair," she said. "I didn't know you were pregnant."

"Would you have stayed if you did?"

I could see her wanting to give the easy answer, to say that she absolutely would have stayed if she'd known. Brett was always a terrible liar, a total open book. If Christa lied to me now, I'd never give her another chance. Maybe she saw it on my face, because she let out a long breath before responding.

"I don't know," she said. "Probably not. I needed to figure myself out. But I might have come back."

"I understand," I said. "But Ethan and I need to figure a few things out, too. I'm still not sure I trust you. He may not want to meet you. But I'll talk to him."

"Thanks, Jess. That means everything."

CHAPTER FIFTEEN

Three days later, I pulled up at the front of Ethan's school before lunch and signed him out for the rest of the day. The receptionist watched me shift from one foot to the other, tapping my fingers on the desk.

"Family emergency?"

That's what I wrote on the sign-out sheet.

"Yes," I said.

"Want to talk about it?" Her tone was practiced, a little too sympathetic. I didn't doubt that if I told her about what was happening, half the teachers in the school would hear about it before lunchtime.

"No."

Ethan rounded the corner and skidded to a halt. "Mom? What's wrong? Is it Grandma?"

Aware of the receptionist's eyes and love of gossip, I put one hand on his back and steered Ethan toward the front door. "Grandma's fine. We'll talk after lunch."

How do you tell your child his father hasn't really been dead his whole life, just kidding, he chose to vanish into thin air? My bedside manner was pretty good, but I didn't have any idea what to say in this situation, how to answer his questions.

On the phone, Teddy's therapist friend had suggested it might be easier for me to tell Ethan on my own before bringing him in. As we sat in the parking lot of a fast-food restaurant, sipping milkshakes, I dearly wished I'd taken him to the psychologist's office first.

"Honey, there's something we need to talk about," I began, setting my milkshake in the drink holder and turning to face him.

"I knew it! Grandma's sick, isn't she?" The accusation in his eyes broke my heart. Any attempts to soften the blow might just make things worse.

"No, honey. Grandma's fine. Honestly, I haven't spoken to her since I picked you up from her house after my trip. She's so busy these days."

"Do you have cancer?"

"No one's sick, Ethan. That's actually the thing." I took a deep breath. "Remember how I told you that your father died on 9/11?"

He nodded, suspicion still etched into every feature. "That's why I get an afternoon off school and a milkshake? Because my dad's been dead for a long time? I'm going to miss practice now."

"No, honey. We're taking the day off because when I was in Quebec last week, I discovered that your father's alive. He never got on the plane that day."

His mouth fell open. I could almost see the wheels turning inside his head as he tried, and failed, to process this information. "What?"

These next few minutes were important. I needed to choose my words carefully. Saying the wrong thing could alienate Ethan, not only from Christa, but from me. Ethan was a few months away from becoming a legal adult, and I didn't want him to start his adulthood full of distrust and anger.

"He was afraid to fly, so he left the airport. Security was different back then—way different. People without tickets used to be allowed to go to the gate to say good-bye to their families or pick people up. He gave his boarding pass to someone else, and the flight crew never realized he wasn't the one in his seat. The records say he checked in for the flight, which he did. And that someone used his boarding pass, which they did. No one knew it wasn't your father."

"Then why didn't he come home? Why didn't he call you and tell you he wasn't getting on the plane?"

"Your father was very confused that day. He had a lot going on inside him, and he wasn't happy with the life he and I built. When he left the airport, I think he intended to come home later. But then the plane crashed into the World Trade Center, and suddenly, the whole world thought he was dead."

Having to explain the situation to a teenager, oddly enough, helped me to understand it better than I had before. "Can you imagine what it's like to feel like you're getting a second chance at life? To go back and undo your mistakes?"

Ethan shook his head. "Not really, no. Not when it means leaving my wife and kid behind."

"He had a good reason for leaving, and I understand." I took a deep breath. "Your father is transgender. He, I mean *she*, moved to Canada, changed her name and started a new life. That's why we weren't happy. Because she knew, deep down, that she was living a lie."

Ethan stared at me, unmoving. My heart pounded in my chest, but I was afraid to say anything else. Then he reached for the handle, opened his door, and vomited all over the parking lot.

Perhaps providing a burger, fries, and a giant milkshake right before dropping a bomb on someone was a bad idea. Ethan refused to go into the restroom to clean himself up, so I started the car and headed toward Dr. Anker's office. When Ethan ignored all my efforts at conversation, I turned up the radio to listen to the news. I should've known I'd screw this up. I should've asked Teddy to come with me to break the news. Or insisted that I tell him while sitting in the therapist's office, ready to go in.

Three blocks down the road, Ethan leaned forward and turned down the radio. "So my dad's alive?"

"Yeah. He is. She is."

"And you've spent my entire life lying to me?"

His words broke my heart. "No, sweetie. I didn't know. I told you what I believed to be true: Your father had a seat on United Flight 175, which crashed into the World Trade Center on 9/11."

"But he wasn't on the plane?" Now he managed to sound both sad and reproachful.

On the floor of the car, my cell phone beeped. Teddy, probably, wanting to know how the conversation had gone or how his ex looked. I wished I could use the speaker and let him have this conversation with Ethan for me. Maybe it would help to hear it from the only father figure he'd ever known.

"No, he left the airport before the plane took off. Flying terrified him. Your father didn't really want to go to the job interview anyway, but I insisted. Sometime after I dropped him off at the airport and went home, he changed his mind about the trip and walked away."

"Why didn't he come home?"

"When the plane crashed, he realized that everyone thought he was dead. And it seemed like a good opportunity to start a new life."

"A new life without a wife and kid?"

"He didn't know about you, sweetie. I didn't even know about you yet. I suspected, but I wasn't sure. My doctor's appointment was scheduled for later that day, and it got canceled because of the attacks. If I'd known—if your father had known—I'm sure he would have stayed."

I wasn't sure at all, actually, but I put as much force into the words as I could, because I needed Ethan to believe it. Maybe Brett would have stayed if he'd known, but more likely we would've kept fighting about money and the future, he would have kept being miserable, and Ethan would have had a front-row seat for a horrible, messy divorce.

Maybe he would have watched his father transition instead of finding out about it after the fact. I had no idea if that would've been easier or more difficult. Kids are more resilient than adults, and the world seemed more accepting than in 2001, at least in Massachusetts. To me, anyway, but what did I know? Maybe instead of any of that, Brett would have gotten on the plane and died that day. We wouldn't be having this conversation.

"So he didn't choose to leave me?" Ethan asked.

"No, honey."

"Does Christa know about me now?"

I paused. "Yes. She wants to meet you. But I asked her to stay away until I had time to think about stuff, process it, and talk to you on my own. It's been just you and me for a long time, kiddo. I didn't know how either of us would feel about a third party joining us. That's not the kind of decision I can make on my own."

Ethan studied me solemnly. "We're a good team, you and me."

"You bet we are. The best team." I leaned over at the stoplight and ruffled his hair. The older he got, the more he complained, but...mother's prerogative. "You must have a lot of questions for me."

"Do I have to meet her?"

"Not if you don't want to. You're almost eighteen, so I won't force you. But I think you should at least consider it."

"Why do you sometimes say he and sometimes she when you're talking about the same person?"

"Good question." I really hadn't found my own peace with any of this, and I had to think hard to use the right pronouns myself. I wanted to give the "right" answer, but maybe it was okay to let him know that I struggled sometimes, too. "It's tough, honestly. This is a new situation for me. Sometimes I have to stop and make sure I'm saying the right thing."

He nodded. "Like when Mrs. Leone asked why I didn't have my math homework, and I couldn't tell her I was reading comic books in my room instead of doing it."

My mouth twisted into a hard line to keep from grinning. "We'll talk about that later."

He ducked his head, so I continued answering his question. "Christa uses 'she' and 'her' to refer to herself, so I do, too. Or at least, I'm trying. Does that make sense?"

He watched a group of pedestrians jaywalk in front of the car. "I guess. There's a senior at school who used to be named Julie, but now goes by Jules and uses the boys' bathroom. Jules likes everyone to use ze and zir instead of he/she or him/her."

Silently, I thanked that unknown child for making this moment easier on me. "What really matters is what each individual person wants to be called. I'm trying to respect Christa's wishes."

I turned the car into the therapist's office, and Ethan leaped out practically before I shut off the car. I trailed him into the building. After Dr. Anker introduced himself and took my son into his room to talk, I tried to read a magazine, but couldn't focus.

My poor son, so confused about everything. He was smart, and mature for his age, but I was a grown woman and I still had questions. I sincerely wished I had all the answers for him, but I didn't even have all the answers for *me*. It was easy to put on a brave face and say the right things, but my emotions were still a big, messy ball of what-the-fuck? If Ethan sensed my inner turmoil, I'd only make everything worse.

There was only one person who could really talk to Ethan about why his father left, help him understand, and make things better. That person wasn't me. The therapist had told me on the phone that Ethan would likely benefit from a meeting, and that doing it sooner could help him come to terms with what happened.

With a sigh, I pulled out my phone and started typing.

I TOLD HIM. CALL ME?

A few seconds after I sent the text, my phone rang. She must have been waiting.

"Hello?"

"It's me." An unnecessary phrase since the invention of Caller ID.

"I know. How are you?" I asked.

"I'm fine. How are you?"

This conversation was painfully awkward. Time to cut to the chase. "I told Ethan."

She knew this from the text. When did I lose the ability to carry on a normal conversation? Mentally, I kicked myself. At least things could only go up from here.

Impatience seeped through the phone when she spoke. "And...? What happened?"

"He's confused, of course."

"Right," she said. Who wouldn't be confused when a dead parent returned to life? Or when a parent comes out as transgender?

"I think he needs to meet you. He hasn't asked me yet, and he might not even know it himself, but meeting you will help him answer a lot of questions."

She let out a huge breath. "Thank you, Jess. That's music to my ears."

I paused. "Honestly, I'm still not sure we're okay. I don't know how I feel about any of this. But Ethan has spent his whole life wondering what it would be like if his dad hadn't been killed by terrorists. He's always felt different from other kids. If meeting you will help him feel better about anything, I can't take that away from him."

"I'm so glad to hear that."

"What are you doing for Thanksgiving?" I asked.

"Next week?"

"What? No—at the end of November. You know, Thanksgiving."

"Oh, right," she said. "Sorry. Canadians celebrate Thanksgiving on Columbus Day. You're welcome to come next week, if you can make it, but I don't usually do much."

"That's too short notice," I said. "Can we come up for a few days next month? We can stay at a hotel. It doesn't have to be the one you work at."

She took a deep breath, tugging at her hair with one hand. "You can stay with me. I have plenty of room."

That didn't seem like a good idea. It could lead to a lot of awkwardness, or worse, if Ethan didn't take to her. But maybe I needed to give her a real chance to make things right. "I'll think about it. He could still say no. I already told him I won't force a meeting."

"I understand," she said. "Thank you."

We said our good-byes, but then I paused. "And Christa?"

"Yeah?"

I summoned my internal Mama Bear when I spoke again, and added a touch of the anger I felt at this entire situation. I wanted my words to slap her in the face. "Ethan's been dreaming about his father since he was old enough to know what a father is. If you fuck this up, neither one of us will ever speak to you again."

PART 3

There's only us, there's only this
Forget regret, or life is yours to miss
No other road, no other way
No day but today

— Jonathan Larson, No Day But Today

CHAPTER SIXTEEN

Christa

The day before American Thanksgiving, I met Jess and Ethan outside the security gates at the Montréal-Pierre Elliott Trudeau International Airport. For agonizing minutes, I scanned the face of every person who walked by, searching for a sign. My excitement was palpable. I drank in everyone's features, eyes moving constantly. Was that my son with the freckles and the red hair? Or that… sixty-year-old Chinese woman? Okay, maybe I needed to get a grip.

And then, finally, they appeared. Jess walked a step in front, but even if she hadn't, I could never question the identity of the young man trailing behind her. Even if he was more focused on the screen in front of him than where he was walking.

My son was the most beautiful, perfect person I'd ever seen in my life. From the moment he and Jess stepped into view, I was enchanted by his long, dark lashes, his dancing eyes so much like Jess's, his dark hair that matched my own. He had Jess's snub nose and my rounded chin.

Had someone Photoshopped pictures of me and Jess from senior year together into one face, Ethan would be the result. He towered over his mother but still needed to look up to meet my eyes. Probably that was because I wore three-inch heels, while he wore sneakers and a Boston Bruins T-shirt. In Montreal. Silly kid. We'd have to talk about not wearing clothing in public that could get your ass kicked.

We embraced briefly, and I kissed Jess's cheek, getting a familiar whiff of lilac from her hair. She seemed a bit stiff, probably as nervous about this meeting as I was.

"Nice to see you again," I said. One wrong move and I feared I'd send them scurrying back to Boston. More formal seemed better.

"You, too." Jess turned toward the young man. She hesitated as if she wasn't sure what words to use. "Christa, I'd like you to meet Ethan. Ethan, this is... your father."

His father. I was a parent. A father, or maybe a mother. Ethan's mother. Something I never thought I'd have a chance to be. I blinked back tears, swallowing, while Jess smiled at me over the top of his head. For a long moment, I felt too overwhelmed to speak. My heart grew three sizes.

"Hey, Ethan." My voice cracked on the words.

"Hey." He squinted up at me. "What do I call you?"

I wondered how Jess would want me to answer. I glanced at her for help, but she shook her head. When I cleared my throat, she spoke up. "It's entirely up to you, kiddo. Whatever makes you comfortable."

I blinked tears out of my vision. Mentally, I cursed myself for forgetting to put tissues in my purse. To give myself something non-emotional to focus on, I directed them toward the parking lot. Jess moved woodenly, uncertainly, as if she wasn't entirely sure why she was here. It hurt to see that she still didn't trust me, but I hoped that in time we could find an easiness, if not our old familiarity.

"Since we just met," I said, "I'd understand if you want to call me Christa. I know this is an unusual situation. Maybe in time, when we're all comfortable with each other, you'll be okay addressing me as a parent. One thing at a time."

Ethan eyed me skeptically before breaking into a smile, and I relaxed. I'd apparently passed.

"Thanks, Christa."

The trip through the countryside was uneventful, with Ethan exclaiming over road signs written in French, the metric system, or both. In the front seat, I pointed out the sights, talking about the countryside and Canadian history.

When I paused to focus on the road, Ethan peppered me with questions. "Do you play hockey? Mom wouldn't let me bring my stick, but I play at the local community center."

"You can't carry hockey sticks on a plane!" Jess protested.

He rolled his eyes instead of answering.

"It's okay." My eyes met hers in the rearview mirror. "I've got a spare. We can go out tomorrow. It's not cold enough for real ice yet, but there's a rink not far from my house. You can rent skates."

"Cool, thanks."

Even after we got back to my house, I kept looking from Ethan to Jess, marveling at the similarities and the differences. At the fact that we created this person. That he'd walked the earth for seventeen whole years, so like me and yet so different, but I'd never had any idea. It was both amazing that he existed and devastating that I'd missed out on so much of his life.

Jess

I leaned back in the car, listening to Christa and Ethan talk. I still wasn't sure how I felt about her, about any of this, but keeping the two of them apart would have been wrong. Overall, I thought I'd done a pretty good job raising Ethan on my own. Still, there was the pang of jealousy at how excited my son was to meet his other mother. What if he decided Christa was so much more exciting than me that he wanted to move to Canada? He was about to start applying to colleges, and McGill had an excellent reputation.

Beneath that lurked a deeper, more sinister emotion: resentment. I'd given up so much to provide for this kid: juggling medical school with raising a child, swallowing my pride and accepting help from my mother because she provided free daycare, giving up my dreams of moving to Los Angeles, missing out on most of the first years of my son's life while I worked toward getting a good-paying job. Not to mention skipping years of sleep during medical school.

Meanwhile, Ethan's father faked his death, moved to Canada, became a woman, and contributed nothing. Not a dime of support, not a birthday card, not a phone call. I wanted to understand, wanted to forgive. But I didn't know how.

During college, Brett and I lived in the dorms. We rarely went to his room because the socks, food wrappers, and other crap that littered the floor presented a safety hazard. Our first apartment had been pretty spartan due to our lack of means, but he'd let me pick out all the furniture. The one time I asked for input on decorations, the response was something like, "I love you, but I don't give a rat's ass whether the sofa cushions are teal or turquoise." We'd lived in apartments because Brett didn't want to do yard work or shovel a driveway.

The memories gave me a little trepidation at the thought of spending four days in Christa's home. Enough that I secretly booked two rooms at a nearby hotel as a backup. So when we pulled into a driveway of a beautiful, gleaming white Victorian house, my jaw dropped. The perfectly manicured front lawn suggested I'd been overly harsh in judging her.

Maybe she had a landlord who cared about such things, and the inside was a mess. Oddly, the thought comforted me.

"Welcome to my humble home," Christa said.

"This is yours?" I asked. "Do you have a roommate who also happens to be an interior decorator?"

She laughed. "I bought it about ten years ago. Still plenty of payments left, but it's partially mine. No roommate, I did all of this myself. Wait until you see the gardens."

Had she mentioned purchasing real estate on Mars, I couldn't have been more surprised at the words coming out of her mouth. My spouse gardened? On purpose?

"Mom, why's your mouth open?"

Suppressing a grin, Christa led us deeper into the house. In the hallway, gleaming hardwood floors led to a staircase in front of us. To the right, a mahogany table filled an elegant dining area. To the left, a brown leather couch sat before classic wooden coffee tables. Throw pillows, an area rug before the fireplace, and other accents added touches of color throughout. Not a dirty sock or a fast-food wrapper in sight. It resembled a page from a magazine.

"Who are you and what have you done with my husband?" The words tumbled out, and I winced at the use of "husband" by mistake, but she put one hand on my arm.

"It's okay. I was your husband. You can say that. I'm not offended. This situation will take some getting used to for everyone."

"Yeah, I guess it will." This whole situation still felt like something in a movie. I hadn't figured out how I felt about anything yet. All I knew was that I needed to keep things together for Ethan's sake.

"Come with me for a second?" She tilted her head down the hall toward a closed doorway I'd assumed was her bedroom. "There's something I want to show you."

Behind us, Ethan exclaimed as he found an Xbox and Play-Station hidden in the console under the TV.

With a glance back at the living room, I lowered my voice and followed her away from the main part of the house. "You can't buy his love, you know."

"I know," she said. "But I didn't know what he liked and... I guess I was trying to buy his love. Sorry."

There it was again. The long "o" in "sorry." Even with my eyes closed, there was no denying how things had changed.

"It's okay, I guess. Just, in the future, run any big purchases by me? He doesn't need dozens of video games or a giant TV or tickets in the first row of sporting events or weekends at Disney World or anything like that."

What he needed was a father who cared about him. Or another mother. A second parent, by any name. I didn't have to say it. My unspoken words hung in the air like icicles between us.

At the end of the hall, Christa opened a door. Her room smelled like apples, but underneath it was a scent I recognized, the smell that lingered in the T-shirt I slept with for six months after 9/11. I waited in the door while Christa walked around the bed, to a nightstand on the far side.

This room was the first one in the house that didn't look absolutely perfect. A tangle of mussed sheets lay across the bed, reminding me of how much Brett used to fidget in his sleep. I'd forgotten.

She opened a drawer and retrieved something before returning to the doorway. "For the past eighteen years, I have slept with this next to me every night. When I've needed comfort or felt alone, I held this and thought of you. I may have left you physically, but you have always been in my heart. I never wanted to hurt you. Running away was something I had to do for myself, and I will always regret how much I hurt you."

Without looking, I knew what she held: the pocket square I made the day before she left. A piece of my wedding dress, significantly more tattered than the last time I saw it. For the first time, I started to think about what I'd found in Christa, rather than what I'd lost in Brett. Something inside me broke, and I dropped onto the bed, silent tears streaming down my cheeks.

"I've missed you so much." My sobs muffled the words, but she got it.

"I missed you, too. Every minute of every day."

She offered me the square, but I waved my hand, not wanting to dirty it.

"Thanks." I kissed her cheek and wiped my eyes with one finger.

Our eyes met, and the remaining awkwardness between us evaporated. I saw something in her face that made my heart skip a beat. So many changes, but the eyes weren't one of them.

When I stared into Christa's eyes, I still saw my best friend, the only person I'd ever loved romantically. Her pupils dilated. Flustered, I moistened my lips with my tongue and looked at the ground.

Ethan's voice from the living room startled me, and I moved away, toward the door.

"Hey, Mom, come look at this backyard!"

"Be right there, honey." To my own ears, my voice sounded thick. Wrong. Hopefully, he wouldn't notice.

Christa ran one hand through her hair but seemed fine. Maybe she hadn't noticed anything weird. It could've been stress or my imagination. She headed through the dining room. I trailed behind her, wondering what just passed between us.

Christa

Wednesday night passed uneventfully, with Jess volunteering

to do the dishes after dinner and me finding myself sitting cross-legged on the floor while Ethan played video games beside me. He seemed easier with me than I expected, but maybe that was because he didn't really see me as a parental figure.

Or maybe it's because I bought pizza for dinner and had his favorite video games on hand. Having once been a seventeen-year-old boy, I prepared pretty well for this visit. Even if on some level, I'd known I was trying to buy his love before Jess pointed it out. I'd missed a lot of birthday and Christmas presents, after all. What harm could buying him a PS4 do? And an Xbox? He seemed happy with them.

Most of Thursday morning was taken up with preparation for dinner. After going to pick up doughnuts and coffee (and one soy hot cocoa) for breakfast, I spent most of the day in the kitchen, preparing the turkey and stuffing and mashed potatoes and bread and mashed turnip. Jess popped in to help a couple of times when she got tired of watching her son play video games.

As the day passed, our bodies fell into old routines our minds had forgotten. We moved more and more easily around each other until we rotated in each other's orbits much the way we did in college. Then, we'd been making Kraft Dinner together, mostly, or Chicken Helper. My cooking skills had improved considerably since I moved to the outskirts of a resort town, miles from the nearest real city, where fast-food restaurants were practically unheard of. But that was where Henny and Val had friends who gave me a job, so that's where I landed.

We didn't talk much while getting things ready, but as soon as the food was on the table, Ethan turned to me with the air of someone who'd been waving his hand at the teacher for twenty minutes and finally got called on to ask his question.

"So, you've known Mom for like twenty-five years, right?" he asked.

"I met her when she was fourteen." I wondered where this was going. Should I point out that I'd been MIA for a huge chunk of that time? Probably not. Instead, I sipped my wine and waited.

"So, you know how old she is now?" Ethan asked. "Because she's sworn up and down that she's twenty-nine for at least five years now."

A guffaw of laughter escaped me. Beside me, Jess choked on her water. Ethan kept glancing between us while we composed ourselves.

"Don't you dare," Jess said.

I turned to Ethan. "How old do you think I am?"

He studied my face for a minute. "Well, you wear a lot of makeup, and it's mostly old ladies who do that, right? So you're like fifty?"

Jess choked on a laugh, and I glared at her. "Did you put him up to that?"

"I swear I didn't."

"No, I'm not fifty. I am actually *younger* than your mother over there."

"You shush," Jess said.

"No way!" Ethan said at the same time.

"Yes, way. Your mother's birthday is in August, and mine's in December. We were born the same year. And your mother is—"

"—I know things about you, too," Jess said, brandishing a roll threateningly at me. "Like how you only got the nerve to ask me out because you didn't want me to date anyone else."

"Is that more embarrassing than the time you farted while on top of the pyramid at the Homecoming game?"

"I DID NOT!" She shrieked, throwing a piece of bread at my face. "That was Clara Chen and you know it."

Instead of answering, I lifted both hands to my mouth and made the loudest farting noise I could.

Ethan snorted and laughed so hard, he fell off his chair. Jess's efforts to pick him up only made him laugh harder. She sighed in fake exasperation before her shoulders started shaking, too.

Hiding my own smile, I went into the kitchen to refill my wine glass and grab more rolls. This first holiday dinner together as a family of sorts was coming along better than I ever could've imagined. Sure, it was a bit awkward at first. But Jess and I had spent weeks video chatting, catching up, her filling me on things I needed to know like Ethan's lactose intolerance and me reassuring Jess for the fifteen thousandth time that I wouldn't be upset if she stayed at a hotel, but I had plenty of room, and I didn't expect her to sleep with me.

You didn't just run into someone you hadn't seen in eighteen years and jump into bed with them. Especially not when one of you had changed genitalia.

Not that I'd mind if she wanted to curl up next to me. When I first left, I ached so much to have her beside me, I couldn't sleep. Dating wasn't easy when you're trans, especially while in the process. I'd had lovers since we parted, but none of them had tugged at my heart the way Jess did. Nothing would make me happier than to take her into my arms and kiss away all the pain I'd caused.

But she'd probably slap me in the face. And she'd be right to. She couldn't possibly love me anymore. I didn't deserve her, not after everything I put her through. Plus, marriages broke up all the time when one spouse's body changed after they got married. Our head housekeeper's husband left because she gained forty pounds. There was no reason to think Jess would be attracted to the person I'd become.

"Everything okay?" Jess asked from the doorway. "Need any help?"

Things had been going so well, I couldn't let these melancholy thoughts spoil an otherwise perfect evening. With luck, Jess and I could one day be friends again. That was all I had a right to ask for. I didn't even know if she was seeing anyone, and it wasn't my place to ask. She might guess I had feelings for her, and she'd get all flustered because she didn't return them. She'd pull back. Then she'd take Ethan back to Boston and I wouldn't see them again unless I sued for custody. I couldn't let that happen.

I ignored her first question and answered the second. "I was planning to dish up dessert in here, but I don't have enough hands to carry everything. If you don't mind grabbing the non-dairy whipped topping from the fridge while I cut the pie, we can both carry it into the dining room."

"Non-dairy? I can't believe you remembered." She popped onto her toes and kissed my cheek on her way to the fridge. My face burned, and I turned my attention to the pie so she couldn't see how that tiny contact got me so flustered.

"Of course I remembered. He's my son."

Jess rooted around in the fridge for a minute before returning to the counter with the fake whipped cream and an unopened bottle of wine. I pointed her at the corkscrew.

"Still, it takes time to learn these things and to remember. You have to want to make the effort." She paused, studying me. "I've seen the way you talk to Ethan, the way you engage him. The little things you did around here to make him feel comfortable, like buying his favorite cereal. I think you're going to make a wonderful parent."

Tears blurred my vision at that point. I wanted to drop the pie plates and throw my arms around her, but now wasn't the time. Appreciating my concern for Ethan didn't equal total forgiveness. Instead, I did the only thing that made sense. With a plate in each hand, I carried the pies back into the dining room, making sure the piece with the most whipped topping went to Ethan.

Jess

After dessert, I leaned back in my chair, patting my stomach. "That was amazing. Best meal I've had in ages."

Christa wiped her mouth with her napkin. "Thank you. I haven't had a real Thanksgiving feast like this in almost twenty years."

Too late, she realized what she said. She flushed, dropping her hands into her lap. Not knowing what else to do, I pushed my chair back and started clearing dishes. Christa touched my wrist to stop me.

"Please don't," she said. "I'm sorry. Let's just enjoy the evening."

A knock on the front door intruded on my intended reply. "You expecting someone?"

"Who would randomly show up on Thanksgiving?" Ethan asked.

"It's not Thanksgiving in Canada," I reminded him. "It's just Thursday. No one knows I'm American, so even if they remembered the holiday, it wouldn't occur to them that I might be celebrating."

"Oh, right." The doorbell rang once, twice. Ethan stood. "Want me to get it?"

"No, it's fine. I'll get it."

He hovered over his chair, while Christa went to the door. The bell rang again.

"What are you doing?" I asked. Whoever was out there, they wanted in badly. I wondered if I should grab the emergency medical stuff out of my bag.

"Sounds important, don't it?" Ethan said.

"Doesn't it," I corrected automatically.

He was right, though, that people who showed up at eight o'clock at night unannounced and rang the doorbell five times usually had something important to say. Probably something I didn't want him to witness.

"If you're done eating, take our plates into the kitchen and rinse them off."

He huffed as he went. I strained my ears to hear the conversation when the door opened. Christa's low murmur evaporated into the air between the front hall and the dining nook, but the response of the person on the porch rang crystal clear.

"Good evening," a female voice said. "I'm Christina McCall. Tina. I think you've heard of me?"

CHAPTER SEVENTEEN

Christa

Christina McCall stood on my doorstep. How? Why?

My entire new life flashed before my eyes. A peek over my shoulder into the dining room at Jess's gaping mouth told me she had heard this woman's declaration.

I stepped toward the porch to continue the conversation privately. "Can we please just—?"

"No, I don't think we can," the woman said. She raised her voice, pitching it over my shoulder, "Actually, *Christa*, I was hoping I could come in and talk to you. Don't your friends deserve to know who you are and what you've been doing?"

Behind me, Jess moved toward the kitchen. I couldn't hear what she said to Ethan but hoped he hadn't caught our conversation. I wavered, not wanting to talk to Tina where they could hear, not knowing what else to do. Dishes clinked in the other room, the faucet started running water.

Jess, creating a sound barrier. Bless her.

The last thing I wanted to do was let this strange woman into my home, but I couldn't risk what might happen if I slammed the door in her face. The house had other doors, and she could easily walk through any of them while I raced to turn the locks.

Holding the door open, I moved backward so she could step into the hallway.

Had I gotten to choose, it would have been difficult to find a woman more my opposite than this Other Christina. Despite standing up straight, chin held high, the top of her head didn't even reach my shoulder. Her curves strained at the buttons of her purple blouse. Long, jet-black hair contrasted with my shoulder-length strawberry blond highlights, and I'd have killed for those high cheekbones.

A million questions flew through my mind, but only one came out. "What do you want?"

She made a sound that might have been a laugh had it held a trace of humour. "Well, to start, I'd like my life back. This is my house you're living in, right? My name on the deed? My social insurance number on your bank accounts?"

My mouth dropped, and I stepped backward again. The wall brushed my backside. Nowhere to go.

"Ironic, isn't it," she said, "that I spent almost two decades living off the grid, hiding from my ex in some shitty American town, only to come back and find that, apparently, he wasn't looking for me at all?"

It seemed prudent not to correct her definition of irony, so I remained silent.

"I've got no money, no job, no friends left, no family, no real prospects for the future, but you're living it up real nicely. Turns out, you're better at being me than I was. But I think you've been me long enough. I hope you've got an extra bed, because I'm moving in."

"What? You can't!"

"Of course I can. It's my house," she said. "The name on the deed, *Christa*, is mine."

My mind raced, but if she was really who she claimed to be, my options had suddenly become very limited. Jess and Ethan didn't know I'd stolen this woman's identity. If she called the Mounties, they could take one look at her ID and toss me, Jess, and Ethan into the street.

Worse, I could go to jail, charged with entering the country illegally, impersonating a Canadian citizen… I didn't even know what else. Jess and Ethan would return to Boston, and I wouldn't see either of them again, possibly for years. When I was released, Jess would never speak to me again.

The only thing to do was find out what this Other Christina *really* wanted and hope she went away. Quickly.

But I couldn't be sure that I was looking at the real Christina McCall. Too much time had passed to say that this woman was the same person who posed for the picture on the passport I used to enter Canada. She'd dyed her naturally light-brown hair, but was the face the same?

Maybe if I sounded sure of myself, it would make me feel more confident. Desperately hoping my voice wouldn't shake, I said the only thing I could that might help make this nightmare go away. "I'm afraid I'm going to need to see some identification. Surely, you understand."

"Of course, *Christa*. After all, ID is everything these days."

She handed me a sheaf of papers, all photocopies: a Saskatchewan driver's license, long expired; a newer passport than the one that sat in a locked drawer in my office; a birth certificate, credit cards, school records, all kinds of stuff. All in the name of Christina McCall. Tina. Her picture, not mine. My heart pounded so forcefully, she could probably see it beating against my chest.

My mouth opened and closed as I looked from her to the papers and back, but no words came out. I couldn't believe she'd found me. Or that she was here, now, at the worst possible time.

"You should probably shut the door. You're letting out the warm air. Also, my bags are still on the porch, so maybe you or that boy you're hiding from me can go fetch 'em." I don't know what she saw on my face, but she softened for a moment. "Don't worry. Play nice, and we don't need to tell the kid who I am. Call me Tina. But I'm here for a few days, at least, until I get what I need. I'm thinking about twenty thousand should be enough to start. Then we're going to talk long-term plans."

My mind raced. I couldn't let her in, have her tell Jess and Ethan everything I'd done. Not now, when we were starting to build a new foundation.

"Please," I whispered desperately. "Can we go get coffee and talk about it there? I promise not to try to stop you from coming back here. I just want to discuss this somewhere more private."

"You don't want the ball and chain and the kiddo to know what you did?" I just blinked at her, and she grinned wolfishly. "I've been outside listening for quite a while. Made some interesting tapes."

"You know it's a crime to record a conversation without the consent of the parties, right?"

"I *had* consent. After all, one of the parties to the conversation was Christina McCall, and that's me, right?"

Her logic probably wouldn't hold up in court, but I saw no reason to argue legalities with the person whose identity I'd stolen. After all, by the time we got to court, I would already be pretty screwed.

At the moment, I just wanted to get out of there before Jess or Ethan wandered out of the kitchen. I pitched my voice to carry down the hall.

"Jess? Ethan? I have to step out for a few minutes. A work emergency's come up. I'll be back as soon as I can."

Ethan poked his head out of the kitchen. "And you'll tell me how old Mom is when you get back?"

Before I could answer, Jess pulled him back into the kitchen and stuck her head out into the hall. "What's going on? Who is this?"

She tugged her left ear twice, hard and shot me a questioning look. Our old signal from when we were kids, to be used only in emergencies. The fact that she even remembered made me more determined to keep her out of this. I'd hurt her enough. I didn't make the return gesture, tugging on my right ear three times.

"I'll tell you later," I said.

She considered me for a moment, still trying to keep Ethan from opening the door further. Apparently, the need to keep him out of whatever was happening outweighed her own curiosity. "Okay."

"I'll bring back doughnuts. We shouldn't be gone long."

Beside me, Tina stepped forward, extending one hand. "My name's Tina. It's a pleasure to meet you."

"Jess." She gave a firm shake before retreating to the kitchen, turning Ethan back at the doorway with a firm, "Dishes. Now."

Tina left her bags in the hallway, and we drove to the Tim Horton's at the end of the block. Neither of us spoke during the ride. Although I racked my brain, I couldn't come up with any way out of this, had no idea what to do. Other than money, what did she want? Why was she here? How had she found me after all these years? And how could I trust this wasn't some elaborate scam?

As soon as we sat down with the coffee I didn't really want, I posed the last question to her and asked to see the documents she'd shoved at me in the hall again.

"I can do you one better," she said, pulling several items from her purse. "I've got an ink pad and paper here, and a magnifying glass. Compare my fingerprints to the ones on my birth certifi-cate. Hell, if you want a laugh, we'll compare yours, too."

"A laugh" would've been awesome at the moment, but looking at my own fingerprints wasn't likely to provide one. Instead, I watched Tina press her thumb into the ink pad, then onto a white sheet of paper. Having never examined a finger-print under a magnifying glass, I didn't have the first clue what I was looking for.

The ink on the birth certificate was smudged, the fingerprints much smaller. I couldn't swear they were identical, but I couldn't swear they weren't. Both looked swirly. I couldn't swear I wasn't looking at a drawing made by a toddler, either. Still, I played the role, peering into the glass as long as I could before things got weird. Weirder. Finally, I shrugged, put it down, and pushed the paper back at her.

"What do you want from me?"

"Easy," she said. "When I decided to return to Canada, I went to a bank to open an account. Imagine my surprise when they told me I already had accounts there! Two of 'em. Checking and a nice, plump savings."

I felt the color drain from my face. She was clearly enjoying this moment, sipping her coffee and smiling at my discomfort. "What did you do?"

"Oh, stop. They wouldn't let me touch the money without your PIN, which I didn't know. But I did ask for a copy of my most recent statement, which they kindly provided. That gave me your address."

"If you don't want money, why are you here?"

"I didn't say I don't want money. But if I just clean out your accounts and walk away, that's not nearly as much fun for me. Besides, I wanted to see my new house, see how you've been taking care of it, find out what other assets you had in my name. This is about more than a few thousand bucks in a savings account."

Yes, it was. It was about losing everything at a time when I'd finally started to feel like I'd regained a part of my old life. When I'd finally reunited with the person who mattered most to me. This woman couldn't simply waltz in and take all that mattered to me.

But I didn't know how to make her go away, or how to stop her from destroying my fragile new family before she left.

Jess

After Christa left with the other Christina McCall, we finished clearing the dishes. Ethan peppered me with questions about the stranger at the door, and I mostly ignored them, not sure how much of what I knew to reveal. As a general policy, I didn't hide things from my son, but this wasn't my secret to tell. Without knowing why Tina had shown up and what she wanted, I couldn't begin to think what to say.

Instead, I directed the conversation toward hockey, and Ethan happily chattered while bringing me plates from the dining room to put in the dishwasher. We moved to the living room shortly thereafter to watch a local game, and that's where Christa found us when she returned, an hour later, with Tina in tow.

We made quick introductions, and I sent Ethan begrudgingly off to bed with strict instructions to keep the door locked and stay out of sight. Maybe I should still take him to a hotel. But he was almost an adult, and I couldn't treat him like a little boy forever. Unless Tina appeared to be dangerous, avoiding her wasn't the answer.

Christa said, "Tina will be staying with us for a few days. Tina, you can take my room, and I'll sleep on the couch."

The way Tina looked me up and down made me uncomfortable. It didn't bother me in the slightest when she went off to take over Christa's bedroom. The less time in her presence, the better. Not knowing what else to do while Christa gathered her belongings, I found sheets and started making up a bed on the couch. That's where she found me, a few minutes later.

"Is everything okay?" I kept my voice low, well aware that little pitchers, teenagers, and adult interlopers all have big ears.

She started to shrug, and then her face crumpled. Quickly, I led her down to the guest suite in the basement, where she could cry on my shoulder in peace. The story came out in bits and pieces, most of it stuff I'd put together on my own while she was gone.

"Did you really steal that woman's passport?"

"She left it in a backpack I bought secondhand. I had no idea who she was or why she hadn't taken it with her. The rest of the bag was empty. I figured no one would ever know or care if I used the passport to cross the border."

"And then you just kept using it?"

"Yeah. It was wrong, sure, but I didn't have any valid ID or a way to get one. At one point, I tried to find out if she was still alive, but the internet wasn't as prevalent then as it is now, and sounds like she was living off the grid. Wouldn't have found her, anyway. I never dreamed she'd show up here."

"What if the whole thing's a scam? She could be just trying to get your money?"

"If she were a scam artist, she'd be calling or emailing in weird English that sounded like it had been run through Google translate too many times, claiming we won the 'Microsoft Yahoo Facebook lottery' or some crap." She gave a hollow chuckle. "No, she's legit. She's got all the paperwork to prove that she's who she says she is. I mean, I'm not saying she's honest or anything—"

"—because she's a blackmailer?"

"Sure. But she really is Christina McCall, and I really have been using her identity since 2001. She could've called the Mounties on me, dragged me away, not given any warning. Then you'd have run, and I'd never get to know Ethan. What-ever happens, I'm glad she didn't do that."

I rested my head on her shoulder. She put one arm around me. We fit together like Legos. It felt right, more comfortable than I would've expected.

"Me, too," I said.

"What am I supposed to do?"

That, of course, was a question I couldn't answer. "Do you have a good lawyer?"

She shook her head. "I'm scared, Jess. I don't want to go to jail. Three months ago, my instinct would have been to take off. Run for my life." She moved a small picture hanging on the far wall, revealing a small safe. With a quick glance at the staircase, she keyed in the combination and opened it, showing me stacks of cash. "It's not much, but it would keep me going for a few months. I've been preparing for this moment for ages."

The safe swung shut, and the picture settled back into place before Christa joined me back on the couch.

"So why aren't you leaving?"

"Isn't it obvious?"

Our eyes met, and the depth of emotion looking back at me startled me, made me uncomfortable. Sure, we'd had that moment earlier, but… it had been a long time. And a lot had changed. She'd changed. I'd changed. We weren't Brett and Jess anymore.

"I can't run out on my son when I've just met him for the first time," she said.

Oh, right. Duh. This wasn't about me. And there was no reason in the world for the pang of disappointment in my stomach. If my husband had been in love with me, he wouldn't have faked his own death and moved to a foreign country in the first place. We were done.

"I'm glad you see that," I said. "Because if you did, you'd have a hard time convincing him to let you back in if you ever showed up again."

"I know. And I wouldn't blame him for shutting me out. I'm not leaving you guys, but you should go. Change your flights."

"I'm not leaving you alone with a stranger who's informed you that she's moving into your house and taking over your life. But first thing tomorrow, I am taking Ethan to a hotel until she's gone. We'll get a cot if you want to stay with us." It was late enough that we'd probably be okay in the house for one night. Ethan and I both knew basic self-defense. He was twice Tina's size, and an excellent tackler.

Still, the mother in me wondered if I should've brought him down here to stay with me. Just in case.

"I'll be fine here. I don't think she's dangerous. I think she's desperate."

"That makes her dangerous."

"She wants money. If she kills us, she'll go to jail, and she can't spend any money." She squeezed my hand. "I should be getting to bed."

My eyes went to the bed on the other side of the basement, which was more than large enough for two. But we'd had enough confusion for one night. Lying next to my dead spouse, listening to her breathe, aware of the space between us... that wasn't something I was prepared to deal with.

If Christa suspected what I was thinking, she didn't let on. Instead, she just leaned over, kissed my forehead, and whispered, "Thanks for everything."

Then she went up the stairs, the door clicking softly behind her, while I tried to dissect the whirling emotions inside me.

CHAPTER EIGHTEEN

Jess

The next morning, I woke up early, showered, dressed and got ready to leave, then knocked softly on Ethan's door. "It's me, buddy. Open up."

It took several minutes of thumping and a couple of muffled curses I pretended I didn't hear before the lock disengaged and the door opened a crack. What on earth had he used to barricade the door? One of Ethan's big brown eyes peeked out at me.

"Mom? What time is it?"

"It's time for you to get up. We're headed up the mountain."

His face transformed in an instant, swallowed by a huge grin. "We're going skiing?"

It was supposed to be a surprise, something for me and Christa to take him to do together. But she was otherwise engaged, and the two of us needed to get out for the day, anyway. As much as I wished Christa could come with us, it seemed better to get my son away from Tina.

"Yup. Gather up all your stuff—we're going to stay at the resort tonight, so we can stop and rest any time we want, then go back out. Maybe I'll let you talk me into snowboarding tomorrow."

He let out a whoop, and the door closed while he dressed.

A quick examination of the kitchen told me that we'd need to stop at a coffee shop for breakfast. Christa's pantry offered about five kinds of fiber-rich and low-fat cereal, but nothing I'd be able to tempt a teenage boy to eat. She'd apparently overlooked one thing in her plan to buy Ethan's affection. And that was okay with me. I'd rather see them getting along than see Christa offer my son fourteen types of sugar cereal to get his love. Even if we were about to eat doughnuts.

Special occasion. Because everyone should get doughnuts when their dead father turns out to be alive. Or something.

While Ethan got ready, I quietly packed up the rest of my stuff. Then I went to the couch where Christa slept. Long brown tendrils fell across her cheeks. My hand itched to reach out, to touch the strands, reassure myself that this person was real and not a ghost from my past. But I knew better. Without the help of mascara, short stubby lashes lay across her cheeks. Her jawline was softer than it had been, her brow more feminine. If I leaned in, would I spot the surgical scars? Would it be weird to have my face so close to hers?

What would it have been like to go to sleep next to Brett and wake up next to Christa?

Shaking my head, I knelt beside her and gently shook her awake.

"Hey," I said softly.

"Hey, yourself. What time is it?"

"It's early. Ridiculously early. Ethan and I are going skiing. I figured it would be better for us to get out while you dealt with everything. Is it okay if we borrow your car for the day? We're going to stay at the resort, but I'll get you a room and come pick you up this afternoon."

She ran one hand through her hair, blinked a few times, and then rubbed her eyes. "Sure. My keys are in my purse." She picked up a bag from the floor beside the couch and handed it to me. "Do me a favor though?"

"Sure. What?"

"There's no way I'm going to remember this conversation when I wake up again. Text me?"

Before I could respond, she'd rolled back over and was breathing deeply. Just like when we were in college. I'd once come home late and found Brett asleep at the table, head on his books. He'd had an exam in the morning, so I woke him up and quizzed him until I was satisfied he could pass the test. Even convinced him to walk to the bed with me. The next morning, he didn't remember me coming home, had no idea how he'd gotten in the bed, and had no recollection of our twenty-minute conversation. He still managed a B+.

Smiling at the memory, I leaned over and kissed Christa's forehead. She muttered something unintelligible in her sleep, one hand swiping at her face like she swatted a fly.

Something in my heart eased at the unconscious gesture. Even when life changed, some things stayed the same.

∞ ♡ ∞

Christa

A horrid screeching jolted me awake sometime later. Someone was singing in my kitchen. Did Jess sound that horrible when she sang? I couldn't remember. The noise sent shards of pain digging into my brain. Or maybe that was the fifth of bourbon I drank after everyone else went to bed. Sunlight streaming through the front windows told me I'd slept pretty late. Unfortunately, I hadn't managed to sleep until my nightmare ended.

Beside me, my phone contained a text from Jess, telling me she'd taken Ethan skiing. A pang hit my stomach when I realized I'd missed my chance to go with them, lost a full day of bonding with my son, because of something stupid I'd done years earlier. I should've covered my tracks better, gotten a legal name change, put the house in the name of a trust or something. At first, I'd planned to, but the more time passed, the more I convinced myself that the real Christina McCall was gone, another victim of 9/11 or killed in an accident or living in America under an assumed name. After a few years, I became comfortable in my skin, and it never occurred to me that the person whose identity I'd "borrowed" might show up, wanting it back. After a while, it was easier to let myself believe she must've died before I got her backpack.

The last thing I wanted was to face Tina and be polite, but stalling and avoiding her would only continue this fiasco. Extending her visit was the last thing I wanted.

She stood in the kitchen, wet hair streaming down her back, cooking eggs and singing a song I didn't recognize at the top of her lungs.

"Why are you doing this?"

"Because you never really know what you're capable of until you're tested. Life took a lot from me, you took my identity. Finding you seems like maybe it's life's way of saying 'Sorry for all the shit, Tina.'"

"You're not the only person who's suffered, you know. It's not like I did this for shits and giggles. Did you ever think what kind of circumstances might have led me here?"

She leaned back and lit a cigarette, taking a long pull before blowing puffs of smoke across the kitchen. I was torn between asking her not to smoke in my house and asking if I could have one. Never in all the years since college had smoking tempted me so much.

"Nope, and I don't care. I'm broke. I'm outta options, and here you are with a fancy house, and you broke the law and you're only doing so well because you're pretending to be me, and that don't seem fair."

Pointing out that, in a fair world, none of this would ever

have happened because I wouldn't have been born in a male body probably wasn't going to help me any. And I somehow doubted that the person blackmailing me would be interested in the fact that I worked and earned the money to buy this house. It wasn't hers, and there was no reason it should be. Instead I opened a beer despite it being morning, offered her one, and sat down at the table.

"Why'd you leave Canada? What happened?"

She eyed me and took a pull from the bottle. "You don't give a flying rat's ass about me. Don't fake it."

"You haven't exactly given me a reason to want to be besties," I pointed out. "I don't even know you. Maybe if I did, this could be easier for both of us. Maybe we've both had hard lives and it would feel better to commiserate a bit. But mostly, I'm just curious where you've been. Honestly, after all this time, I thought you were dead."

She still seemed suspicious, and I didn't really know why I wanted to talk to her, but it seemed better than sitting around and wishing she would leave. Maybe she'd say something that would help us connect, help me convince her to leave me and my family alone.

"When I was real young, real stupid, I got involved with this guy. He was good-looking, a sweet talker, but mean as a rattlesnake when he got drinking. And some days, he got drinking enough for two people. I had no job, no money, no education, nowhere to go."

"What about your family?"

"They disowned me when I ran off with Harvey. Insisted I was making a mistake, and I was too proud to go home and tell the truth."

I pictured telling my older brother, Brad, who'd spent most of my teenage years teaching me to "be a man," that I'd transitioned. Today, I could probably do it. But I remembered the fear that seized me before I left and knew I'd never have been able to tell him if I hadn't gotten the opportunity to escape. The fear of telling Jess, the certainty my parents would disown me…

"Yeah, I know that feeling," I said.

"So, one day, I took off. Found a trucker driving down to Boston who agreed to take me as far as Albany. Hitched a ride. We stopped at a motel as soon as we crossed the border. I was young and stupid, he'd been nice to me, so I let him fuck me. When I woke up, he was gone. So was all my stuff. How'd you get it?"

"I bought the backpack at a second-hand store in Boston. Guess the trucker sold it when he got where he was going. Your passport was in one of the pockets."

"So why'd you take it?"

I took a deep breath. She could be recording this conversation. But if she wanted to turn me in, I was in trouble anyway. Identity theft in Quebec could be punished by up to five years in jail. So could using a fake social insurance number to get a job. So could several other things I'd done. I'd looked it all up when I moved here. And I had no defense. It would be easy enough for her to prove what I'd done.

"On September 11, 2001, I was supposed to be one of the passengers on United Flight 175," I said. She widened her eyes, telling me she knew what that meant. "Had a panic attack at the last minute and didn't board the plane. When it hit the World Trade Center, I had the perfect opportunity to start a new life. Everyone thought I was dead. But I couldn't get across the border without a passport. We had similar coloring, and Canadian border patrol wasn't that concerned with citizens returning to the country, so I decided to give it a shot. I had nothing to lose."

She shook her head. "Maybe we're not that different. Tell you what: You leave, give me the house keys, never show your face in Quebec again, and I'll forget all of this ever happened."

That sounded simple, but the house was worth over $250,000,

and I bet Tina knew that. Even if she took on the remaining mortgage payments, she'd be getting a lot of money.

"How long do I have to think about it?"

"I'll give you one week. I've been living in a commune near Albany for the past sixteen years, working hard without any modern conveniences. I need to relax. I'm going to book a stay at a spa—on you, of course. When I get back, we'll talk more."

After a quick trip to the basement safe, I pushed a wad of cash at her. Then I named my hotel. "You stay away from Jess and Ethan, or there's nothing else. I lose them, I don't care what happens to me."

She snatched the bills from my hand without hesitation. "Deal."

Jess

About an hour before lunch, Christa texted me that Tina was gone and wouldn't be back for at least a week. We hadn't checked into the hotel yet, and Christa was confident that she was gone for now, so we returned to the house for the evening.

Dinner was a quiet affair, with Ethan worn out from going up and down the mountain all day and Christa and I both lost in our own thoughts. I wondered if she regretted running away. If she was thinking about running away again now. What would happen when Ethan and I returned to Boston? Would she really stand by her word and continue her relationship with Ethan? With both of us? Did I even want her to? Everything happened so fast, and I kept moving forward, reacting without really thinking.

When we finished eating, I told Ethan to help with the dishes and went to sit on the back porch, rocking back and forth and staring out over the frozen landscape. I didn't know how much time passed before Christa found me there.

"Hey. Mind if I join you?"

I scooted over to the side of the bench without looking up. "Plenty of room for two."

She sat, our shoulders touching. I thought about when we were kids, sitting on my parents' front porch, looking up at the same stars we saw now. Never in a million years would I have guessed we'd wind up here, not like this. When we were kids, I didn't even understand what "transgender" meant, and faking your own death was reserved for Christopher Pike novels. Throw in an unplanned pregnancy and a bit of identity theft, and I couldn't believe this was my life. I didn't have the slightest idea what to do or say anymore.

Part of me longed for the days when everything made sense. Tomorrow morning, I could pack up my son, fly home, go back to my practice, fix up my online dating profile, and pretend that all of this had been a dream. Ethan and I could live a good life, without Christa. And Christa wasn't my problem. She'd made her bed, and she would have to learn to live with those choices. She'd forfeited the right to my love and help the day she'd let me think she was killed in a terrorist attack.

But... you couldn't control how you felt about someone. Love wasn't about rights and obligations. The girl inside me who'd spent day and night with her best friend, with the only person who'd understood what it was like to be constantly at war with her father, who'd spent eighteen years feeling like half of her was missing, couldn't walk away.

Plus, as confusing and frustrating as all of this twas, we still had a connection. Our old easiness was still there, along with buried emotions that needed to be explored. I needed to figure things out. Walking away and abandoning her wasn't an option.

"Is she gone?" I asked.

"Yeah, she's gone. For now. But she says she'll be back in a week. I don't think we're lucky enough for her to just vanish."

"What are you going to do?"

"I don't know. My options are pretty limited: I can go to jail, I can pay a blackmailer for the rest of my life, I can disappear somewhere up north and hope she doesn't find me a second time. A realtor can sell the house and send me the money when it's all over. There's a lot of land in Canada, not a lot of people once you get closer to the Arctic Circle."

At those last words, my blood ran cold. If she took off, I'd never see her again. Ethan would never have a real relationship with his father. All of my indecision about helping her vanished when the sheer terror of losing Christa a second time hit me. It was too soon. Even if I couldn't forgive or learn to trust her enough to be friends again, and even if we never regained the intimacy we had when we were kids, I needed more time with her.

"What's she asking for?"

"She wants the house. And before she left, she asked for twenty thousand dollars—Canadian. That's about fifteen thousand U.S., I think."

"I have the money," I said. "If all she wants is fifteen thousand dollars, I can give it to her."

"I can't take your money, Jess."

"Sure you can. We're still legally married. Part of it technically belongs to you, anyway." She started to reply, but I stopped her. "Your 'death' gave me the money to go to medical school. I'd have nothing without you."

"We'd have found a way to make it work. You'd have gotten loans and been just as successful."

"Maybe," I said. "Or maybe you'd have resented me for the fact that you had to work long hours to support us, and we'd have wound up going through a bitter custody battle."

"I doubt that," Christa said. "More likely, we'd be living

together, me silently hating myself but still loving you, and hoping my self-loathing didn't drive you away."

I squeezed her hand. "Never."

"So you forgive me?"

"Don't press your luck." My smile took the bite off the words. In truth, I understood why she had left. It hurt, and understanding maybe wasn't the same thing as forgiveness, but it went a long way.

"You've got a great kid, you know. Ethan's in there doing the dishes. I didn't even have to ask."

He'd never once voluntarily done the dishes at home. I swallowed back a sarcastic reply. "Thank you."

Even after our time apart, Christa still knew me better than anyone else. "You okay? You seem a bit too laconic."

"Just thinking about things. You and Ethan and holidays and how we're going to do this."

"Whatever makes you comfortable," she said. "I'd like to get to know him better, but it's ultimately up to you. You know that."

Deep down, under the frustration and resentment, I did know that. The person I used to know wanted me to be happy, first and foremost. She'd never fight for half my earnings, not after everything that happened. Even if she wound up losing her house. The million-dollar question, of course, was: What would make me happy?

We swung back in forth in silence, lost in our thoughts.

Finally, I spoke. "What are you going to do about Other Christina McCall?"

"I don't know." She sighed. "She said she'd leave me alone if I paid her off. But what's to stop her from asking for more? When does it end? Will she show up at work, get me fired? Try to take over my job? Decide she wants hush money each month?"

"Maybe," I said. "And do you have to change your name? Get new ID, a new job, everything."

"Yeah, I guess so. Fuck. How do I even do that? Who am I? What do I do?"

The panic in her voice brought tears to my eyes. All I wanted was to make her pain go away. Without even thinking about it, I said the last words I ever expected to hear myself utter—but what seemed like the most natural solution in the world.

"You should come home with us."

CHAPTER NINETEEN

Christa

"You should come home with us," Jess said.

I hadn't set foot in America since I left. Watching Bo get beaten, knowing that it wasn't really the Land of the Free for people who weren't born straight, or cisgender, or exactly as society wanted them to be, terrified me. The world had progressed, sure, but it also took a huge step backward at the end of 2016. It would take a long time to repair that damage. Also, I didn't have a U.S. passport anymore.

"I am home. I have friends and a job and a life here."

"You know what I mean. You've made a good life for yourself, but this isn't *home*. It's not where your family is, where you grew up."

"Home is where the heart is, right? I feel safe here." I'd never feel safe in America again.

"Things have changed since you left. Massachusetts is far more advanced than most of the rest of the country."

"But I'm dead," I said. She couldn't argue with that.

"Actually, you won't be for much longer," she said.

Her words sent a shiver down my spine. I blinked at her for a long moment. "What the hell are you talking about?"

"After I ran into you in September, I started the process to have your death certificate rescinded. You're alive, and your name shouldn't be listed on the plaques with the victims of 9/11. It's not fair to everyone who lost someone that day."

She had a point about that, but still, anger flared within me. "You can't do that! You don't have any right—"

"I have every right," she said. "In the eyes of the world, I'm your widow. But I'm not. I have a living spouse, which means I'm legally married. If I want to date anyone else, have sex, have another baby, all of those things would make me an adulteress. Getting remarried would make me a bigamist. That's a felony, and I don't want to go to jail."

"The odds that anyone would ever find out, that they'd report you, are—"

"About as good as the odds that the real Christa McCall would turn up on your doorstep?"

I flushed, but couldn't refute her point. It didn't matter. This wasn't a tit for tat situation, where my lie justified her taking action without my knowledge. I had a right to make decisions about my own life.

She continued. "It's not just that. I received a settlement as a family member of a 9/11 victim that I'm not legally entitled to. That money needs to be repaid. I can't stop you from vanishing again, can't make you come home and tell everyone the truth, but I needed to get you declared *un*-dead so I'm not living a lie. It'll take time, but I needed to get the ball rolling."

I fumed. "Still, you should've told me about it first. What if the insurance company wants the money back? I don't have a quarter of a million dollars lying around!"

"I do," she said quietly. "I'm an orthopedic surgeon, remember? My partner and I run a successful practice."

She'd said earlier that she was a doctor and doing well enough, but I hadn't dreamed she'd become wealthy over the years. Good for her. Still, I started to protest. She interrupted me.

"Anyway, it doesn't matter. My lawyer said because so many

years passed, the insurance company can't sue for it now. The money's mine. Ours, I guess."

"No," I said. "It's yours. Life insurance money is for the survivors."

"You survived. In fact, you did better than that. You prevailed. And now you're in a tight spot, and you need some-place to go. Come home."

Her words lit a beacon of hope inside me. Could it be that easy? Go home, change my name legally to the one I'd been using, start a new life? Spend time with my son and my best friend, even if she no longer wanted to be my wife? It sure beat spending twenty years in a Canadian jail for identity theft and fraud.

I squeezed her hand before settling back onto the bench. She leaned against me, and I put my arm around her like I'd done a thousand times when we were kids. My mind never allowed me to remember those days, but my heart stirred at the feel of Jess nestling against me, the scent of her shampoo, the touch of her face against a shoulder that had far less muscle than during my football days.

With a start, I realized how much I still loved her. No matter how much I'd changed over the years, we had a history that couldn't be ignored. That I didn't want to ignore. Jess had always been my soulmate. When we started hanging out in high school, it wasn't because I wanted to date her—we'd been friends for years before I felt anything romantic toward her. Our relationship naturally developed and became physical over time, but our love was rock solid before that happened.

When I asked her to marry me, it was because I loved her and wanted her by my side for the rest of my life. Leaving Jess had been the hardest thing I'd ever done. I didn't want to do it again.

Asking her to take me back could prove to be harder. If not impossible.

"This is nice," she mumbled.

I agreed. "I've really missed you, Jess."

"I missed you, too."

With one hand, I stroked her hair. She looked up at me, and our eyes met. Could she still read my every expression the way she used to? "You know, I never stopped loving you."

She sat up slowly, eyes roaming over my face. She stroked my hair, my ears, as if re-memorizing my features. Or trying to reconcile the woman in front of her with the man she married.

"I tried," she said. "I wanted to stop loving you. Everyone fixed me up—my mom, my partner, everyone. I set up online dating profiles, I went on a lot of first dates. A couple of times, I tried to force myself to feel something I didn't. But it was always wrong. Like, on some level, I was waiting for you to come back, even though I knew it was impossible."

As if in a trance, she leaned forward, placing her lips within a hair's width of mine. For a heartbeat, we almost kissed. Indecision froze me in place. The last thing I wanted was for her to back away, but I didn't want to make any move that might scare her. It had been a long time since I'd been this close to anyone. Much, much, too long.

She licked her lips, and I gave in, pressing my mouth to hers, just for a heartbeat. When she didn't pull back, I kissed her again. This time, her lips definitely moved beneath mine. I cupped her face, giving in to the temptation to show her all the feelings I'd been holding back since the moment I first spotted her.

After a minute, the intensity of what we were doing overwhelmed me. I pulled back, our foreheads touching.

I whispered, "Is this okay? Is it too weird?"

"Honestly, I don't know," she said. "It's weird. I'm not sure I forgive you, and so much has changed, but you're still the person I used to love."

"But I'm a woman now."

"Yes. I am also a woman."

"And you're straight," I said.

"Am I? You know me well enough to say that I've never felt any desire for a woman? Never dated a woman? You assume I'm exactly the same person I was in college, just like you are?"

"Point taken," I said. "Have you ever dated a woman?"

A flush touched her cheeks. "Well, no. But my point remains valid."

I chuckled. "You're right."

"I mean, think about how long it took for us to start dating after we met. When you died, I tried dating, and it was impossible for me to find anyone I wanted to get physical with. I was really turned off by guys making sexual innuendo early on, or sending me dick pics—"

"That's because unsolicited dick pics are disgusting. When someone sends me those, I use Google images to send one right back. Usually a bigger one."

She smiled. "Eventually, though, I concluded that I have to get to know someone—male or female—before I'm capable of feeling anything romantic, any sexual feelings. I'd just started to think there was something wrong with me when I met a patient who was demisexual. And all of a sudden, everything fell into place."

"So you're attracted to men and women?" I asked. It wasn't something that ever occurred to me when I knew her, but she'd never been one to comment on the attractiveness of celebrities or other guys, even when we were just friends. I'd always thought she was just being considerate of my feelings.

"I'm attracted to a *person*. To their insides."

"So you're okay with this? With…us?"

She nibbled on her lower lip, something I'd seen her do a thousand times. It had never been more endearing. "I'm not sure I'd go that far. We still have a lot to work out. But…I've missed you. Kissing you feels nice. Right now, that's good enough."

She leaned forward, lips curving into a smile. I pulled her against me, and my mouth found hers. As soft and supple as I remembered. She shifted, and I ran my tongue across her lower lip. Her tongue met mine, hesitantly at first, but then more eagerly. A sigh escaped me.

My hand found her waist, and she trailed her fingers down my back. I shifted so I lay on the bench with Jess atop me. She moaned when my hands found her perfect breasts. We still fit together like pieces of a puzzle.

I needed more. Needed to feel her burning skin against mine.

One of Jess's hands moved to my breast, and she stiffened. I pulled back. "Are you okay?"

Her face turned bright red. "I don't know. This is really new. But I made a vow. Until death do us part, right?"

A wave of disappointment hit me. If she was only doing this because she didn't believe in divorce… "The man you married died, remember?"

"I know. Really, I do. But I never stopped loving that person. And now that you're sitting here in front of me…I *want* to be okay with it. We just need to take things slowly, if that's okay."

I pulled her toward me, rested my chin on top of her hair. "Of course it's okay. How could I expect you not to need a little time? This is a major adjustment, for both of us. It's not like you adding blond streaks to your hair."

With a chuckle, she reached up and twirled a highlighted strand around one finger. "No, I guess it's not. But…my heart beats faster when you're around. I'm more alive. I just want to…"

She tilted her face up to mine, and I leaned forward. We closed the gap between us, parted lips meeting eagerly. I cupped her face, moved my hands into her hair, reveling in the touch, taste, and feel of someone I never thought I'd see again. Someone I never even dared dream would let me touch her if she found out the truth.

Jess shifted, pulled me closer and sweeping her tongue into my mouth. If there was a God, I'd found my heaven. I never wanted to spend another second without this woman. I moaned.

She stiffened a second time, and I cursed myself for getting carried away so easily. Then she leaned back, and I realized what had made her pause.

Over Jess's shoulder, the patio doors stood opened. Ethan stood in the opening, mouth agape. Fragments of glass littered the floor around him: one of my plates. I'd been so caught up, I hadn't even heard it.

Before I could move, Ethan found his voice. "Mom? Christa? What are you doing?"

Jess

Oh, shit.

Ethan's voice sent a wave of panic through me. Caught by my own son, when I didn't even know what I was doing. Not knowing how to explain things, I immediately went on the offensive. Time to change the conversation.

I bolted to my feet, ran one shaking hand through my hair, and put my fists on my hips. "What are you doing up so late, young man?"

He snorted. "Nice try. I'm going to be eighteen soon. I'm not a child." He eyed me, Christa still lying on the couch, then me again. "Are you two sleeping together?"

"No! Absolutely not." It was Christa who answered, but my cheeks grew warm. Sure, we hadn't made it that far, but who knew where things had been headed? Certainly not me.

"It's none of your business, Ethan," I said.

My son turned to Christa, who'd risen to a sitting position. When she was nervous, she played with her hair. Brett used to do it, too, tucking longer strands behind his ears, but it was more noticeable now that Christa's locks tumbled down past her shoulders. It was adorable. Not the point.

Ethan asked, "Do you have any idea how fucked up this is?"

"Language, Ethan," I said automatically.

"Of course we know. There's a lot of history here, and a lot of feelings to unpack." Christa's words came out in a rush like they did when she was uncomfortable. "Let's talk in the morning. Your mom and I got a little carried away walking down memory lane, but we still have a lot to discuss. Why don't you head to bed?"

"It's only seven-thirty."

D'oh. So much for that. My son probably hadn't gone to bed at seven-thirty in about ten years.

"Okay, then," Christa said. "There's a Coffee Crisp on the kitchen counter, and you can watch whatever you want on the TV in the basement."

"I don't drink coffee," he said. The wary look on his face hadn't budged an inch. In that moment, I felt very much like the child, not the parent. And I couldn't get my warring emotions under control enough to do anything about it.

"It's candy," she said. "If you don't like it, there's other stuff in the bag. I didn't know what you'd like, so I bought a bunch. Help yourself."

Ethan's slitted eyes grew rounder. "I'll be in the kitchen, checking out the candy. And *listening* to you two."

The door slid shut behind him, and feet pattered across the wood floor toward the kitchen. I raised one eyebrow at my spouse. "He can watch anything he wants?"

She shrugged. "Canadian TV is different from American. He's not going to find anything he hasn't seen before. Besides, I don't have cable. He'll probably wind up watching my Star Wars Blu-rays unless he finds a hockey game."

"We love Star Wars." I held out one hand. "Want to join him?"

She studied my face before taking it. "Do you want to talk about what just happened?"

Leaning forward, I kissed her softly on the cheek, without

passion. "Later. I have a lot to think about. Right now, it's more important for us to spend time with our son."

"But you're okay with this? With… everything?"

My stomach churned, but she didn't need to know about that or the roiling thoughts in my head. Christa remembered my parents, my upbringing. We were light years away from my comfort zone. Tonight, after the lights went out, I'd lie alone in the bed in the guest room, staring at the ceiling and wondering what on earth was going on. But now, my son needed me. Needed both his parents. Everything else could wait.

"Not yet," I admitted. "Not entirely, anyway. But I will be."

PART 4

I didn't run away to come home the same.

— E.L. Konigsburg, From the Mixed-Up Files of Mrs. Basil E. Frankweiler

CHAPTER TWENTY

Christa

Crossing the border had been much easier before 9/11. It certainly wasn't as easy in 2019 as it had been for me to cross into Quebec. Especially because not only were the border patrol agents on the U.S. side stricter, I no longer possessed a valid passport: the one I'd found in 2001 expired years earlier. Not intending to leave Canada, I'd never renewed it.

Flying was out of the question. Even if I'd had the right ID, my fear of giant metal death traps in the sky only grew stronger after my intended virgin flight wound up killing more than two thousand people, including everyone aboard. I had never set foot on a plane, and I never would. Nope, nope, nope. If God wanted humans to fly, he'd have given us wings.

We agreed to leave the house and let Tina stay for now. As long as she had a roof over her head, she was less likely to press criminal charges against me—and since she'd be pissed to find out that I vanished with all the money in the bank and all the too-large clothes she'd been eying when she thought I wasn't looking, the house was the least I could do for now. Someday, after I was declared legally alive, maybe I'd find a way to sell it.

Jess cancelled her return flight to ride with me, although I tried to tell her I'd meet them back in Boston. She wouldn't even consider leaving me alone. She pretended it was more about emotional support, but I'm sure she thought I was going to disappear again if I had a chance, going somewhere I'd never be found. I'd be lying if I said it never crossed my mind, but after spending only a few days with Jess and Ethan, I couldn't stand the thought of not being part of their lives. I'd lost too much time already.

Her suspicions were clear in the way her eagle eyes watched me, the tilt of her head, and the timbre of her voice when she spoke. The way her hands shook when folding laundry. She spent hours sitting on the back deck with me, shivering but not talking. She knew me too well. And I knew her too well. She accompanied me to the bank when I went to close my accounts, volunteered to make coffee runs as if she worried I'd never stop driving. So when she insisted on sharing a car back to Boston with me, I didn't argue.

Once that decision was made, it was time to figure out how, exactly, I'd get across the border now that I didn't have a valid passport. I certainly couldn't ask Tina to borrow hers—especially since we planned to be gone before she got back from her spa vacation. Instead, I phoned an old friend for help.

Before I left, Henny had mentioned they had ways to get people across the border. I hadn't pressed for details, thanks to Tina's passport, but now that it had expired, the women who ran Tranquility were the best hope I had of getting back into the U.S. other than being deported for identity theft and fraud. We'd call that Plan B. My heart pounded as the phone rang, hoping one of them would answer instead of some random helper.

"Tranquility Cooperative Bed and Breakfast," a familiar voice said. Older, more frail, but familiar. "How can I help you?"

"Henny?"

"This is Valerie. To whom am I speaking, please?"

I swallowed. Val was okay, but talking to Henny would've been much easier. "My name is Christa. I stayed at Tranquility almost twenty years ago. I really need to talk to Henny if I could, please."

"Sorry, dear. Henny died back in 2017. No one left but me and the dust bunnies."

My heart dropped. By the time I'd left Tranquility, Bo and I had fixed up most of the exterior, and more people showed up every day. In my mind's eye, I'd seen it turning into a thriving establishment, a new way of doing business, and of helping other kids who came through Vermont for generations to come. I'd envisioned Val and Henny running it side-by-side until both were well over a hundred years old, maybe with some grand-children running around, collecting eggs and feeding the chickens.

"I'm sorry, Val. I didn't know."

"Can I help you? If you just wanted to chat, I've got animals to feed and some leaky pipes to fix. Lots of work to do around here." She paused, but my mind was still processing everything she'd said. "Well, lovely to hear from you then. Have a good day."

"Wait! Years ago, you and Henny helped me when I needed to leave the U.S. and start a new life in Canada. I'm here now, and it's time to cross back into the States, but I don't have a pass-port. I need your help."

If I'd thought her voice seemed hard before, it turned to steel now. "Lady, I'm afraid you've got the wrong number. We're not caught up in anything illegal here."

Desperate to prevent her from hanging up, I let loose a flood of words. "When I stayed at Tranquility, I went by Chris. I was there for the entire fall of 2001. My friend Bo showed up a few weeks after I did. We were attacked by homophobes outside a bar. They beat me pretty badly, but he spent three weeks in a coma." Sitting beside me, Jess squeezed my hand. She didn't know about any of this. I avoided her gaze but my voice cracked, anyway. "That night, I was wearing Henny's silver wedding shoes that she'd loaned me. I still have them. A few days later, you and Henny helped me escape so I wouldn't be part of the news footage. You called me the day Bo woke up and we cried together for half an hour. Please don't hang up, Val. I'm desperate."

She sighed. "You know, we never got that wedding. We wanted to wait until it would be legal in the whole country. Stupid. By then she was too sick."

"I'm sorry." I hoped she heard the sincerity in my voice. "I've been hiding in Canada for so long, I don't have any way to get home now. If there is anything at all you can do to help, I'd very much appreciate it. I'm prepared to make a generous donation to Tranquility."

I glanced at Jess out of the corner of my eye. We hadn't really talked about that, but she nodded. If Val couldn't help, I'd be hiding in the trunk of a rental car, so we'd do almost anything for a better plan.

"Okay, listen. I have a friend who owns a ranch that straddles the border. Most of the property's in the U.S., but part of it crosses over into Canada. You can get to it from the Quebec side before you get to Customs. Have someone drop you off at the ranch, then they drive across the border and meet you at the rest stop on the other side. You walk across the property to my friend's house, about five miles, give her a hundred bucks in greenbacks, and you can get picked up at the front. You won't go anywhere near border control."

My entire body exhaled a sigh of relief. "That's perfect."

"Well, it's a little more involved than that. I'll send you the details. And if you tell anyone about this, I will find you and kill you in your sleep."

"Thank you so much. I owe you."

"Don't I know it," she grumbled. "Bring me back the shoes on your way through."

"I'll bring you whatever you want. Just email me the directions to the ranch." I gave her the address, and she repeated it.

Voices rose in the background. "Thank you for your reservation with Tranquility. That'll be two hundred dollars. We look forward to seeing you on November 30. Don't forget to bring cash."

The line went dead. Jess turned questioning eyes on me. I related what Val told me, ending with, "We cross the border on Wednesday."

Two days later, we were on the road, headed through winding back roads according to the map Val had emailed me. Beside me, Jess gave Ethan a long lecture on the importance of following the law and respecting authority. He nodded along, rolling his eyes, too smart to point out what hypocrites we were.

If we lived closer to this ranch, I somehow suspected he and his friends would be visiting weekly as soon as they turned eighteen, which was the Quebec drinking age. Not because they wouldn't have passports, but because danger's fun at that age. Heck, if I'd had access to a place like this when I was a teenager, I'd have tried to talk Jess into having sex with me on the Border. Partly for the experience, and partly because my brother would've done it, too. I did a lot of things because Brad would've done them before I realized that was no way to live.

Under ordinary circumstances, the sprawling ranch would have been impressive. Instead, I wondered which country would throw me in jail if I got caught.

"Relax," Jess muttered out of the corner of her mouth. She gripped the steering wheel with white knuckles.

"You're one to talk."

"You failed to mention that there's barbed wire surrounding this place," she said.

"Of course there is. You think you can just have a property half in the U.S., half in Canada and let people wander across at will?"

She groaned. "Please don't tell me any more about this plan. Where do I let you out?"

I pointed to a small grove of trees off to the side, near the fence, and she pulled over. When Ethan hopped out to climb into the front seat, I hugged him. "Now remember, if anything goes wrong, you've never seen me before, okay? Do you remember how to say 'Officer, I don't know that woman' in French?"

After making them each repeat the phrase three times, I promised I'd see them in about two hours and waited for the van to pull away. Part of me expected the Mounties to burst out of the trees, but nothing happened other than a rustling in the brush. Jumping, I whirled around and suppressed a scream before realizing that whatever made the noise was too small to be human. Much too small to be a moose, so I forced myself to relax.

Once the van disappeared, I walked further into the trees, following the fence. After about a kilometre, I found a yellowed link about a foot off the ground, just like Val described. Most people would pass right by it without paying any attention. Checking around for anyone watching, I pulled on the link, and a section of the fence lifted. There wasn't much space, but it was enough for me to squeeze through. Once I went through the gap and replaced the fence on the other side, I stood on American soil for the first time in eighteen years.

It took probably an hour of walking across the ranch, following Val's directions, before I stopped expecting police to storm out of hiding and arrest me. For the first time, a spring entered my step, my hunched shoulders fell, and my head lifted. I stopped, lifted my face to the sun, and let it all sink in. Tina couldn't hurt me now. I wouldn't be arrested and sent back to Canada. Maybe, just maybe, everything would be okay.

No one was at the ranch house when I arrived, so I dropped the envelope of cash into the post box next to the front door and kept going down the driveway. Turning left when I reached the main road, it wasn't long before I found the rest stop Val had mentioned.

Although doctors were trained to perform well in high stress situations, crossing the border took a toll on Jess's nerves. This wasn't exactly the same as performing surgery. She drove to the rest stop as planned, but got out and insisted I spell her at the wheel. She crawled into the back and promptly started snoring, while Ethan joined me in the front seat.

He shot a couple of glances over his shoulder while playing on his iPad, as if he had something to say that he didn't want his mother to hear. Instead of pushing him to speak, I turned up the radio and sang softly under my breath. On the third song, Ethan joined me, sneaking me a glance across the console. Our voices blended, filling the car, and breaking the ice.

When the song ended, with another glance back at his mother, my son finally told me what was on his mind.

"Do you ever wish you'd been born a woman?"

"I didn't understand it when I was younger, but I *was* born a woman," I said gently. "A trans woman."

Although the size of a grown man, he was still a kid, so I couldn't expect him to grasp all the nuances. Less than three months ago, he'd thought his father was dead. Finding out that I was a woman wasn't the sort of confusion that evaporated after a good turkey dinner and a duet.

He shrugged, making me wonder if I underestimated how much a seventeen-year-old knows and understands. "Sure. But if you could go back, would you put yourself in a woman's body to start?"

I thought about this for a moment, because he deserved a real answer, not a flippant one. "I don't know. If I'd been born any other way, I might not have the strength and resilience I have now. Your mom and I might have been friends, but we might've been too scared as teenagers to fall in love, and I wouldn't give that experience up for anything. And then we wouldn't have had you. Definitely, you make it worth all the shit I went through. I'm so glad to have met you."

We sat in silence for a long time.

"How's school?" I finally asked. "Have you made any decisions about college yet?"

"Harvard, if possible," he said. "Or BU. I'm going to be a

surgeon when I grow up. E/R, though. Orthopedics is boring. All sports injuries and old people."

A doctor. My son, the doctor. Ethan Cooper, M.D. My heart swelled with pride, although I didn't raise this child and deserved no credit. For all I knew, if I'd been around, I'd have screwed everything up.

"Are you two going to be a couple now? I mean, are you going to be my moms and be married and stuff?"

"I don't know." When I first transitioned, it seemed like I was supposed to date men, but it never felt right, and I'd only been with women for the past few years. Jess loved me, but I wasn't sure if she was ready to dive back into our marriage, and I couldn't speak for her. "Would that bother you?"

"Not really. Lots of kids at my school have two moms or two dads. Erin's dads bought everyone bee.....I mean, um, milk-shakes, at her New Year's Eve party last year."

He looked at me nervously. I made a mental note to suggest Jess have a talk to with Erin's dads, but decided to lecture my son on underage drinking later. "Oh, yeah?"

"Yeah. There's this kid in my calculus class, and his moms have a bakery. He gives me stuff when I help with his home-work. He doesn't need much help, but the cupcakes are good, so it's cool."

Ah, to be a teenager again and have your impressions of people based on whether they bought you cupcakes or threw good, illegal parties. Things used to be so simple.

"Things were a lot different when I was your age."

"I know." He paused for a moment, biting the inside of his cheek the way I used to when thinking. "I'm the only 9/11 baby I know. People treat me different because I don't have a dad. Last year, one of the sixth graders lost her mom. I didn't know her, but everyone wanted me to talk to her, anyway. She told me it wasn't the same, because I'd never met the parent I lost." He paused for a moment, so I leaned over to ruffle his hair.

"Strangers have treated me different my whole life. Things will change, but it don't really matter. I'm still me."

This poor kid. Without even knowing it, I'd forced him to grow up so much faster than he should have. "I'm sorry, Ethan. I had no idea Jess was pregnant. If I'd known—"

"You'd have stayed and been miserable and it woulda been my fault. No, thanks."

Another look into the backseat. Jess always slept like the dead, so I wasn't overly concerned with her hearing us. Besides, we'd said nothing I wouldn't tell her later, anyway. But Ethan lowered his voice.

"What would bother me," he said, "is if you hurt her again. She's been happy the last few weeks, ever since we scheduled this trip."

"She's been the most important person in my life since I was fourteen. I've never loved anyone the way I love her, even when I was gone."

"Then why'd you leave?"

"Because I couldn't be the partner she needed when I was denying part of myself. It wouldn't have been fair to either of us."

"Why didn't you try? Coach always says you can't win without trying."

His words were a knife in my gut, and I didn't know what to say. My seventeen-year-old, who I played no part in raising, was smarter than me. "I'm afraid it's not that simple. Sometimes, even when you love someone, you can't be with them. The world was a lot more prejudiced before you were born."

"It's been pretty bad since the election. Lots of hate crimes."

My heart clenched at the words. "I'm sorry you have to see that. But I want to try to make things right with your mom."

"Does that mean you'll stick around?"

"Yes, I'm sticking around, for as long as the two of you will let me. As a friend or a parent or whatever."

"We'll see," he said. "If she's happy, we're cool. If not… I'm pretty strong."

His protectiveness of his mother only made me love him more. I vowed to do my best to keep her happy, then went through a drive-through for donuts to seal the deal. In the backseat, Jess woke up long enough to accept a bag of doughnut holes, apparently oblivious to the agreement Ethan and I forged.

Hours later, after a stop for lunch and another seat rotation, we pulled up at the Tranquility Cooperative Bed and Breakfast. It looked nothing like I remembered. Weeds grew wild near the road, nearly obliterating the entrance to the dirt path that used to be a gravel driveway. Jess drove right by it, backing up only when Ethan spotted a tiny sign I missed.

Potholes pitted the road, reminding me what Val said about leaky pipes. Tranquility wasn't doing so well since Henny died, apparently. The front porch sagged. Crooked blinds hung in several of the windows, but only a dim bulb shone through here and there. Vines grew up the sidewall.

"Is this place even open?" Ethan asked. "Mom, can we stay at the Best Western? They have HBO and Wi-Fi. I want to watch Game of Thrones On Demand."

Jess's eyes were on me as she replied. "This is the right place, kiddo, but we're just going to say hi to an old friend. We won't be here long."

Tears blurred my vision. Never had I imagined, even after talking to Val, that Tranquility had fallen into such a sorry state. Whatever I expected to find here, the red "FOR SALE" in the window slammed a lid on those hopes.

Grabbing my purse, I opened the door and got out. "Why don't you guys go to the Best Western and check in? Come back for me when you're done."

The door creaked open, and a familiar woman appeared in the doorway. "Don't be ridiculous. You're all staying here. Come in, come in."

CHAPTER TWENTY-ONE

Jess

The thought of my husband hiding in this dilapidated, moldy old building while I lay on the couch, crying, and eating cheese-flavored crackers all day filled me with despair. Something about seeing it for myself changed everything. I'd let myself believe that Brett left for a better life, but it was impossible to wrap my head around this place being that better life. Instead, it felt like my husband abandoned me to hide out in a filthy slum and avoid responsibilities like having a wife and a real job.

Behind me, Ethan exited the car and wrinkled his nose. "What's that smell?"

"Chickens and cows," Christa said. "There's a barn around the back. Tomorrow morning, I can show you how to milk a cow, if you want."

"Cool."

All I wanted was to dive back into the car and keep driving, but I forced myself to place one foot in front of the other. When the porch steps didn't disintegrate beneath my feet, I breathed a little easier. Although I never thought of myself as a snob, my entire body screamed for me to run away from this place. There must be spiders hiding in every corner.

Instead, I called on my bedside manner and greeted the plump, grandmotherly-looking woman standing inside the doorway. "I'm Jess. Nice to meet you. This is my son, Ethan."

"Val."

The inside made me feel a little better about the accommodations, if not my situation. The front room was homey, if not luxurious. Fresh pine scent filled the room. Gleaming wood floors led to a staircase that curved up and out of sight. The scarred front desk and lumpy old couch had seen better days, but so had the furniture in my basement. We could stay here. As long as my room wasn't full of spiders.

Christa took our bags upstairs to our rooms while Val explained what "cooperative bed and breakfast" meant. Ethan perked up when Val mentioned picking apples, mashing them, and learning to make donuts and cider. "We'll need someone to taste test and let us know when we've got the consistency right. Know anyone who might be interested?"

"Heck yeah," Ethan said.

All questions about Wi-Fi and free HBO stopped. Good thing, since he'd watch Game of Thrones over my dead body.

He followed Val down the hall toward the back of the house, peppering her with inquiries about apple types, how to reach the high branches, and how many bushels you needed to make a gallon of cider. A couple of days here might do my son some good, after all. It couldn't hurt to see how other people lived, how much work went into creating the food that appeared like magic on our table at home.

Upstairs, I found Christa putting sheets on a double bed. "Where did you learn to do that? Think of all the time I could've saved having you make the beds when we were married!"

"I learned it here, back in 2001." She flushed, keeping her eyes focused firmly on the bottom sheet as she smoothed it across the mattress.

We navigated such awkward emotional ground, neither of us knew what to do or say when the conversation drifted into "unsafe" territory. Awkward silences didn't feel like the answer, but I wasn't even ready to think the "d" word, much less have a conversation about ending our marriage. Or not ending it. I still didn't know which I wanted.

"You learned a lot here, right?" I picked up a pillowcase and smoothed it over a softer pillow than I expected to find here. "Hotel management and housekeeping and stuff?"

"Yeah. I learned how to cook and garden, which was good for me. But I also learned how to manage a front desk and do check-ins and a lot of stuff that helped me find a job later." With the fitted sheet stretched smoothly across the double bed, she moved on to the top sheet. I grabbed the other side to help. "And… this is where I met Bo."

The name she mentioned when talking to Val about setting all this up. I overheard enough of the call to gather that something horrible had happened, but was waiting to bring it up until we got settled. Or until Christa gave me the perfect opening.

"Who's Bo?" I asked.

"The only friend I had after I left."

Her words slapped me in the face. My natural instinct was to lash out, remind her that she had a friend in me, that it was her own fault if she'd been alone. But that wasn't what she meant; she wasn't trying to hurt me. Reestablishing our connection and getting to know each other again was more important than my pride. I bit my lip and waited for her to continue.

"Oh, Jess," she said, noting the look on my face. "That's not what I meant."

"I know. It's okay."

"No, I mean, when I walked away, I was lost without you. I didn't know what to do. I had no one to talk to. I hid in a hotel room, shaved my beard, bought some crappy clothes so I'd look like a student. Wandered Boston for a few days—"

Her words sparked something, deep in my memory. "Oh my God. That was you!"

"What are you talking about?"

"A few days after the attacks. They were interviewing people on one of the local news stations, and someone shoved a mike in this young guy's face, and I thought, 'He looks kinda like Brett.' But you were dead, and I hadn't seen you without a beard in years. I figured it was just hormones and the stress of losing you making me hallucinate. I never dreamed… I should've known. I should've kept looking until I found you."

She walked around the bed and put her arms around me. "No, you shouldn't have. Where would you even have started? I left Boston the next morning. Besides, if you'd started looking, I'd have kept running. You're my best friend, and I love you with all my heart, but this was something I needed to do on my own."

"You mean, with Bo." My voice still held a trace of jealousy that I hated.

"Well, yes, but—"

"What happened to him?"

"The two of us went to a bar—as friends—and we were jumped by two rednecks. They were offended by the idea of men dressed as women, assumed we were gay, and freaked out." I gasped in horror. "I was pretty strong, and I fought off the one who attacked me. The other one smashed Bo's face into the pavement, knocked him out, put him into a coma that lasted weeks."

My heart broke for her. "I'm so sorry."

"Thank you." Her eyes glazed over, and when she spoke again, she was lost in memories. "Bo arrived at the hotel a couple of months after I did. I'd been keeping to myself—milking cows, collecting eggs, chopping wood. I stuck to manual labor so I wouldn't have to talk to anyone. But it's like he recognized me for how broken I was, and made it his mission to fix me."

"It's nice that you had someone."

"Thanks. Bo worked as a drag queen, with this great character he needed to retire. He was hanging out here to save money while he came up with a new act. He recognized that I wasn't happy. He showed me how to use makeup, taught me that it was okay to wear women's clothing." She blinked and swallowed. "Showed me that being myself, no matter how difficult it was, beat living a lie."

"And that's when you changed your name?"

"I chose the name when I started venturing out in women's clothing. But after we got attacked, I didn't want to be here anymore. Vermont was always one of the more liberal states in the United States. If Bo could be almost killed for being a drag queen, if I could get beaten up for walking around in makeup and a dress here… no place in the country felt safe."

"You would've been safe in Boston."

"Maybe. Or maybe I'd have gotten off the T in the wrong neighborhood one night and we wouldn't be having this conversation. I didn't want to find out."

I nodded.

"And I couldn't risk running into you. I needed to get away, figure things out somewhere safe. Tina's passport was still in my backpack, and our basic features were similar enough. Henny helped with my makeup. Then I drove Bo's car as far north as I could, hitchhiked across the border, and got a job working in a small inn outside of Montreal. The owner was a friend of Val and Henny. Hired me right away, no questions asked."

"Henny helped you a lot. I'm sorry I never got to meet her."

"Me, too. She had a kind soul."

"So what happened to Bo after you left?"

"The hospital wouldn't give me any information, but Val eventually found out that his parents moved him to a place near their home in Buffalo to recover. He woke up a few weeks after I left, but he never had a cell phone, so I couldn't call. His parents hung up on me, and I'm assuming they didn't deliver my messages. I don't know where he wound up, but I'm sure he didn't stay with them."

Something in her story sounded so familiar, I wondered if I'd read about the attacks in the Boston papers at the time. Or maybe it just reminded me of Brokeback Mountain or Matthew Shepherd. Bo's story was sadly all too common.

"I'd guess he went to New York City, probably, or Chicago. Maybe Los Angeles. Bo liked the big cities. But when I checked Google a few years ago, I couldn't find anything. Not knowing her new stage name didn't help."

"I'm sorry that you lost touch." I leaned forward and kissed her, gently. Not with passion, but with friendship and understanding. "I should go find my room."

"Will you stay here with me?" Her tone may have been casual, but the pleading in her eyes gave away her true feelings. "Just for a bit. Being around you makes me feel better."

I kicked my shoes off and leaned back on the bed, reaching for her with one hand. "Of course."

She wrapped her arms around me, and I sank back into her, just like when we used to watch TV together as kids. The rightness of being in her arms made all the strangeness of this day, of this place, fade away. After a few minutes, I rolled over, put one hand on Christa's hip, and kissed her. It felt like coming home again.

Outside that room, the world was chaos. We stayed in what was really a crumbling hostel, no matter what we called it, with a woman who had helped traffic people to/from Canada, now teaching our son how to milk a cow. That had to be the weirdest sentence ever.

Christa could face criminal charges, at home or back in Canada, and I had no idea how to tell my conservative, religious mother that my dead husband returned to life as a woman. But inside that room, the only things that mattered were me and the individual I'd known and loved since the ninth grade.

CHAPTER TWENTY-TWO

Christa

Tranquility gave me new life twice. I'd happily have remained there, cocooned with Jess and Ethan forever. The farm work could've kept Ethan fascinated for weeks, and being able to rediscover Jess was the greatest single experience of my life. I loved tracing her stretch marks, marveling at the things her body had done.

But, alas, real life intruded. Jess couldn't abandon her practice, and Ethan needed to be back at school on Monday. On Sunday morning, we cleaned up our rooms, and I mowed the lawn while Jess and Ethan weeded the garden. Then, having left the place better than we found it, we said good-bye to Val, thanked her again, and continued our trip southeast to Boston.

For the first couple of days, I drifted. No one knew I was back, other than Jess and Ethan. She cancelled dinner with her mom the night we got back, preferring to talk to her one-on-one rather than spring me on her out of nowhere. The last thing we needed was to give the poor old woman a heart attack. I may have never agreed with her on a lot of topics, but she'd taught me a lot. Jess's mom was a good person, and I loved her nearly as much as my own mother.

My father died in 2006. I didn't attend the funeral, of course, didn't even know it happened until I looked my family up online years later. Jess went with Ethan, the only grandchild, who was too young to understand or appreciate what was happening.

Jess explained that my mother developed Alzheimer's not long after Dad passed, going downhill pretty quickly. She didn't say that losing me and my father contributed to her decreasing health, but I wondered. Mom now lived in a nursing home as nice as many five-star hotels. When I left, Dad was doing very well. Apparently, he'd left Mom plenty of money to care for herself.

Knowing in the back of mind that, somewhere, I still had family and they had mourned me and would probably want to know I was alive wasn't the same as picking up the phone and calling them. I didn't even know if Mom would recognize me if I showed up.

When I tried to call my brother, paralysis gripped me. He wouldn't understand. He might be glad to hear I was alive. He might be pissed that I ignored all of his "Be a man" advice. He might be high and not even care about anything. You never knew with Brad. So I stalled. But I was well aware that, at some point before Ethan graduated college, I needed to reach out to my brother. He deserved to know the truth.

Days turned into weeks. The longer we were home, the more frustrated Jess got at my sitting around, doing nothing.

"You should at least go see your mother," she said one Saturday. "She doesn't have a lot of time left."

"Seeing me as I am now could kill her. I'd rather not have that on my conscience."

She sighed. "I hate to say it, but she probably won't recognize you, even if you looked like Brett. We stopped going because she doesn't know Ethan. Sometimes she thought he was you, which was even worse. She has good days, but..." She shrugged. "You of all people should understand how fragile life is."

"But she thinks I'm dead. She mourned me once."

"Then maybe finding out you're alive will bring a sick, old woman some happiness. At least talk to her doctors and see what they think."

Finally, I went. When I told her about my decision, Jess offered to go, to bring Ethan, but some things in life needed to be done on your own.

Jess nodded like she understood, but I saw the fear in her eyes. She was glad I'd come home, she wanted me there, but she still didn't trust me. Deep inside, part of her thought I'd bolt every time I got into the car. Thought something would go wrong and I wouldn't come back.

I didn't even know how to assuage her fears. I didn't have a U.S. driver's license yet. If pulled over, a Canadian license could get me extra questioning from the cops, and I couldn't produce a visa or valid passport. A little investigating, and I could still be charged with identity theft and fraud. For all I knew, faking your own death was a felony.

Everyone said Canada didn't request extradition for minor offenses, but how minor was pretending to be someone else? Besides, my crimes extended north and south of the border. Usually, I avoided this problem by making Jess drive. When I got behind the wheel on my own, I exercised the kind of care all licensed drivers throughout the world abandon the moment they passed their driving tests.

With white knuckles on the wheel, I pointed the car toward Connecticut. What I'd say to my mother completely escaped me. I didn't even know if I'd have the guts to tell her who I was. Maybe I should put on gender-neutral clothes and hide my hair under a hat. Not much I could do about the boobs, though. Besides, I was done living a lie.

My stomach twisted in knots the whole way there. Twice, I pulled over, a panic attack making it difficult to focus on the road. I hated myself for putting the people I loved in this posi-tion in the first place. My parents may have been strict, narrow-minded, and unyielding, but they gave me life. I still loved them. The idea of hurting them so much killed me. The only thing that might hurt my mother more than my death was the life path I'd taken after we last saw each other.

The time spent fretting could've been put to better use. When I arrived at the facility, more a resort than a nursing home, the receptionist asked for my name. Moments later, Christa McCall was ushered down the hall to my mom's apartment. There was no sense in giving my legal name: Explanations would have wasted time and benefitted no one when you had to present ID during check-in.

Somehow, I expected Mom to look exactly the way I'd last seen her at the wedding. Beaming with pride, short brown hair artfully arranged into a more stylish helmet than usual, hazel eyes twinkling. The woman who greeted me barely resembled the mother I remembered.

She sat hunched in her chair, peering at some kind of needlework. Not a single brown hair remained on her head. She seemed smaller, somehow, as if the disease had eaten her body as well as her mind. Or maybe it was that she'd lost a lot of weight in the past fifteen years. I hovered in the doorway, uncertain.

The nurse went ahead. "Helen? You have a visitor. A friend of your daughter-in-law."

Her face broke into a smile. "Jess? How is Jess?"

When I approached, her eyes met mine, and I stopped in my tracks. People had always said I favored my mother, and I nodded along, not really paying attention. But now, the similarities took my breath away. We'd always had the same eyes. My long hair was now the same length and texture as hers, even though she'd gone grey. My chin, softened by surgery, was a mirror reflection of hers. At first, I couldn't speak.

After a moment, I gathered my courage and approached, shaking one of her bony hands. "My name's Christa. It's lovely to see you. Jess is fine."

"Do you know Ethan? A lovely boy, so much like his father."

My heart leapt into my throat. "Yes, he's a great kid."

"What brings you to see me, dear?"

All the answers I'd practiced on the drive flew from my head, leaving me only with a version of the truth. "She asked me to drop by and see how you're doing. I was in the neighbourhood."

"I'm fine. Your voice sounds so familiar. Are you sure we've never met?"

I shook my head before realizing her vision is so poor, she couldn't see me. "No, ma'am, I don't think so."

"You talk like Jess. Do you know Jess?"

Of course I did. Years of voice training, and I taught myself to speak like the female who'd had the most influence on my life. I'd thought about her all the time until my therapist pointed out how unhealthy and unproductive that could be.

Not a word of that could be shared with my mother, and I couldn't point out that the nurse had already told her I knew Jess, so I simply nodded. "Yes, Jess is a lovely woman."

"Yes, she is. My son loved her very much, before he died. Did you know Brett?"

Did *you* know Brett? I wanted to ask but didn't. "No, I don't think I did. Why don't you tell me about him?"

She patted the seat beside her. "Such a wonderful boy. God took him from us much too soon. Sit down, and I'll tell you a story."

For the rest of the afternoon, I listened to her relate long-forgotten stories of my childhood, telling the history of my relationship with Jess, as tears streamed down my cheeks. Then she told me about the first time she saw Ethan, the similarities she saw between her son and grandson.

Finally, I got up the nerve to ask the question that had been in the back of my mind for weeks. "What about your other son, Helen? How's Brad?"

"Oh, he's wonderful! We were so proud when he joined the military after his brother died. He knew the country was going to war, and he had a thing or two to say to those terrorists who killed Brett. Served two terms in Iraq before a broken leg sidelined him for a bit. He threw himself from a moving Jeep to save a young woman from a sniper. Now he's stationed in Japan."

Wow. Of all the things I'd thought about Brad, it never occurred to me that he would've grown up and gotten an adult job, much less joined the military and become a hero. He'd certainly figured out how to "be a man."

"You must miss him terribly," I said, hoping my voice didn't crack.

She shrugged. "Kids grow up, they move away. Life goes on. He married a nice Japanese girl and settled down a few years back. I'm happy for him."

For years, I'd tried not to think about my brother, to wonder what he was up to. I was startled to realize that I was happy for him, too. That I hoped one day to see him again, meet his wife.

Before I left, we embraced for a long time. Part of me never wanted to let go. Jess was right. I'd needed to do this, even if I couldn't tell my mother the truth. But when I pulled away, she gazed into my eyes, and I realized that she must've known all along. What a fool I'd been. Jess recognized me instantly. How could I have thought my own mother wouldn't do the same?

Mom squeezed my hands and kissed me on each cheek. "Thank you for coming to see me. You've brought an old lady some happiness."

Jess

The Saturday after we returned home, with Christa out of town for the day, I sent Ethan to play Laser Tag with his friends and invited my mother over for brunch. Before she arrived, I "taste-tested" about a bottle and a half of champagne. I mean, a couple of mimosas. The enthusiasm with which I greeted my mother could only be found in the bottom of a bottle with twelve percent alcohol content. She greeted me with equal warmth and breath that suggested she'd had a nip or two herself, "to ward off the cold," as my father used to say. I wondered what made her nervous about spending the afternoon with me.

After exchanging pleasantries, we dug into the food. It both steadied my nerves and calmed my buzz enough to remind me that we had things to talk about, and soon. Christa wouldn't be gone all day. When my knife scraped the last bit of Hollandaise sauce onto my fork, I pushed the plate away and started the speech I'd been working on in my head for several days.

"I'm sorry we missed Thanksgiving, Ma. I know how much you looked forward to having us over."

"Nonsense. For the first time in fifty years, I didn't have to waste an entire day cooking while people talked about football in my living room. Did I ever tell you I hate football?"

My jaw dropped. "Are you serious?"

"What a stupid game. All that running back and forth and falling down and rolling around on the ground, trying to get your neck broken for no good reason. At least basketball takes some skill. But don't tell Ethan, I'm always rooting for him." She sipped at her drink, which I refilled hastily. This was the best conversation we'd had in ages, and I wanted to keep her a bit tipsy until I finished what I had to tell her. "But if you could talk him into playing some other sport in college, well, that would be okay with me. Or maybe he can do baseball in the spring."

I chuckled. "I'll see what I can do. He plays football because his dad played football."

Ma clucked with her tongue. "Well, I'm sure Brett would be proud of him."

"Funny you should mention that."

She leaned over, patted my arm. "You look so happy, dear. Did you have a nice time away? I said to Nancy at the Y, 'My Jess has met some new guy, mark my words. Nothing else would take her away over the holidays.' Now that you're back and I see the sparkle in your eye, my guess is that she owes me ten bucks. You've lost the look of someone who hasn't gotten any nookie in way too long."

My jaw dropped. "Who are you and what have you done with my mother?"

She waved a hand. "We're all adults. Life's too short to be so uptight. The world's changing. Anyway, tell me about this new guy."

"There's no new guy," I said with one hundred percent accuracy.

"Nonsense. What else could have your cheeks flushed like that?"

I started to point out that I was on my sixth or seventh glass of champagne, but we needed to move this conversation along while we were still alone. Instead, I took a long swallow, savoring the taste while I gathered my courage.

No way to possibly say what I needed to say without just spitting it out. I didn't know any way to ease someone into "your dead son-in-law is now your live daughter-in-law."

"It's Brett."

"Brett wouldn't mind you seeing someone new at all, dear. It's about time, if you ask me. Long past, really."

"No, it's not that, Ma. Listen. Brett is alive. He didn't get on the plane that day. He's been living in Canada, and when I was there in September, I ran into him."

Her fork clattered onto the plate. "Dear, that's not funny. What would Ethan say if he heard you talking like that?"

"Ethan and I just spent a week in Canada. He knows."

"Is this some kind of joke? Am I being—what is it you kids say—Punk'd?"

It had been at least fifteen years since that show aired, so I couldn't begin to guess where she heard about it. We never had MTV when I was a kid. "No, Ma, I'm serious. Brett is alive. I know it's hard to accept. It took me a long time, but I'm learning to be okay with it."

As I spoke, her face lost ten years. Her eyes lit up. "That's wonderful news, dear! Why didn't you tell me sooner?"

"You're not mad? Angry that he vanished? Upset that he used a national tragedy for his own purposes? Confused at all?"

"Life's too short for grudges." She sipped her mimosa. "I assume you've worked through those issues or you wouldn't be looking so happy. That's not the face of someone who just found out her husband has a new wife with multiple kids or has been in prison for all these years. I just wish you'd mentioned it earlier, so I could help you work through your feelings."

Behind me, the kitchen door closed. The click-clack of high heels on the tile told me instantly who had returned home earlier than expected. I shot to my feet, unsure whether to go to her, to stop her, to finish getting my news out before Christa entered the kitchen. The champagne hit me, and I gripped the table to steady myself.

Hesitation cost me precious seconds. Before my brain even began processing the options, Ma's eyes darted behind my shoulder. I stepped to the side, but my five-foot-four-inch frame wasn't about to block Christa's six feet of height. She rested her chin on the top of my head easily and put her arms around me. "Hi, honey."

That wasn't the best way to do this, but we'd run out of time. I tilted my face upward and kissed Christa on the cheek. "Hi, yourself."

The whites of Ma's eyes nearly swallowed her face. She put one hand on her chest, and for a moment, I thought she was going to have a heart attack. "Brett? Jess, is this some kind of joke? What…?"

I stepped forward. "It's not a joke. Brett changed his name after he left. This is Christa."

"No. No, no, no, no," she muttered, shaking her head.

I glanced at Christa, who appeared saddened by this reaction, but not surprised. Of course. What on earth had I been thinking, introducing my Bible-thumping mother to my transgender spouse without preparing her for it first? I realized now how stupid I'd been, that I should've taken her out to brunch, to a public place where Christa couldn't accidentally interrupt us.

Christa stepped forward and held one hand out to my mother. "I know it's hard to accept, but I'm home. I'm here to help raise Ethan."

Ma pulled herself to her feet, wobbling slightly. I didn't know if it was from the alcohol, the shock, or both. Then she took two steps away from the table and slapped Christa so hard her head jerked backward. I gasped. "What could you possibly know about raising a son? What could you know about being a father? You're not even a man anymore. You're... I don't know what you are."

"She's Christa. My spouse," I said. "The woman I love."

"This is wrong," she said, digging in her purse. "All wrong. I have to go."

"You can't leave like this. You're drunk." I reached to take her keys, but she slapped my hands.

"I'll get a cab," she snapped. "You stay away. Both of you. I don't know what you're trying to do to me, but that's clearly not Brett. I don't want to talk to either of you ever again. What a cruel thing to do to an old woman."

We stood in shock as she stormed out, the front door shaking the house. For a long minute, Christa and I just stared at each other.

"I'm so sorry," I began.

"Don't be," she said. "You thought she'd mellowed. And I should've warned you that there was a high probability she'd react this way."

"Still, this is all my fault."

"No, it's my fault. I'm the one who left. I'm the one who came back. Do you want me to go after her?"

I let out a sigh. "No. She'll come around. Or not. It might take some time for her to wrap her mind around everything, but she'll be back. She loves Ethan too much to walk away from me for long."

My words were largely bravado, said as much for my own benefit as Christa's. I wanted my mother to be okay with everything. What if she never spoke to me again? Had I made a huge mistake in telling her? In bringing Christa home in the first place?

CHAPTER TWENTY-THREE

Christa

In the internet age, gossip traveled a thousand times faster than wildfire. Once our son told a couple of friends about his new mom, news of my return spread through the community faster than a meme gleefully extolling the number of divorces among "pro-family values" politicians. When Jess and I left the house together, whispers surrounded us. There was no escape. I stayed off social media, but people found Jess and Ethan, asking questions we couldn't or wouldn't answer. After a few days, they gave up and deleted their accounts.

Yet, when Ethan told me his football team was in the state championship, no power in the universe could've kept me away from the game. The high school season usually ended before Thanksgiving, but a fortunately timed early October blizzard and the Trojans' amazing defense meant I'd get to watch my son play in his final game of high school, the State Championship, while television cameras rolled. The game might even air on ESPN 3 or 4.

"Serendipity," I called it.

"Plain dumb luck," Jess said. Either way, I was glad to be at the stadium.

Red and gold banners swayed in the breeze. A different high school, different home team, different state. Still, it felt like coming home again. The same smells filled the air: grass and hot dogs and, closer to the field, sweat and male bravado. Bleacher seats contained no more padding in 2019 than 1996, but Jess had brought these awesome heated pillows she kept in the back of her car. The marching band played the same old songs. If I closed my eyes, I was a high school senior again, standing right back on the sidelines, waiting to go out on the field and win the final game of my high school career and walk away a champion.

We'd lost that game, a solid 35 to 3 trouncing. Half my passes were intercepted. Hopefully, Ethan's team would do better than the Lancaster Lions had.

Until that moment, I didn't realize how much that legacy meant to me, how badly I wanted Ethan to follow in my footsteps or, more accurately, to do better than I had. I suddenly wanted him to win more than I'd ever wanted anything in my life. Jess and I bought foam fingers, wore red sweatshirts, and cheered at the top of our lungs when our son came running out.

The man in front of us turned around at the commotion. He wore a red baseball cap with white letters. "You Ethan Cooper's mom?"

"We're both his moms," I said.

His eyes widened. The woman beside him coughed.

Beside me, Jess said, "Christa, this is Franklin Hudson. His son is the second-string quarterback."

"It's nice to meet you," I started to say, before being cut off.

"It just isn't right," Mr. Hudson said. "Two women shouldn't be raising a child together. Nowhere in the Bible does it say that's okay."

"It also doesn't say anywhere in the Bible that it's okay to harass a couple of people at their son's football game, just looking to have a nice time," Jess said. "So how about you leave us alone?"

"A boy should have a mother and a father."

"Says who?" I asked. "Which Bible verse says that?"

"Ephesians 6:2. 'Honor your father and mother.'"

"That doesn't say all people need to have both. What about single parents? Kids with a deceased parent?" Jess said.

"What about Luke 14:26? Any man who does not hate his father and mother cannot be my disciple?" I asked. "Does your son hate you?"

Franklin turned red but said nothing.

"When did you become such a Bible expert?" Jess whispered.

"It was the only book I had in the days after 9/11," I said. "Took it from a hotel."

In front of us, Franklin stood, clenching his fist. "What I don't understand is why you two *freaks* are still here."

"It's a public stadium. Everyone is allowed to watch the game," Jess said. "C'mon, Christa, let's find other seats."

He reached for her arm. "I said, you need to go. Get out of this stadium, leave us God-fearing folk in peace, or there will be consequences."

"Are you threatening my wife?" I stood, too, moving in front of Jess and forcing Franklin to release his grip.

All around us, necks craned in our direction, our discussion far more interesting to the other parents and students than the introduction of a bunch of kids who'd been bused in from the other side of the state.

The woman beside Franklin, who had to be a second wife since she wasn't nearly old enough to have a high-school-aged child, stood and nudged him, whispering in his ear. She tugged at his hand, but he ignored her.

"All I'm saying," Franklin said, "is that you and your kind have no place here. Maybe you should go sit somewhere else."

"Happy to! Where's the 'no bigots' section?" Jess asked.

Second Wife's face grew red. "Who are you calling a bigot?" She swung wildly at Jess, but I caught her wrist.

"Lucky for you, I am a fucking lady," I said. "And I would never hit a woman, or you'd be missing teeth by now."

Franklin stepped up onto the bleacher, looming over me. "Get your hands off my wife." He swung at my head, but I ducked.

The movement caused me to let go of Second Wife's wrist, and she teetered backward. Standing, I grinned at Franklin. "I'm glad you did that."

"You think I'm scared of you?"

My fist collided with his jaw, not as strong as when I played quarterback, but with plenty of force behind the throw. "I think you should be."

His eyes fluttered shut, and he dropped to the ground.

Pandemonium broke out. Franklin's wife started screaming and swinging her purse at both of us. Something struck me from behind. Out of the corner of my eye, I saw a fist land in Jess's stomach. She doubled over from the impact, gasping.

I flashed back to that moment in the bar, of watching Bo get beaten, hearing his nose crack against the pavement. If I lived a hundred years, I'd never forget that sound. My breath came in gasps, the world started to close in on me. I couldn't go through that again. Spots danced at the edge of my vision. Panic threatened to close in, so I twisted and spun like an animal, trying to land a punch anywhere, on anyone who might be threatening Jess.

This couldn't be happening. Not again. I couldn't lose her now. I never should've come back.

A cup of ice dumped down my back brought me back to reality. With a growl, I turned and swung wildly at the college-aged kid standing behind me, holding an empty cup. Someone's older brother, probably. Then I grabbed Jess's hand and shoved to the end of the row, fighting frantically to get her out of there before things got worse.

We made it about halfway down the stairs when two police officers stepped into view. We stopped and turned, but another officer stood at the top, blocking the exit that way. On the field, whistles blew, halting the action. So much for trying to have a nice, quiet evening watching football.

Beside me, Jess squeezed my hand. "It'll be okay," she whispered.

"I don't have ID," I whispered back. "I'm still dead, remember?"

Jess

There was no escaping the stadium. Christa looked around desperately, but I clutched her hand and waited to face the music. Running would only make police think we were hiding something. They'd come after us. Ethan didn't need to witness his parents being tackled and tasered by police because they evaded arrest after starting a brawl in the bleachers. I hoped he hadn't seen the fight itself from his vantage point on the field. What a stunning example I was turning out to be for my teenaged son.

Once upon a time, I worked hard to instill good values in my child. Teaching him to respect others, think for himself, use table manners. This year, apparently, I'd decided to teach him about faking your own death, illegal immigration, and brawls. Mother of the Year, that was me.

When we got to the bottom of the stands, four police officers herded everyone out of the stadium and into a corner of the parking lot created by three cop cars. We all stood, glaring at each other, while they took witness statements. I eyed each of the officers, trying to guess who might be the most sympathetic to our plight while we tried to figure out what on earth to say.

"Just tell them you forgot your ID, right?" I whispered out of the side of my mouth.

"Sure. And what's my name?"

"Ch… oh, shit."

It wasn't illegal to walk around without identification, since I'd driven to the stadium and she wasn't drinking. But giving a false name to a police officer was a crime, which we'd both learned when we started researching the legal ramifications of faking your own death. Brett Cooper had not yet been declared legally alive.

"Maybe they'll just ask a few questions and let everyone go? We were the ones attacked, right?"

"I love your optimism, Jess, but I'm not sure what part of this evening makes you think good luck is on our side."

"Well, the universe owes us a break, right?"

Her positive attitude was sweet yet naive. As if good things happened simply because you wanted or needed them to.

Before I could respond, a young woman in a blue uniform approached. She couldn't have been on the force more than a year or two. "Name, please?"

"Jess Cooper."

"You got ID, ma'am?"

"Right here." I fished it out. She examined it with a flashlight for a long moment before returning it.

"Thank you, ma'am. And you?"

Christa swallowed. "My legal name is Brett Cooper."

The policewoman squinted at her long hair, the T-shirt stretched across her breasts. "You don't look like a Brett."

"No, ma'am." Christa lowered her voice. "I've completed gender reassignment but not legally changed my name."

"That so?" We both nodded. "Do you have ID, Mr. Cooper?"

"No, I'm afraid I don't. I wasn't driving."

She looked at me. "Will you vouch for your husband?"

I started to correct the noun use, but the look on Christa's face reminded me that now wasn't the best time for political correctness. "Yes, absolutely. I've known Brett Cooper since I was fourteen years old."

"Good enough for me. As long Mrs. Cooper drives home, I have no reason to keep the two of you here. Let me see what I can do to speed things along here." She leaned forward. "I think, under the circumstances, it's better if the two of you disappear into the crowd. It's clear to me that someone else started this fight."

Relief flooded me. We started to thank her, but then another, older police officer approached, and my heart sank. He didn't look nearly as sympathetic as the officer we'd been talking to. His lip curled when he looked Christa from head to toe.

He placed one meaty hand on the woman's shoulder. "I'm sorry, ladies, but we're going to have to take you both downtown."

Christa

Jess and I, along with twenty-five other parents, high school students, and family members, piled into two police vans waiting to take us downtown. No one spoke. Jess settled into the seat next to me, staring stubbornly at the ground. When I reached for her hand, she pulled away. With an inward sigh, I leaned back against the wall to look at the other parents, all of whom avoided my gaze. This wasn't my fault. No one else would see things that way.

What the hell was I thinking? I should have stayed in Canada. Where I would've been arrested. Maybe I should've gotten on the damn plane in the first place. Dan would be alive; I would be dead. Jess wouldn't be getting arrested right now.

At the station, they lined us up and took us in one at a time for fingerprints and mug shots. The officer asked if I wanted to use my one phone call, but with Jess behind me in line for booking, I hadn't the first clue who to call. Too bad my brother was in Japan, or I could've asked him for help.

That would have been an interesting call. *"Hey, Brad, it's me, Brett! Guess what? I'm alive now, and I go by Christa, and I have a vagina. Also, I'm in jail. Can you come bail me out? Thanks, Bro!"*

Nearly an hour after we'd climbed into the van, an officer ushered me into a holding cell filled to what appeared to be nearly double its maximum capacity. Everyone moved out of the way when I entered. Ignoring their stares, I plopped down on a bench in the corner and waited, trying to remember if anyone I'd known in college went on to law school. A few minutes later, Jess joined me. At least she wasn't so pissed she was pretending she didn't know me.

"Are you okay?" I asked.

"Yeah," she said. "Sorry about before. I just… was too furious with myself to let you comfort me."

"…with yourself?"

"I shouldn't have lost my temper. I should have been prepared to deal with these assholes. I should've—"

"Shh!" I put one arm around her. She stiffened but didn't pull away. Another parent glared at us, but I ignored her. "You couldn't have known. I should've prepared you better for the way people might react. This is my fault."

She sighed. "People are such assholes."

"Yeah." There didn't seem to be anything else to say.

"Anyway, I made a call," she said. "We should be out of here soon."

"Thanks," I said. "How's Ethan?"

"The officers said all the players who weren't picked up after the game went to the coach's house until someone with legal authority arrived to pick them up. He should be fine. Embarrassed, but fine."

"That's good, but I mean, who won the game?"

Jess's lips pressed together into a thin line. "This is your biggest concern at the moment?"

"It's an important game, Jess."

She sighed and shook her head in overly faked exasperation. "We did. Final score, 21-14."

I let out a cheer that earned me some surprised looks from the crowd until I shared the score. Then the entire cell erupted, united in our victory for a brief moment until the officer came in and told us to keep it down.

"At least Ethan had a good night before he found out about us," I said. "I'll start thinking about how to explain to him what happened."

"You got attacked by bigots. I defended you. End of story." That was nowhere near the end of the story; it barely scratched the surface. Without thinking, I'd set my son up for a life of bigotry, discrimination, and being forced to defend my decisions. That wasn't fair to him.

"Jess?" A voice called from the other side of the bars. "Jess Cooper, where are you?"

She stood and jumped to see over the crowd. "Teddy! Hold on!"

My wife pushed her way through the crowd, and I fell into her wake, murmuring "Excuse me" to each person we passed, until I found myself pressed up against the bars looking at a very tall, dark, and handsome total stranger. Even after our fight, I expected Jess to have called her mother to come get us, but this wasn't my mother-in-law.

"You know, I'd have bet good money that if we ever found ourselves looking at each other through a set of bars, our positions would be reversed," the man said.

The man, presumably Teddy, was all perfectly chiseled muscles and gelled black hair that clearly hadn't been in a riot. His smile revealed the kind of perfect white teeth that made me want to punch him, especially after I saw how Jess gazed at this schmuck like he was her knight in shining armor. I was supposed to be her knight in shining armor. Her protector.

"More likely, you'd be in here with me, and I'd be alternating between calling myself a dozen types of asshole and cussing you out." The two of them chuckled.

Who was this guy? Had Jess been hiding a boyfriend all this time? Even when we…?

I stepped toward the bars, about to say something, but Jess beat me to the punch. "Christa, this is my partner, Teddy."

Her partner? She was seeing someone, and she never mentioned it? I'd just been swung at, hit with a purse, had a Big Gulp poured down my back. I sported a black eye, a split lip, and what I hoped weren't bruised ribs. None of that compared to the pain knifing through me when Jess said, "my partner" referring to someone other than me.

As if he saw my pain, the man on the other side of the bars spoke. "Oh, no. She means I'm her *business* partner. The two of us started the practice together a few years ago."

Oh, right. Duh. She must've mentioned his name at some point. My face grew warm, and I looked at the ground.

"Teddy and I met in medical school," Jess said. "He decided I'd been grieving long enough and needed to experience the world again, so he forced me to join his study group. We've been *platonic* best friends ever since."

I released a breath. "Okay, sorry. Of course I've heard of you, Teddy. It's just been a long night. It's nice to meet you."

"I can only imagine. Now, Jess, I've posted bail for you, and you should be out once they finish processing."

"Thanks," she said. "I owe you one."

"No shit. I also called my sister to go get Ethan so your mom wouldn't have to hear about this from me. Unfortunately, she must've seen it on the news, because she pulled into the parking lot as I was waiting to post bail. I had to flirt with the front desk officer a LOT to stall her… and he makes Gilbert Gottfried look like a hot, young stud."

Shit. Jess's mother was the last person I wanted to face from behind bars, especially when I'd been the one to put her daughter here. And considering that the last words she'd spoken to me were, "I never want to see you again." Maybe I should just stay here, let Jess talk to her alone.

"Mom came?" Beside me, Jess sounded hopeful. "I thought she was pissed at us."

Teddy shrugged. "Well, she's here. Maybe she's here to gloat. Or maybe she's not mad anymore. Anyway, I'm running out of time. Christa, I tried to bail you out, too, but… there are some issues."

"What kind of issues?" I asked.

"You mean because she doesn't have ID?"

"No, it's actually good she didn't have ID," Teddy said. "The problem is, according to your fingerprints, you're dead. I asked if they're in the habit of jailing dead people… and they suggested that if I didn't shut up and come get Jess, I might be joining both of you in there."

My heart sank. One stupid moment of losing my temper, and everything was going to come out. We should've just moved seats.

"Hey," Jess said, "stop beating yourself up. That other jackass swung first, remember?"

Before I could answer, a police officer entered the hallway. "Jess Cooper?"

"That's me!" Jess waved one hand over her head to be seen through the mass of other parents. "Right here."

"You're all set to go. You'll get a court date in the mail." The metal door swung open. The officer put one hand on his nightstick, daring anyone who wasn't Jess to step forward. Teddy was right: with that scowl, he really did resemble an older Gilbert Gottfried.

She hesitated and bit her lip, studying my face.

Officer Gottfried glanced between us. "It's no skin off my nose if you'd rather spend the night in here, sweetheart. But you've got three seconds to decide before I lock this door again. It's going to be a long night, and I don't get paid enough to deal with your personal issues."

"It's fine," I said. "Go. I've slept in worse places."

The sadness that slashed across her features told me that was the wrong thing to say, but she took a step toward the open door. Teddy reached forward and grasped her hand. "It'll be fine, Jess."

She didn't take her eyes off me. "I'll start calling lawyers first thing tomorrow morning. We'll get you out of there as soon as we can."

That might take a while, especially if police figured out I was wanted in Canada. But I forced my lips to stretch into something that resembled a smile. "I know. I'll be fine."

The door clanged shut behind her, and the lock clacked back into place, reinforcing that we were all stuck in here. Jess and Teddy walked down the hall behind the officer, arm-in-arm to the main door.

A chill went down my spine. If the police sent me back to Canada, I might never see Jess—or my son—again. And I'd have no one to blame but myself.

$$\infty \; \heartsuit \; \infty$$

Jess

Of all the places to run into Ma again after the biggest fight we'd ever had, jail was by far the least desirable. For a moment, I thought about putting my jacket over my head, racing out to Teddy's car before she saw me, and asking him to floor it.

Unfortunately, that plan would have required running her over. When we stepped out into the sunlight and headed for the silver bimmer, she was leaning against the hood, reading a book. I stopped dead, looking for another way home, but Teddy pulled me forward.

"You'll have to face her eventually," he said. "At least here, if she tries to strangle you, police will intervene."

Always the optimist. Half walking, half being dragged, I approached the car, keeping my eyes down. Teddy unlocked the car and dove inside, but the locks clicked again before I could make it to the passenger door. Not knowing what else to do, I stopped in front of my mother.

"Hey," I said.

"Hey yourself."

Ours wasn't the most expressive family. "So… read any good books lately?"

She snapped it shut and dropped the book into her cavernous beige purse. "I miss my grandson."

Right. She wanted to see Ethan. Of course. "That's why you came to the jail? Because you could've called if that was it. Or you could've gone to the coach's house and picked him up."

"No, that's not it." She sighed. "You're not making this easy on me."

I nodded and waited. Yes, I'd given her one hell of a shock. Three, really, between Brett turning up as Christa and me being arrested. But knowing she might react badly and emotionally preparing for it were two different things.

When I didn't respond, Ma said, "I shouldn't have said the things I did. You know that I love you, and that I loved Brett like a son. I'm delighted that he's not dead. Everything else… is strange for an old lady like me."

"I know. It was strange for me at first, too. Sometimes it still is."

"Are you happy?"

Was I happy with the looks and the whispers and the snide comments? The side eyes, people moving out of our path on the street? Or was I happy to have my spouse back?

"It's a bit of an adjustment," I finally said. "We're still working a few things out."

"Do you love him?"

"Her," I said automatically. "I really do. I never stopped."

"Then I'll figure out a way to accept her," Ma said. "I'm sorry for the way I acted."

"I'm sorry we told you the way we did. I wanted more time to ease you into the idea, and everything got messed up somehow. I love you."

"I love you, too."

She stepped forward, wrapping her arms around me. At first, I stood woodenly, but then I remembered the wide range of emotions I felt when I first saw Christa. Ma's words may have been hurtful, but we'd blindsided her.

Through the windshield, I saw Teddy wipe a tear from his eye.

Christa

Spending a weekend in a holding cell wasn't so bad. Sure, the piss pot in the corner stunk to high heaven, and using it in front of a bunch of people felt extremely awkward. But at least they moved me into a cell full of women. Once most of the other parents cleared out, I had a lot of time to think. Time to wonder what my next step should be, time to make a plan for getting my name changed.

On Saturday, the guard informed me that I had a visitor. A short, pudgy man in an expensive suit stood at the front of the now-nearly-empty holding cell, carrying a brown leather brief-case. The officer escorted us to a tiny, windowless room so we could talk.

"Hi, Christa," he said. "I'm Robert Bradford, Esq. You may have heard of me?"

"I'm sorry, no. But I have been out of the country."

The corners of his mouth twitched. "I meant, your wife may have mentioned that I'd be coming to visit. She called me to come in and discuss your little problem."

"Thank you. It's good to see you." I hesitated. "Not to sound rude, but why am I still here?"

"They ran your prints through the system and it came back with a death certificate. Now, being dead isn't a crime, but identity theft is, so they're keeping you until they can verify who you are. Jess gave me all the paperwork. I have your birth certificate, your marriage certificate, an old photocopy of Brett Cooper's driver's license, and the court paperwork she filed on your behalf. They're doing some processing now, but you should be out of here soon. Just sit tight."

Moments later, I was once again a free woman. I didn't know where to go or what to do, and I was a little nervous about leaving the one place I was reasonably likely not to get attacked again, but I was free. If being paralyzed by fear and indecision qualified as freedom. Really, I'd just traded a literal jail cell for one constructed in my mind.

In the parking lot, a couple of TV cameras waited. Must be a slow news day in Boston. I lowered my head and covered my face with one hand, but a familiar sense of dread filled me. What if the incident wound up on the news? What if Tina found us again? We locked up the house, hadn't left her a key, no money when we took off. I was sure she'd broken in, but she must be pissed. If there was any chance she'd reappear, I'd be so tempted to run again, but I couldn't leave Jess.

Seeing my response to the reporters, my lawyer said, "No comment" repeatedly until we reached his car.

"Get in. I'll call your wife to meet us down the street."

"Thanks," I said, sliding in and buckling my seat belt. "What do I owe you?"

"Jess already paid me. You'll get something in the mail confirming all the charges have been dropped. It's ridiculous for police to think they could hold you for not having any identification on you while attending a football game."

"What about disturbing the peace?"

"Twenty witnesses saw the two of you get attacked. Those charges will be dropped, too. You never should've been taken into custody in the first place."

That was a relief, at least. But there were still other things I needed to take care of, and maybe Mr. Bradford would be able to help with some of it. I considered him carefully for a minute before speaking. Any lawyer who dressed like that, carried that briefcase, and carried himself like a rock star had to be pretty good at what he did.

"If my wife hired you, does that mean you have to tell her everything we talk about?"

"Legally, you're my client. I'm prohibited by the rules of ethics from telling your wife about our conversations without your consent. Attorney-client privilege transcends death—real or faked."

I cracked a sardonic smile at the words. "Good to know."

"As far as I'm concerned, this matter is closed. Is there something else you wanted to discuss?"

"Yeah." The word somehow extended to about three syllables. I'd been thinking a lot over the past couple of days, and this was no way to live. I couldn't be constantly in fear of what might happen. Something needed to change.

Out of the corner of my eye, I spotted a familiar crossover vehicle turning into the parking lot. "Can I make an appointment for later this week?"

"Sure thing. From what Mrs. Cooper told me about your situation, I may be able to help." Mr. Bradford handed me a card. "Feel free to contact my secretary. I'll see you soon."

"Thank you, sir." I shook his hand, palming the card. The car stopped beside me, and I climbed in.

Jess threw her arms around me. "Are you okay? Was it awful?"

"It wasn't the worst night's sleep I've ever had. Thanks for coming to get me."

"How sad. We need to get you a current ID. We need to file for your name change with the courts. And we need—"

"Jess. I just spent almost twenty-four hours peeing in front of other women. I slept on a cement floor with a piece of stale bread from dinner as a pillow. Can we please talk about this later?"

She fell silent, chewing her lip. Her stiff posture told me she was upset, but I couldn't worry about her right then. I needed to figure out my next steps, and as much as I loved Jess and Ethan, what was best for me might not be what was best for them.

CHAPTER TWENTY-FOUR

Jess

Christa hated being home with us. She didn't complain, but her discomfort showed in the way she avoided people's gazes when we left the house, in the set of her jaw and the square of her shoulders every time she introduced herself as Ethan's other mother. Introducing herself as his father only made things more awkward. Neither of us was ashamed of our relationship, but explaining your life over and over to people who had no business asking got exhausting fast. Refusing to answer questions always somehow made Christa feel like the asshole.

She came to bed later each night, tossing and turning until I wished I could ask her to sleep in the guest room so I'd be awake for surgery the next day. During the days, she delayed looking for a job, delayed returning the paperwork needed to reinstate her social security number, delayed doing anything useful.

I could tell that she was miserable, but I didn't know how to help. In Canada, she had a job, she had friends, she had a life. Here, she had only me and Ethan. Increasingly, I worried that we weren't enough for her. She needed something to do, a reason to leave the house every day. Sure, she could do the grocery shopping, but after the brawl, I knew she was scared even to do that.

"Hey, Christa?" I asked one day, flipping through the online statement for the credit card I'd given her.

"Yeah?" She and Ethan sat on the floor, playing some game that involved stealing cars and dealing drugs. Christa and I were apparently tied for Mother of the Year.

"What's PeaPod?"

She didn't answer, just leaned forward and squinted, focusing intently on the game. "Christa?"

"Just a second."

"Can't you pause it?"

Beside her, my son hit a button on his remote and looked at me. "It's where you order groceries online and they deliver them for you. So people don't have to leave the house if they're busy or something." Ethan turned to Christa. "I told you she'd figure it out."

"What are you talking about? Are you not leaving the house at all?" How had I missed this? I knew she wasn't happy, but I'd never dreamed she'd turned into a hermit.

"You know, I have to work on my college applications." In the blink of an eye, Ethan set down his controller and vanished into his room.

Christa watched him go, her lips twitching into a smile. "Maybe we should argue in front of him more often."

"Is that what we're doing? What's going on?"

Finally, she turned off the television and faced me. "You remember what happened to my friend Bo, right?"

I nodded, realization dawning.

"After we got attacked again," she said, "I guess... I've not been feeling like going out. Much. At all."

My heart broke for her. "So you've been sitting in the house, hiding from the world?"

She nodded, looking miserable. "I'm sorry. I don't know what's happened to me. It's just... too much. I worry about Tina finding us. I worry about bigots. I worry about everything."

"Of course you're worried," I said. "All you do is sit inside all day and think about everything that could go wrong. Why didn't you tell me?"

"I didn't want you to think I regretted coming home with you."

It killed me that she was so upset and that I'd not only missed it, but I had no idea how to make things better. With a sigh, I kissed her forehead, her cheeks, her lips. "I didn't make a mistake. We just need to figure out how to get you back into the swing of things. Hiding in the house, playing video games, and cooking for me isn't living."

She sighed. "You're right. So, what do we do?"

"Well, first, we're going to bundle up and go for a walk. You need some fresh air. Then, we're getting you a job."

Finding gainful employment in the United States after being dead for eighteen years presented several logistical problems. First, all of Christa's recent work history was in a foreign country, and although my spouse actually worked those hours, a certain very pissed-off Canadian might have something to say about it if Christa tried to work under that social insurance number in the United States. Even if she changed her name legally. We didn't need any more problems. After we snuck out in the middle of the night, we couldn't be sure what kind of reference Christa would be able to get from the hotel, anyway.

Second, I didn't want to be involved in fraud. Using Christa's name on legal documents without legally changing it was out of the question. Third, Brett Cooper couldn't explain the gap in his employment history. Nor did dead people keep up on technological advances, so even if Christa were willing and able to apply for jobs as Brett Cooper using his college degree, she lacked any of the knowledge required in 2019 for the types of jobs Brett was qualified for in 2001.

Not to mention that it wouldn't be legal for Christa to work in the United States until Brett Cooper was legally declared alive. Any employer that did a background check would promptly show her the door. We were working on ironing out all these issues, but things took time. All things considered, I might be supporting her for at least the next few months. Not that I minded, but having something to occupy her time would probably make Christa feel much better than sitting around at loose ends, playing Grand Theft Auto or Fallout 4.

I'd known it would be hard, but after a few weeks, I worried the adjustment was too much. That I'd wake up one morning and find she'd taken off again. The only thing more difficult than faking your death, it seemed, was coming back to life.

Christmas approached, but no one thought about decorating our home. In college, Brett and I would go into the mountains and chop down our own tiny tree, finding the perfect spot to place it in my dorm room. We'd never had a Christmas together as a married couple. After Ethan was born, I bought a fake tree, which was much easier. Still, getting it out of storage required too much effort.

Ethan didn't say anything, either, but stopped talking about school. His friends didn't come over after school anymore. Poor kid. I scheduled another appointment with the therapist, but his moms and a doctor weren't substitutes for friends his own age.

In our liberal community, people were accepting of many things, but they didn't know what to make of us. A week after we returned, a For Sale sign went up on the house next door. Sure, they were a pretty conservative couple, but their oldest baby-sat Ethan when we first moved in.

Not long after that house sold, an identical sign appeared in the Christian family's yard across the street and to the right. Since they'd proudly boasted several Trump/Pence signs, we weren't that surprised. But still, Ethan played with their kids every day when they were in grade school.

If you ever want to know who your friends really are, enter a sexual relationship with your dead husband turned queer lover. That'll send the fakers away pretty quick.

The day before Christmas Eve, I took the afternoon off work to go Christmas shopping. This should have been the happiest

Christmas I'd had since Ethan was born, but not even the cheesy piped-in holiday music I secretly adored or gingerbread-flavored donuts could raise my spirits. I shopped quickly, not paying much attention to my purchases. Ethan wanted a new iPad, I knew, and that was already hidden safely in my closet, having been delivered to my office shortly after Black Friday. But this year's stocking stuffers might not wind up the most exciting. I had no idea what I bought.

When I arrived home, I left the packages in the car before checking to see if the coast was clear. The undecorated tree sat in the corner, once again waiting for Christa to put up the garland and the lights so we could all hang the ornaments together. The sight of the naked tree sent a pang of depression through me, although I didn't know why. I hurried past it, refusing to look at another reminder that nothing this year was working out the way it should have.

Ethan sat in the backyard, on the frozen old swing set I never bothered to take down when he outgrew it, staring at the ground. Colored lights twinkled from the apartment building across the street. Christa was nowhere to be found.

"Where's your mother?"

"Out."

"Thanks, Sherlock." I grinned, but he avoided my eyes. "What's wrong? Where is she?"

"Nothing. I don't know."

I sat beside him, turning his head so he'd meet my eyes. Then the reason for his attitude hit me like a fist in the gut. Blood smeared his nose and upper lip. His nose puffed out to twice its normal size, and one eye was swollen shut. My hand lifted even as a gasp escaped me.

"What happened?"

"Nothing. I'm fine." I glared at him, not bothering to point out the obvious lie. "It's not a big deal. I quit the basketball team."

"You...oh." The reality behind those words hit me like a ton of bricks. "I'm so sorry, honey. Come inside, let me get you cleaned up."

"No. If they're going to treat me like a freak, I'll look like a freak."

My heart broke for him. He didn't ask for any of this, but kids were cruel, and he bore the burden of the choices his parents made. Both of us. I may not have been involved in Brett's decision to leave, but I certainly encouraged Christa to come back. In doing so, I'd turned our son into an outcast.

Neither of us asked his permission, not really. We just acted, expecting our child to deal with whatever consequences arose. And we were ridiculously short-sighted, thinking that just because we lived in a liberal community, in a state where same-sex couples could marry, no one would have a problem with our choices.

Ignoring his words, I went into the house and returned with the first aid kit. He winced when I dabbed at his face with cotton, clearing off the blood, but knew better than to argue. Thankfully, his nose wasn't broken, all his teeth remained in place, and it wouldn't be worth the hassle of trying to get him to agree to stitches. Instead, I put a couple of butterfly closures across one eyebrow and threatened to change the password for the Wi-Fi if he removed them before the next morning.

"I'm so sorry this happened, Ethan."

"You should see the other guy." He attempted a smile but winced when his split lip stretched open. I reached for another butterfly closure.

"I'm calling the school first thing tomorrow morning. This isn't okay."

"Please don't, Mom. You'll only make things worse. They hit me, I fought back, we're good. The other guys know now, just because I have two moms, I'm not a wuss. This is how guys work things out."

I wasn't so sure, but I'd never been a teenage boy. I made a mental note to talk to Christa about this later. She'd have a lot of insight. Maybe we could even talk about that time she beat up Aaron Porter when we were in high school. I never got tired of that story.

Inside the house, the front door closed.

"Please don't tell her," Ethan said.

"What's she going to think? You fell and hit a doorknob with your face?"

He swallowed. "I'll do it. Just not yet. Give me a few minutes?"

With a sigh and a squeeze of his shoulder, I went into the house to greet my wife. She looked drawn, haggard. When I'd re-met her, she'd been so vibrant, so alive. Had I done this to her? Maybe Christa would've been better off in Canada, living someone else's life.

Until she went to jail, I reminded myself. But still, if I hadn't been there, if Tina had arrived at Christa's house on a day when Ethan and I weren't sitting around the dining room table, our lives right now could be very different. I'd thought this was the best solution, but the choices I'd made less than a month ago now seemed naive at best. It was foolish to think we could pick up our lives as if nothing ever happened.

Nothing was working out the way we'd hoped. What were we even doing? Were we stupid to think we could recapture a high school romance, decades later? Maybe there was a reason so many first loves wound up divorced at forty or fifty, once the kids were grown.

CHAPTER TWENTY-FIVE

Christa

After breakfast on Christmas Eve, Jess told me to get dressed up and get in the car without asking questions.

"What about Ethan?"

"That's a question," she said.

"Okay… So I'm just going to assume we're ditching our son on Christmas Eve, the first time we'll have all spent the holiday together in his lifetime."

She stuck her tongue out at me. "He's going to Ma's. We'll be home before midnight, and we'll be with him all day on Christmas. Now get your ass in gear. We're going to be late."

Late for what? That was a question, though, so I kept my mouth shut and went to get dressed instead. An hour later, we hugged Ethan good-bye and left him in the care of my mother-in-law.

Jess handed me a blindfold. "Put this on."

"Why?"

"No questions."

"Okay, but if my mascara smudges, it's on you."

"That's a risk I'll take. Now hush."

The radio started blasting a recent musical, making any

further conversation futile. I couldn't see to turn it down, even if I thought it would be likely to help. Instead, I leaned back in my seat, wondering where we were going. When the musical clicked around to the first song for the second time, I realized this wasn't a quick trip. Were we going to visit my mother in Connecticut? Up to Vermont to surprise Val? I hadn't planned to spend my Christmas Eve chopping wood, but if she needed us, I'd help.

Finally, when my bladder was about to explode, the SUV stopped. Jess took my hand while I alighted from the vehicle, hushing all my attempts at conversation. I managed to squeak out the word "bathroom," but that was about it.

The smells of fried food and garbage and people and urine and dirt hit my nose: the unmistakable mishmash of odors that signaled we'd arrived in a city. Did Jess drive in circles for three hours just to wind up in downtown Boston?

"This way," she urged. "Careful, there's a doorway ahead. I'm holding it open for you."

My heels clicked against pavement before moving onto what felt like tile. Jess maneuvered me until we wound up in a place that absolutely smelled like a bathroom.

"The stall door is in front of you. Take one step, then you can take off the blindfold. Put it back on when you're done."

Okay, this was getting ridiculous. Where were we? Why the secrecy? I studied the interior walls of the bathroom stall as if the secret to the meaning of life was written on them, but all I gleaned from the addresses was that we were somewhere near New York City. I'd always wanted to skate in Rockefeller Center, to see the big Christmas tree in person, but that seemed like an experience Jess would've wanted to share with our son.

Soon, we were back in the hall, the blindfold once again leaving me in frustrating darkness.

"Just another minute," Jess said. "We're almost there."

I grumbled under my breath, but secretly I was touched she'd gone to so much effort to do something special for me. We went through another doorway, then Jess stopped walking. "Wait right here."

Where was I going to go?

Heels clicked away from me. Great, now I was blindfolded and alone somewhere in New York City, with my cell phone in my purse in the car. If it had been anyone but Jess orchestrating this stunt, I'd have been out of there.

Still, I tapped my foot to let her know I preferred not to wait forever for the big reveal, whatever it was. It didn't take long.

A voice rang out behind me, sending a chill down my spine. "Why, if it isn't the bitch who stole my best blond wig."

Not even daring to hope, I removed the blindfold. Posters lined the cinderblock wall, telling me we stood in an old theater. Slowly, I turned, seeking the person who'd spoken. It couldn't be. How…?

In front of me towered a gorgeous Asian woman with long black hair, dressed from head to toe in red leather and wearing an aggravated expression I'd seen a dozen times. When our eyes locked, her faux frustration evaporated, and she grinned widely.

Mouth open, I looked from her to my wife and back. Jess just beamed at me, looking like she'd won the lottery.

"Don't just stand there gawking. Get your ass over here and give me a hug!"

The words shocked me into movement, and I closed the distance between us. Nina wrapped her long arms around me, and I clutched her as if she were the last lifeboat on the Titanic.

"Don't start crying now, or you'll ruin my makeup," she said.

I chuckled and pulled back. "I'm sorry. It's just so good to see you."

"You, too. I'm glad you found yourself. I wish my husband were here to see you."

"You're married?"

"That's right. To the hottest man you will ever meet. We've got two kids, 7 and 9. Gorgeous little rug rats. We're all ruled by a gorgeous Siamese cat. Unfortunately, Leroy's home wrapping presents and putting out snacks for Santa Claus, so he's not here tonight. Oh, I wish I could invite him."

"We'll come back," I said. "I'd love to meet him. And this is Jess."

"Oh, I know Jess. We go back DAYS." She blew a kiss at the air behind me. "But look, I gotta go do my show. You two meet me around the back after?"

"That sounds awesome."

She sashayed away, and I marveled at how she hadn't changed a bit. Part of me wanted to chase her down the hall, worried that if I let her go, I'd never see her again. But we were only going to the front of the theater, and security guards were everywhere, and she'd be fine.

Beside me, Jess touched my hand. "How're you doing?"

"I can't believe you did this! How did you even find her?"

"When you told me Bo's story, it sounded familiar. It took some time, but I finally figured out why. There was a queen on *America's Top Drag Model* a few years ago named Tabby Rangoon. She told a heartbreaking story about how she was gay-bashed, and how her parents never accepted her. I went back and watched the season again, and it all checked out. So, I contacted the show, told them my story, and asked where Tabby was working now. I was prepared to travel anywhere, but luckily, she landed in New York City. Then I just had to convince her manager that I wasn't some kind of crackpot and he got us permission to go backstage. Knowing her real name helped."

She made it all sound as easy as ordering takeout, but I marveled at the amount of time and effort this surprise must have taken. "I can't ever possibly thank you enough."

"You don't have to. The look on your face when you saw her was thanks enough. Merry Christmas, Christa."

CHAPTER TWENTY-SIX

January 2020

Jess

Six weeks after moving back to Boston, Christa still hadn't found work. Our son's bruises may have faded, but he was becoming quieter, more withdrawn. He went out less, stayed in with Christa more. He decided not to apply to Berkeley because it was too far away. I should've been glad they were bonding, but their shared isolation worried me. All I wanted was a way for the three of us to be happy together. I'd thought taking Christa to see Bo, to show her that he was doing well, would help. For a few days, maybe it did, but by the time New Year's rolled around, she was back to spending most of her time playing video games.

One Friday, after receiving a phone call at work, I told Teddy I'd be leaving early. Knowing what this meant, he agreed with an air of resignation and a hug that left me gasping for air.

"I'll be fine," I said.

"I know. Good luck."

After a quick stop, I drove home, wondering how Christa would respond to what I had to tell her. A manila envelope sat beside me, thick with a sheaf of papers. This would be best for everyone involved. Things just weren't working out the way we thought they would. Something had to change.

After I pulled into the driveway, I watched snow fall onto the windshield. Although it was early, dark clouds obliterated the sun. Some days in January, the sky never lightened at all.

With a sigh, I shut off the engine. I loved this house, this neighborhood, the life I created for Ethan. But that wasn't the life I now found myself living. Everything was about to change. We couldn't go on like this.

No one greeted me when I entered the house. I called Christa's name, checking the kitchen, my office, even the guest room. Nothing. Halfway up the stairs, I heard her answering call.

"In here!"

"There's something I need to…" The words died in my throat when I reached our bedroom door.

Clothes lay strewn across the bed, the floor. A sock hung over one lampshade. It took a moment to find the suitcase beneath the mound of crap on the bedspread. Clicking hangers and swishing garments directed me to Christa in the walk-in closet.

Did she know? Had she somehow guessed what I'd come home to say?

"Did he tell you?"

"Did who tell me what?" she asked.

"Ethan. He's… well, I've… Maybe we should sit down. We've got some things to talk about." I held up the envelope still gripped in one hand.

We moved to the bed, and I handed it to her. She opened it and pulled out a sheaf of papers. Her expression changed from confusion to joy to sadness as her eyes scanned the page. "You bought Tranquility?"

My heart in my throat, I nodded. "We need to start over. A new beginning. Ethan loves snow and skiing, you've got experience in hotel management, and, well, there's a need for doctors everywhere. I started in general practice before switching to orthopedics. I can go back. It's not as lucrative, but with the farm and the lower cost of living, we'll be fine."

She sniffled. "This is amazing. Jess, you didn't have to do this for me. We could've made things work here."

"No, we couldn't. You're miserable, I'm frustrated, and Ethan feels the tension coming from both of us. Something has to change, and this seemed like the perfect solution. Besides, I got an awesome deal. Val's already on her way to Florida, and she couldn't be happier."

"Thank you!" She threw her arms around me. "I love you."

I held her for a minute, but then my eyes returned to the clothing strewn over the bed. Releasing her, I moved backward. "If you had no idea we were moving, why are you packing? What's going on? Where are you going?"

She choked on her words, swallowed, and reached for my hands. I batted them away and stood.

"Stop, Jess," she said. "It's not what you think."

"So you're not the same asshole who ran out on your wife years ago when things got tough?"

The doorbell rang. She didn't answer, instead glancing helplessly in the direction of the front door. I wondered who stood on the other side: a divorce lawyer? Movers?

"Oh, my God. You really are leaving me. Were you even going to say good-bye? Or were you planning to fake your death a second time?" With tears blinding me, I stumbled toward the doorway.

"Jess, wait!"

"Fuck you," I said.

At the bottom of the stairs, I flung the door open, running past a wide-eyed man in a black cashmere overcoat and a top hat. My feet skidded on the ice beneath the snow, my arms reeled, and I fell backward into the stranger, knocking us both to the ground.

∞ ♡ ∞

Christa

When Jess ran out that door, my heart jumped into my throat. I'd spent days planning how to tell her, weeks even. Every detail in my head was worked out perfectly, but I'd failed to anticipate what would happen if Jess returned home before I was ready for her. If she figured out what was going on before I managed to break the news to her gently.

I also hadn't considered her reaction fully. With all that happened, until the hurt filled her eyes, part of me wondered if Jess was really happy I'd come back. Sure, we'd hugged and kissed and snuggled and talked, but we seemed more like old friends than spouses most of the time. The sex was fantastic, yet infrequent. We were more like roommates who shared a bed than wives.

She defended me in public, but was distant and brooding when we were alone. Part of me wondered if Jess was really okay being married to a woman, or if she was just doing what she thought I wanted, or what she thought Ethan wanted. Fear of hearing her answer made me delay asking.

The second she ran out that door, all of her distance since I'd come back made sense. Jess wasn't holding back because she didn't love me, or because she wasn't attracted to me, or because she was only doing this for our child. She was afraid she wasn't enough for me, that she wasn't what I wanted, and that I'd leave her again. She'd been holding back to protect herself.

Stupidly, I'd made plans without talking to her, thinking I'd fix everything. Instead of creating a solution for us to be together, all I'd done bring her worst fears to life.

Cursing myself a hundred different ways, I took off behind her. She got a good head start, but my longer legs quickly ate up the space between us. When she opened the front door, I'd have caught her if she'd slowed at all to go around the person standing on the porch. Instead, she plowed right into him, and both went down.

Stifling the urge to laugh at the tangle of woman and lawyer on the ground before me, I plunged into the cold to help them up, forgetting that I was barefoot and not wearing a coat. My feet went numb when I hit the snow, but there was no going back. If I couldn't catch Jess, couldn't help her understand what I was doing and why, I'd lose her again. This time forever.

If that happened, I'd never be able to forgive myself.

∞ ♡ ∞

Jess

Christa knelt beside me, taking me back to the day I found her at the resort. How things had changed. I'd gone from a youngish widow, a single mother, to a married bisexual on the verge of being abandoned by the person she loved. Again.

Tears welled in my eyes. My ankle throbbed, so I focused my attention on it, wondering how I could possibly salvage my dignity and get back to the car before Christa realized how she'd made me feel. Fool me once, shame on you. Fool me twice…

"Jess, please listen to me," she said. "I'm not leaving you. Not exactly."

Behind me, the man I'd nearly forgotten about cleared his throat. "Is this a bad time?"

Christa stood, handing my purse to him. Great. She was leaving me and robbing me. Exactly what I needed.

"Jess, I'd like you to meet my lawyer, Mr. Robert Bradford of Bradford & Associates. You spoke on the phone after the football game about bailing me out of jail. What you don't know is that we've been working together ever since."

For the first time, I looked at the stranger standing on my porch, getting more snow on his coat by the second. It had been years, but everyone remembered the face of the man who defended one of the most notorious murderers Boston had ever seen. I'd called him because his name jumped out at me when I skimmed through the lawyer listings online, and because I knew he was good.

What was he doing on my doorstep?

Mr. Bradford leaned down, offering me a hand. "Pleased to meet you at last, Jess. I've heard a lot about you. May I help you up?"

I grasped his smooth, warm palm and rose. The longer I stood in the cold, the more numbness replaced the throbbing in my ankle. It also replaced my manners, because instead of introducing myself or thanking him, I blurted out the one thought moving through my head. "You're not a divorce lawyer."

"No, I'm not," he said with a glance at my wife. "Really, if this is a bad time, I could come back."

Christa stepped forward. "Jess, Robert is a criminal lawyer with associates in Quebec. He helped connect me with a law firm there."

Things started to fall into place. "Tina."

Robert said, "We've convinced the prosecutor to reduce the charges against your wife in exchange for her spending six months in a minimum-security women's detention center. Once her time is served and she leaves Canada, she will not be permitted to re-enter the country."

"That's it?" After all this time, worrying and living under this black cloud, I couldn't believe things would be resolved so easily.

"Not entirely," Christa said. "I had to get a legal name change, and get a passport in that name. That's what I've been working on, when you thought I was just playing games online and doing nothing."

Not an online affair. Not regretting coming back. No plans to leave again. A wisp of hope fluttered in my stomach.

"You changed your name? To what?"

"Christa Cooper."

Cooper. My name. No, our name. Christa and Jess Cooper. Christa, Jess, and Ethan Cooper. If ever I needed a sign that she loved me, that she wanted things to work, this was it. For the first time in months, things were finally coming together. I leaned forward and kissed her slowly, trying to put as much love as I could into it.

"Thank you," I whispered, with tears in my eyes.

"There's more," she said. "I also have to forfeit the money in my social insurance account, since it was earned under someone else's name and number. I have to pay a fine—me, with my money, not you—and pay five thousand Canadian dollars to Tina as restitution. Once that's done, we'll be free. The house is still mine, as long as the mortgage gets paid, and I'll be allowed to sell it. Tina's agreed to move out, in exchange for not being charged with extortion."

"So you're not leaving me?"

"I am, but I swear, it's only temporary. I have to go back to Quebec for a while."

"But I bought the Tranquility…" Weak, I knew. My brain wasn't processing words the way I needed it to.

"I know, and that was a wonderful, sweet, caring thing to do. I love the way you want to take care of me. But I caused this mess, and I'm the one who needs to fix it."

I gestured to Robert, who'd pulled out his phone and was tactfully pretending he couldn't hear every word. "Were you two going to just leave? You weren't going to tell me?"

"Part of me thought you'd be happier without me around. But, yeah, I was going to tell you. Robert and I weren't planning to leave for a few hours." Christa pulled me into her arms. Her lips lingered on mine with a heat that seared away the numbness. "I have to do this. I have to go. But I promise, I'll be back here as soon as I can."

Even knowing she was right didn't make it easier. "Don't come back here," I said. Her face fell. "Meet me at Tranquility."

"I will," she vowed.

"I hate long good-byes," I said. "So let's not. Just tell me you'll see me again soon, and that you love me."

"I love you, and I'll see you as soon as I can. I'd stay if I could. I'll write to you every day."

We hugged and with one last kiss, she walked away, following Robert to his car. Tears blurred my vision. I wanted to scream, to rage, but my heart knew that walking away was for the best. Only leaving me now would allow Christa to stop running, for the first time in her life. By going to jail, she would finally be free.

READ ABOUT JESS AND BRETT'S FIRST WEDDING

Want more? Sign up for my newsletter and get a free bonus scene! To start, visit:
https://BookHip.com/HCVATXP

AUTHOR'S NOTE

Twenty years ago, I had the pleasure of working with a trans woman while she was transitioning. Back then, trans people weren't highly visible in the media other than Chandler's father on *Friends* (who was the butt of far too many jokes). I didn't know anyone else trans that I was aware of. Didi and I were surface-level friends, a step beyond acquaintances primarily because we worked similar shifts and took our smoking breaks at the same time. She was just a person, like me. She loved her wife and her kids. She worked hard to provide for them. Just by being herself, Didi opened my mind and changed me in many ways. Her story stayed with me, and the idea of being in love with someone both before and after transition never left me. Thus, Finding Tranquility was born.

Thank you so much to everyone who assisted with this project. I owe a huge debt of gratitude to all of you who read and assisted with early drafts, especially to Jami, Owen, and Lex. Any mistakes in representation are my own.

And thank you to my readers. I couldn't do this without you.

ANNA'S GUIDE TO GETTING EVEN
PREVIEW

What does a woman do when her ex-boyfriend posts nude picture of her on the internet and sends them to everyone she knows?

Check out ANNA'S GUIDE TO GETTING EVEN

My name is Anna. That's Ahn-a, not Ann-a. People hear my story, they say, "Oh, that's awful." They

> *think it would never happen to them. I thought it*
> *would never happen to me, either.*
> *But it did.*

Chapter 1

November 10, 2018

The newscasters spent days repeating dire warnings most people didn't believe. After all, we'd made it through ninety-nine percent of hurricane season without any storms traveling anywhere near us. Early November wasn't exactly known for its tropical weather in New York City. Still, as Mamá used to say, it's better to be prepared *por si las moscas por si las moscas*, or just in case.

Just in case, I stocked up on eggs, milk, and bread (as if I'd be making French toast in a storm), grabbed a box of strawberry-flavored toaster pastries for good measure, froze blocks of ice in plastic containers, and filled my bathtub with water. This basic nod at preparation seemed more than sufficient. It never occurred to me to cover the windows or anything like that.

When the storm hit, the entire northeastern seaboard realized the newscasters hadn't been overreacting for once. Winds howled and shrieked, shaking the house. Rain obliterated the satellite signal to my television early in the evening. Soon there-after, I cowered in the basement of my three-bedroom house with a battery-powered lantern from an old camping trip and Hermione, my roommate's brown tabby cat. The two of us huddled in the spot furthest from the row of tiny windows under a sea of blankets as the storm raged overhead. Not long after sunset, my house lost power. The dots of light provided by street lamps winked out at the same time. My phone provided a lifeline to the outer world for almost an hour before the service stopped working. At least the lantern gave off a steady glow.

Alone, scared, and bored, I unfairly cursed my roommate for

not being with me. Tara was in the middle of nowhere, taking care of her sick mother. She lived in a tiny trailer with no TV, cell service, or Internet in one of those squarish-type states that started with a vowel. Tara probably would prefer to be with me, storm or no. If she even knew about the storm, isolated as she was.

Still, sitting alone in my basement listening to rain beat against the windows was no fun. My boyfriend, Jay, got stuck working late. By the time he left the office, the Mayor of New York City asked all residents to remain home unless absolutely necessary, keeping the roads clear for emergency vehicles. The last time I talked to him, Jay was about to walk the twelve blocks home to his loft apartment through a downpour so thick he couldn't see five feet beyond the circle of his umbrella.

Thunder crashed overhead. A streak of lightning lit up the room before the roar ended. I shivered and rearranged my covers. Using my phone as a flashlight, I picked up one of about five dozen old copies of *Forbes* magazine stored in our basement. My own face smiled up at me from a sidebar on the cover. When the magazine ran its feature on "Up-and-Coming Executives Under Thirty-Five years Old," I'd warned Tara that my friends and family would read it online, but she insisted on buying all the hard copies she could find. At least Tara's mother appreciated not having to drive thirty miles into town to read about me. The rest collected dust down here, in case the zombie apocalypse came and I needed a reminder of my old life or a way to start a fire.

The house shook, distracting me from reading about "No. 17: Katherine Ashcroft." A lovely woman, by all accounts. I saw her at a networking event a while back, but we didn't talk. I distracted myself by trying to remember the name of her company until thunder crashed on top of me. Rain beat against the windows so loudly, I double-checked the latches. Something banged against the roof. Cringing, I pressed my hands against my ears. The sounds of the storm grew louder, and Hermione squirmed closer against my chest, purring. The basement door rattled in its frame.

Another crash, followed by a bang. A siren wailed next to my ear. It took a moment to realize that the blaring sounded eerily like my car alarm. Uh-oh. Hopefully the wind set it off, and I could turn the blasted thing off from where I sat. Except I'd left my car keys on the kitchen counter. Upstairs, beyond the safety of the basement.

For fifteen minutes, I sat listening, regretting my decision to let the salesman talk me into buying the extended battery. The darn thing would blast all night if no one shut it off. He hadn't been exaggerating. Putting my hands over my ears was about as effective as trying to put out a forest fire with a Dixie cup of water.

Finally, I couldn't take it anymore. With a sigh, I threw off my blankets. Hermione glared at me before tearing off toward a pile of crap in the far corner. For her sake, I hoped it was quieter under there. My legs tingled after so much time cowering on the concrete floor. I rubbed them, one at a time, while I willed myself to go deaf. When the feeling returned to my lower limbs and the alarm still blared behind me, I drew a deep breath, pulled myself upright, and told myself there was no reason not to venture into the house for a minute or two. I'd be perfectly safe.

My prosthetic left foot sat against the wall where I'd left it when Hermione and I settled in for the night. It wouldn't take long to strap it on, but I couldn't stand the thought of another single unnecessary second listening to that siren. I'd hopped up the basement stairs before, I could do it again. The kitchen lay directly across from the basement door. Less than twenty feet of open space separated me from silence. Lots of windows, lots of potential for broken glass up there, but I had no choice. My shoes were also in the kitchen. Perhaps I should've shown the newscasters a little more respect.

A sturdy banister helped me to the top of the stairs. The basement door stuck, especially on humid days. Apparently, "humid" days included hurricane days. I shoved with all my might. The wood didn't budge. I tried again, with the same lack of results. On the third attempt, I braced my shoulder against the door, rested the bottom of my calf against the step, and slammed my full weight against the wood. The door opened— and whipped away from me. Without the support, I stumbled out into the hall, tripping over the top step. My palms and knees slammed against the ground, knocking the wind out of me.

The kitchen wasn't overly large, and my keys hung from a hook between the French patio doors and the door to the garage. I braced myself against the gusts, wondering how many windows broke to create this wind tunnel in my hallway. Still, I needed to move forward. Either I turned that alarm off, or I'd lose my mind by morning. With a deep breath, I started across the kitchen floor as quickly as I could.

Before I made it two feet into the room, I came to a dead stop. "*¡Dios mio!*"

Wind slapped my face, tearing the words from my mouth. Water drenched my hair and clothes. Shivers immediately followed. Surprised, I glanced toward the glass doors. The panes weren't broken. They weren't there at all. Neither were the doors. Or the walls, or the kitchen, or the roof. I stood, shivering, in the middle of the storm, surrounded by granite countertops, peering through the sheets of rain at our beautiful old oak tree, which lay across my newly topless Infiniti, alarm still blaring.

By the time the winds died down and the rain slowed, my phone's battery had long since crapped out. The moon finally peeked through the clouds, sending streaks of white light through the miraculously-still-intact basement windows. I lay huddled in the blankets, wishing for the warmth of the traitor cat that still lurked somewhere in the depths of the basement. I managed a couple of hours of fitful sleep by the time the sun peeked over the horizon.

My first hysterical thought upon opening my eyes was, "I'm going to be late for work." Of course I was. I also wasn't likely to make it at all, since the storm smashed the roof of my car in and whisked away my kitchen. I didn't even know if the house still contained my closet. If not, the only thing I had to wear, other than my navy blue sweatpants and Yankees T-shirt, sat folded in a box of Halloween costumes we stored in the basement. The idea of showing up at work dressed as Slutty Cop brought a ghost of a smile to my lips.

Ugh.

I forced myself to sit up and reached for my prosthetic.

"Mwar?"

"Hey, sweetie." Now that the danger passed, Hermione was more than happy to rub against my legs and accept petting until I remembered my obligation to feed her. One problem: we stored the cat food in the kitchen. Which could be somewhere over the rainbow for all I knew.

I picked her up and rubbed my face against her soft fur. My own stomach reminded me that I hadn't eaten, either. "Let's see if Mother Nature left us anything in the fridge. Or a fridge."

Talking to the cat soothed me. I kept up a constant stream of chatter while I found my phone in the tangle of blankets, plugged it in, confirmed that the power remained out, and headed upstairs to assess the damage.

"Well, Hermione, it appears that we lost the kitchen. Luckily, we still have a fridge." It lay on its side on the ground, and the cord dangled uselessly down the back, plug no longer attached, but I did *have* a refrigerator. "You like three-day old burrito, right?"

"Mwar?"

Gingerly, I opened the door, thankful at least that the side with the handle landed on top. A tangle of condiments lay against the fall wall, most of the containers still intact. On the top shelf, several plastic containers created a haphazard pyramid. Grabbing the top one, I pulled out a chunk of ground beef, wiped off the rice, and offered it to the cat while I kept digging. "Old lunch meat?"

She stood on her back legs when I opened the package, so I dropped a slice on the floor and grabbed a second for myself while I explored the rest of the house to assess the damage. The spare room, naturally, seemed more or less untouched.

Pretending I wandered someone else's home was the only thing holding me together at the moment, so I held my head high and tried to imagine an invisible realtor leading me on a tour...of a very water-logged house owned by a messy homeowner.

Not much happened in the bathroom, other than a pile of broken glass in the tub and the complete lack of hot water. I shrugged and shut the door to keep Hermione out before moving on. Then I stood for a long time, surveying Tara's room, delaying the moment before facing my own. I refused to allow myself to think about what I might find behind my closed door.

My best friend's room always looked like a hurricane hit it. Truly, I couldn't tell the difference until I spotted the puddles. Or, I wouldn't have, if the roof had been attached. Instead, sunlight streamed into every corner of the room as if mocking Tara for spending three hundred dollars on blackout curtains she never opened. My lips twitched upward when I realized the curtains themselves still lay perfectly in place, not even ruffled by the winds. Too bad she wasn't here, she'd appreciate the irony.

Finally, I turned to my room, on the same side of the house as the kitchen. As the missing pantry. The bedroom window five feet from my smashed car.

The door wouldn't open. With one shoulder braced against the wood, my hand tightened on the knob. I shoved as hard as I could. For my efforts, the door moved an inch. Something brushed against my face. I screamed and jumped before realizing it was only a tree branch. A branch with no business in my bedroom. Wonderful.

The door wasn't budging, so I abandoned my bedroom and continued my exploration. I felt nothing. Somewhere, deep inside, shock numbed my emotions, kept me from feeling the brunt of the pain.

My feet carried me from one room to the next as my mind took in, but refused to process, the damage. Windows shattered. Broken glass everywhere. Plaster coated every surface. A soaked couch in the dining room. Something soggy touched my right foot. I jumped, then realized it was a scrap of paper.

Thick, heavy paper, part of something once much larger. The letters on the front now spelled "Colum—." This could be either my diploma or Tara's. It didn't matter. Below it, I found a soggy mass of blue and red fabric. It took a minute to realize this wad of filthy sateen used to be horseback riding ribbons from my childhood. Shaking my head to ward off the onrush of emotions, I dropped everything into the rubble and continued picking my way toward the door.

Outside, movement caught my eye. Hermione dashed across the lawn, chasing a squirrel or something. Oh, no. I should've locked her in her carrier before doing this. Assuming I could find her carrier, which in my defense, was a pretty big assumption.

A wave of despair welled in my chest. A familiar old emotion I thought I'd long since conquered. I needed to get out of here.

If only I'd been wearing shoes when I went to hide in the basement the night before, escape would've been easier. I poked along the floor the best I could, trying not to step on nails or broken glass until I got to my "picking up the mail" slippers near the front hall. I slid on sunglasses I found dangling off the chandelier in the dining room, a pair Tara lost before she left for her mom's. She'd be glad to know I finally found them. With a deep breath, I headed outside to assess the rest of the damage. I just needed a plan. First a plan, then I could be sad.

One glance at the trunk of my shiny red Infiniti sticking out from under a tree broke through my emotional barriers. I blinked back tears as if when I hit the hundredth blink, my car would magically be restored. My pride and joy was a total steal at seventy-two payments of four hundred fifty dollars. Two payments down, only seventy to go. Random stuff covered the lawn: the lid to my cast iron skillet, what looked like an old prescription pill bottle, the remote for a window air conditioner I'd recycled years ago. Not knowing where to start, I bit my lip and forced my gaze toward the curb.

Across the street, the house belonging to my favorite elderly couple mirrored mine—half the front room lay in ruins, the garage decimated, but the other side more or less intact. Thankfully, my neighbors already left for Florida for the winter, so they would be fine, but I needed to call when the networks cleared to let them know. They unfortunately didn't know how to text.

No one else was in sight, but I called out, looking for anyone trapped inside their homes or needing an extra pair of hands. Only my voice broke the eerie silence.

Downed power lines to the east and the storm-created swimming pool next door in what used to be Mrs. Everling's living room persuaded me to head west, up the hill, toward a gas station on the corner. Walking past the house to the west, I marveled at the lack of damage. One front window was broken, the hole shaped suspiciously like a baseball.

The shouting match that had carried across the yard the day before and the sulking teenage boy who'd offered to mow my lawn for twenty dollars suggested the storm had little to do with the damage to my next door neighbor's house. That conversation felt like a lifetime ago.

Most of the other houses on this end of the street were fine, untouched. The sun still hovered near the horizon, filling the air with tinges of color. If I didn't turn around, only the eerie stillness would give any indication a storm occurred. I couldn't think about that. Focusing on the road ahead helped staunch the rising panic in my chest.

A week ago, the fact that the gas station owner still maintained a working pay phone had been a running joke throughout Red Bank. Now, the archaic device reeled me in like a lifeline. Me, and half the town, apparently. I stood in line with neighbors I'd seen a million times and never spoken to. Everyone wore the same sunken-eyed, slack-jawed expression on their face. If I'd possessed a mirror, I suspected the same dead eyes would peer back at me. We were haunted. No one spoke above a whisper.

The woman behind me poked something in my back. I whirled around before realizing she held a crumpled granola bar. "You hungry, honey?"

My stomach rumbled, but the thought of eating didn't appeal to me at the moment. I shook my head.

She shoved it into my hand. "I walked by your house, your kitchen's gone. Take it for later."

The woman's sincerity touched me, even as I struggled to remember how she knew me. Finally, it hit me: a week after I bought the house, her dog got loose. We'd met when I returned him, exchanged pleasantries, and not spoken since. "Thank you. Are you okay?"

She laughed. "Ain't nobody okay around here, but I'll live. I'm doing better than you, I think."

The sun rose higher. Our voices dropped away as we each processed the extent of the storm. I inched closer to the phone, wondering if anyone was trying to reach me.

When I finally reached the booth, my fingers fumbled for a minute. Change. How had I forgotten I needed change? Once upon a time, Mamá made me memorize her calling card number for an emergency such as this one. If someone asked me two days ago, I'd have been hard pressed to recall what a calling card was.

A voice rumbled behind me. "Make a call or get out of line, sweetie."

I didn't acknowledge them. Instead, I grasped at a distant

memory and dialed the operator. "I'd like to make a collect call, please."

Less than a minute later, my boyfriend's voice filled my ear. "Anna, thank God! Are you okay?"

"I'm fine, but the house is destroyed. My car's smashed. Phone's dead. I can't possibly get to work today. Or all week, probably. I can't even get my clothes. We've got no elec—"

"Don't even worry about that, sweetie. My place is fine; the storm passed right over it. I'll come pick you up, we'll pack your stuff together, and you can stay with me until you get everything settled."

A three-thousand-pound weight lifted off my shoulders. "Thanks, Jay."

"Where are you calling from? I'm on my way."

"Just come to the house. I'll be sifting through the rubble all day." I thanked him again and hung up.

With the condition of the roads, I didn't expect to see Jay any time soon, so I headed back. The insurance company would send people to help with clean-up eventually, but I needed to do something to keep my hands busy. I couldn't just sit here and stare at the mess. The scope of the damage overwhelmed me. For a long time, I stood in the kitchen doorway, just staring and hoping Hermione would bound across the lawn.

Deep breaths, Anna. One thing at a time. Just do one little thing. Then do one more little thing. That was manageable.

All those leftover magazines from the basement turned out to be useful, after all: I used them to divert water away from the main hallway, back into what used to be the kitchen. I spent several seconds watching the water seep into my image on the cover before flipping the top one over and dumping more slick pages on top. Not quite as good as a door, but at least Hermione could hop over the stacks when she returned to get into the house. My treasured ribbons, memories of a lost youth, went into a trash bag with chunks of plaster, broken picture frames, and something furry that might've been a drowned rat. Sniffling,

I added the now-beheaded, one-legged ceramic horse Tara made me when I gave up riding to the trash pile.

I wiped my eyes. "Goodbye, Sir Maxwell."

The last time I saw the horse was twenty years ago, and I hadn't been in a saddle since. But saying good-bye to the figurine hit me almost as hard as the day I quit. Tears flowed freely down my cheeks. Ignoring them, I continued to sift through the rubble, looking for anything that could be salvaged. Tara's favorite Blu-ray, our picture from prom, both of us sporting "the Rachel". I sniffled again, wondering if a bit of music could lift my spirits.

The lack of a phone, computer, router, or electricity made streaming music impossible, but I rooted around in the basement until I found an old battery-operated CD player with my other camping stuff, along with some tarps that could come in handy.

"Hello? Anna?" Jay's voice emanated from the general direction of what used to be the kitchen.

The moment I saw him, my facade of bravery broke. An armload of tarps tumbled to the ground. My chin quivered, and a sob escaped me. He held me, the boom box cradled awkwardly between us, for a long time. "I'm so sorry. It's okay. We'll rebuild together."

"Thanks," I sniffled. "How did you get here? And what time is it?"

"I borrowed a scooter from my neighbor. I couldn't leave you to deal with this alone. Traffic is backed up all the way into the city. You don't want to go out there if you don't have to. Trees blocking lanes, power lines down, flooding everywhere. About three blocks over, water's up to people's doorsteps. But I'm here now."

I smiled up at him and leaned forward to give him a kiss. "Thank you. *Te amo, mi vida.*"

"I love you, too. Let's get to work."

Eventually, everything would need to come out while contractors did the repairs, but at least I could try to avoid more water damage until I got a truck and a storage unit. I turned on the boom box while we got to work. We needed to move as many of my belongings as possible to the basement, since I could lock that door. Tarps would hopefully protect things we couldn't move and what used to be the kitchen entrance from the elements for a few days. At least we might be able to keep out the local wildlife, although I hoped Hermione would come back.

"Just out of curiosity," Jay said as Ace of Base filled the room, "When was the last time you listened to your boom box?"

I thought for a minute. "A little over a year ago, maybe? Tara and I went camping around the time I met you."

"Not that I don't love 'The Sign,' but do you have anything more recent than, say, 1993?"

"Nope," I shot back. "When was the last time you bought a CD?"

"Touché. I don't even own any CDs anymore. Donated 'em all years ago."

I gestured toward my room, swallowing a lump in my throat. "I had some yesterday."

A heartbeat later, Jay wrapped his arms around me. "Hey, it'll be okay. I'm here with you. We'll both take a couple of days off work to clean this mess up. They'll manage without us. The whole office is closed. You can't stay with me until this place is rebuilt. A few weeks, several months, it doesn't matter. Okay?"

I nodded, trying to quell the growing panic inside me. Everything I lost was stuff. It wasn't me. Stuff could be replaced. Breathe in, breathe out. "Thanks."

We moved to the living room and sat on the couch. From this angle, with the wall blocking my view of the blue tarp, I could almost pretend things were normal if I didn't let my eyes wander toward the pile of debris Jay'd swept into one corner. Perhaps any light in the room would've helped the illusion. Or maybe it would've made everything worse.

No puedes tapar el sol con un dedo, as Mamá used to say. *You can't cover the sun with one finger.*

Unfortunately, now I possessed a perfect view of the mantel. Where Tara and I once displayed our favorite pictures.

I got up and sifted through the stuff on the floor.

"Ahn? What are you doing?"

Ignoring him, I kept digging until I found what I wanted—the only gold framed picture in the room. Mamá always hated silver, thought it looked cheap. In the frame, she and I stood before the house, with our identical long dark hair and smiles. Her white sundress made her seem half her age; I wore a light blue cap and gown. Glass showered onto the floor when I lifted the frame. Dirt and gook streaked our clothes and faces. We gave the impression less of mother and daughter at college graduation, more like survivors of a disaster movie.

"This is the last picture of us together." My voice cracked. "Now it's gone, too."

A tear dropped off my nose, making a clean spot on the snapshot.

"It's going to be okay. Your dad probably took a hundred pictures that day, right?"

I nodded.

"We'll call him when we leave here, tell him you're okay, ask him to send you another one. Good?"

It wasn't good. We hadn't owned a digital camera back then, and Papa probably didn't keep the original negatives. Still, I nodded, knowing if I didn't put on a brave face, I'd never get through the rest of the house. "Okay. Thanks."

When the waning light made further work impossible, we walked into town to see if anyplace serving food was open. One of the sagging power lines had given way under the weight of a tree during the afternoon, blocking access via the route I followed earlier. Jay and I picked our way through fallen trees, soggy leaves, broken glass, and puddles until we reached the end of the street. The bistro at the corner now offered outdoor seating in the back, but I suspected the owners would've preferred to build a patio over losing the rear walls. Employees milled around, moving chairs and boarding up the broken windows. I waved, offered condolences, and kept moving.

We weren't picky: restaurants, fast food, a gas station. Since my stove was in the kitchen, and the kitchen was no longer attached to the house, all foods requiring any preparation whatsoever were out of the question. Luckily, the nearby pizza shop used a wood-burning oven and a back-up generator. The line stretched for a couple of blocks around the corner, out of sight.

Jay pointed at a bench across the street, partially hidden from view by a green Acura stopped in traffic. "You've been on your feet all day. Do you want to rest?"

I hesitated. As much as I hated to show weakness, my left leg throbbed where the end connected with my prosthetic. The only thing I wanted more than my bed and my house back was to sit and remove the device. Jay touched my chin, forcing my gaze back to him. "Hey. You've had a rough day. There's no shame in sitting down."

Puddles littered the path between me and the debris-covered bench. Still, sitting seemed more appealing than standing in line. My heart warmed at his thoughtfulness. "You're right, thanks. I'll take—whatever they have, honestly."

About an hour later, Jay returned with a large pepperoni pizza. Although the wind carried a bite, we ate on the bench, as if this were an ordinary day and we were just another couple enjoying a pizza for dinner in the middle of a disaster zone. We shared a tender, cheesy kiss under the stars.

Cars packed the center of town. As we tried to decide whether we wanted to fight traffic to get back to Jay's, I realized the green Acura I'd walked past to get to the bench still idled at the end of the street, waiting to turn onto the main road. If this tiny town was gridlocked, trying to get to Jay's house in midtown would take hours at best. Considering the amount of work left to us the following morning, we decided to unpack the rest of the camping gear and spread it out in the basement.

We picked our way up the hill, detouring around more tree

branches. Two college-aged guys in a raft offered to take us up one of the side streets, but the road to my house wasn't totally underwater, so we declined and gave them each a slice of left-over pizza. Emergency crews hadn't made it anywhere near our neighborhood yet. Between the rubble, the flooded areas, and the lack of street lights, walking home took nearly twice as long as the trip into town.

On the way back, I insisted we knock on a couple of doors to see how the neighbors were faring. The only one who answered seemed more concerned with feeding me than the tree lying across her living room. I asked her to keep an eye out for Hermione and convinced her that we had enough leftover pizza for the night.

Although part of me wanted to take the scooter back to Jay's for the night, I hoped the cat would return if I stayed. On top of everything else, I couldn't stomach telling Tara I lost her beloved pet. I couldn't even call her with the news about the hurricane until I knew Hermione was safe. Jay put bowls of food and water on what used to be the back porch while I scoured the house for usable pillows and blankets.

The next day passed in much the same way, except we finished securing the house before dark. Hermione remained out of sight. News reports told me that traffic into the city had light-ened up, so I went to a neighbor whose house was mostly okay and offered him some free samples of our new product line in exchange for borrowing his truck. He agreed, and even helped me load up a few boxes.

"You ready?" Jay asked after he loaded the last of the stuff.

I shook my head. "I can't leave without Hermione."

"I'm sure she's fine. You know how cats love to hide."

"I do," I said, "and she's probably in the basement. But I'm not going anywhere until I'm sure."

Jay surveyed the resolute line of my mouth, the determina-tion in my eyes. He'd seen it before at many a board meeting, and he knew what it meant. After a long moment, he sighed. "I'll pack up the food and kitty litter, then get the carrier. Check the basement again, and if you don't see her by the time I'm done, we'll go for a walk."

"Thank you. I really appreciate it."

He nodded and disappeared into the house. After a moment, I followed. Hermione did love to hide in the basement when Tara or I opened the door to do laundry. With luck, I'd find her squished behind the water heater.

Ten minutes later, I'd scoured the entire basement and determined that if the cat hid there, I would never discover her hiding place. With a sigh, I grabbed a bag of cat treats from a drawer in what used to be the panty, and went outside. Jay and I walked up and down the block, shaking the treats and calling her name, until finally, a meow answered us.

"Hermione?"

The fat cat bounded out of the bushes, absolutely soaked, and catapulted into my arms. I'd never been so happy to see another living creature. I snuggled against her, cooing until Jay pointed out that it was dark and we'd need close to an hour to get home.

We didn't have a towel, so I dried Hermione off as best I could with my sweater before bundling her into the carrier for the trip into the city.

By the time we reached Jay's apartment, I barely had the presence of mind to plug my phone into the wall before I collapsed into his bed, exhausted. Nearly three days of emails, texts, and unanswered calls awaited, and I didn't possess the strength to even turn the device on. It could wait until I got to work the next morning. Even Tara shouldn't have heard about the hurricane, tucked away at her mom's, and I'd better be able to convince her everything was okay in the morning once I believed it myself.

A good night's sleep did wonders for my health and mental well-being. Jay and I arrived at the office in high spirits. I was halfway through the door of the ladies' room before I remembered my phone had been off for almost three days. Funny how, after years of treating the phone as an extension of my hand, a few days without power or service made me almost forget it existed.

When I turned the phone on and finally got my three days of messages, I wished I'd never remembered it. A flurry of email notifications flashed across the screen, blurring together. My voicemail beeped, and then a text popped up on top of everything.

SLUT.

Click here to read on

MORE BY LAURA HEFFERNAN

The Reality Star Series

America's Next Reality Star: Jen went on a reality show to compete for the $250,000 grand prize. But when she finds herself battling another woman for co-competitor Justin's love, she finds herself wondering what the true prize is.

Sweet Reality: After a killer competitor threatens her new business, Jen sets sail on a new reality show adventure to save the day. But Ariana's back, and she's determined to end Jen and Justin's relationship once and for all.

Reality Wedding: After retiring from reality TV, Jen receives an offer she can't refuse. The Network wants Jen and Justin to film their wedding to fill an empty time slot—and if they refuse, the Network will get Justin fired.

The Gamer Girls Series

She's Got Game: Gwen's dedicated to becoming the American Board Games Champion, and she never ever mixes gaming with pleasure. But when she meets Cody, trying to resist his charm becomes a losing proposition.

Against the Rules: For years, Holly has harbored a secret crush on her best friend's dad. Nathan is young, he's hot. What's a little harmless flirtation while playing games? But when she discovers that Nathan returns her feelings, Holly may have to choose between two of the most important people in her life.

Make Your Move: Shannon's more interested in designing games and rising to the top at work than dating. She's surprised to find herself falling for her roommate, Tyler. Worse, he's dating her boss's daughter. If she makes her move, Tyler's girlfriend could get Shannon fired.

~

Push and Pole Series

Poll Dancer: A delightfully modern twist on *My Fair Lady*: When a promotional video for her pole-dancing classes goes viral, Mel comes under fire from a local politician running for senate. Desperate to save her studio, Mel decides her only option is to launch her own campaign — and win!

The Accidental Senator: After accidentally finding herself elected state senator, Lana Chen is determined to prove her worth. But when a mistake aids the passage of a bill that's going to put her best friend out of business, Lana has to find a way to set things right before it's too late.

~

Retail to Riches Series

A Royal Farce: After years of secretly crushing on her friend Pierre, Lila is thrilled when he proposes they start a fake relationship. For weeks, she finds herself hoping their farce could turn into the real thing—but Pierre's hiding a secret of royal magnitude.

A Royal Pain: **Coming Soon**

~

Standalone Books

Finding Tranquility: Jess Cooper lost her husband on 9/11. Just not the way she thought. On September 11, 2001, Brett enters Logan Airport bearing a ticket for a flight that crashes into the World Trade Center. Jess knows her husband is gone. She doesn't know he never boarded that plane. Years later, Jess is shocked to meet Christa and recognize her spouse. She's more shocked to realize their love may have survived.

Anna's Guide to Getting Even: Anna's perfect life has turned into a string of disasters: After a hurricane destroys her house, her ex publicizes private photos of her — which costs Anna her job and her current boyfriend. And after hitting rock bottom, she decides that revenge is the only way forward…

Friction: Britt's always avoided relationships. Then, weeks before she's set to move away, she meets Colin. To her surprise, she finds herself wanting more.

Time of My Life: She's a poor dance teacher. He's her rich student. If they can only overcome their differences, this could be love. A gender-flipped update of *Dirty Dancing*.

ABOUT THE AUTHOR

Laura Heffernan is the award-winning author of fun, witty romantic comedies and women's fiction that touches on some of society's most important issues. After a few years of practicing law, she realized that she much preferred arguing with her characters than other people. It's easier to win that way. She lives in the northeast with her husband, the world's most active toddler, and two furry little beasts.

Laura loves connecting with readers. Find her at http://www.lauraheffernan.com, on Facebook or on Twitter, where she spends far too much time tweeting about reality TV, current events, and Canadian chocolate.

BOOKS WRITTEN AS ADA BELL

Welcome to Shady Grove...

Aly doesn't believe in psychics. Too bad she just had a vision.

Future scientists don't have visions. Aly's got enough on her plate, with finishing her degree and taking care of her nephew and starting her new job at the antique store while drooling over the owner's gorgeous son. No visions.

Alas, the universe doesn't care what Aly believes. When she turns 21, she starts to feel psychic impressions left on objects. A disorienting power for someone surrounded by antiques. Then cranky customer Earl is killed, and Aly's new boss Olive is the prime suspect. Who hated Earl enough to kill? Police would rather make a quick arrest than investigate, so it's up to Aly to clear Olive's name.

Shady Grove is reeling from the first murder in decades. If Aly can get
her hands on the murder weapon, she should be able to solve the crime.
Can she learn to control her visions before the killer sets their sights
on her?

Mystic Pieces

The Scry's the Limit

Sight Seering

Mystic Treasure

Seer Today, Gone Tomorrow